I0690047

Alpine Destiny

Henry Melton

Alpine Destiny

Henry Melton

Wire Rim Books
Hutto, Texas

WRB

Printing History
First Edition: March 2022
ISBN 978-1-935236-87-0

ePub ISBN 978-1-935236-88-7
Kindle ISBN 978-1-935236-89-4

Website of Henry Melton
www.HenryMelton.com

Cover art by HMT STUDIOS Manila

Printed in the United States of America

Wire Rim Books
www.wirerimbooks.com

Acknowledgements

I often tell people that story ideas come together in pieces. Ideas are all around and you plug them together like Legos™ to make an interesting shape. This story of a far future Luna and the people who were trying to make it better came together from a number of disappointments. There was the only book I've ever tossed into the trash half-read (don't ask, I don't remember the title or author). There was the moment when I walked out of the **Apollo 13** movie and stared at the distant full moon in the sky and ached for a return. Other ideas and needs combined to create this story that I wanted to tell. I wrote it for me. I can just hope that other people can enjoy it as well.

I dearly want to thank the people who have stood by me for years, helping to shape my rough text into a better version. Thank you all;

Jim Dunn, Lynda Elliott, Todd Hartman, Mike Lynch, Scott McNay and Tom Stock

Contents

The 48–Hour Lunar Day

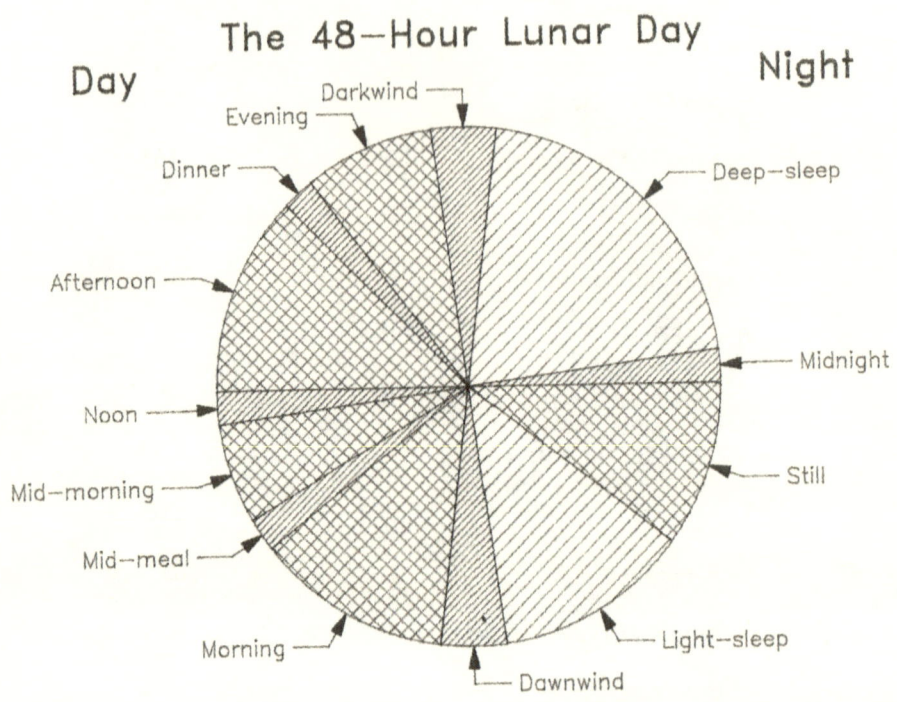

Day

Night

Darkwind

Evening

Dinner

Deep–sleep

Afternoon

Noon

Midnight

Mid–morning

Still

Mid–meal

Morning

Light–sleep

Dawnwind

Northeastern Luna

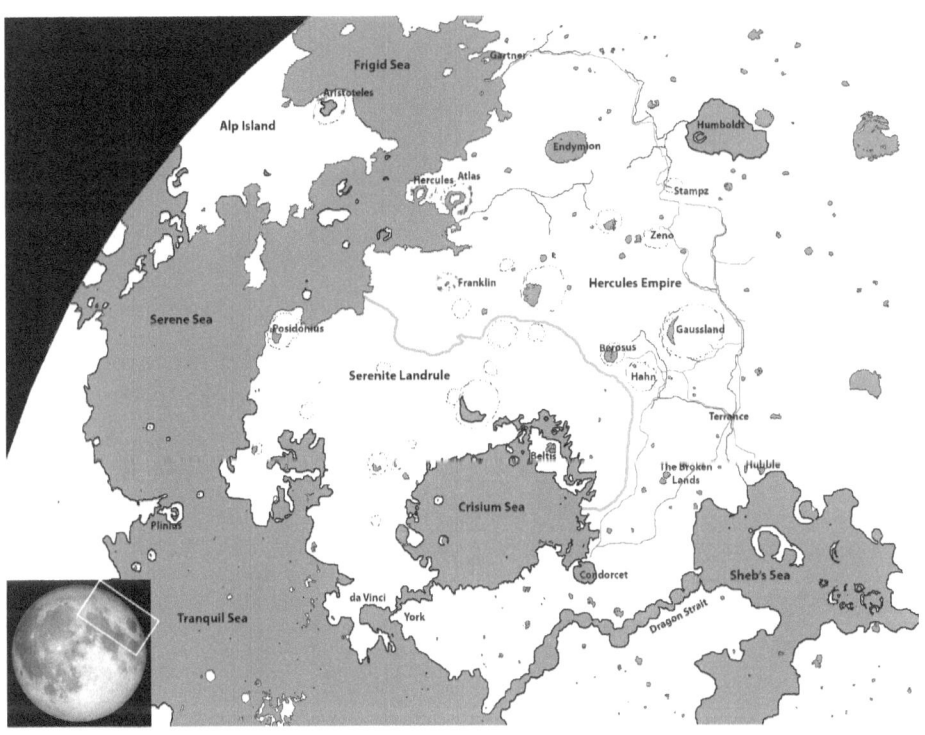

Cis-Terran Space

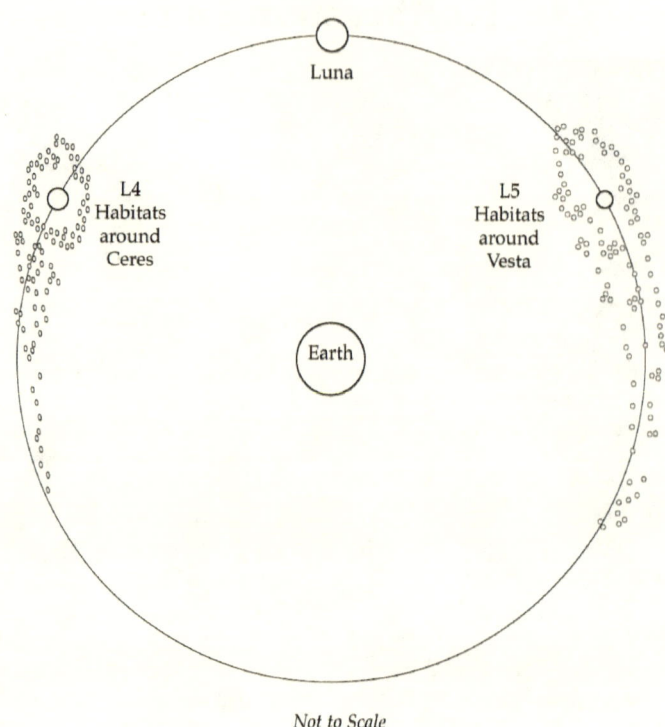

Not to Scale

The Prophet

Charles Fasail walked into the little fishing village as the dawnwind died out and the most isolated people on Luna came out of their huts to start the day. To Charles, this was another world, with people living in wooden huts that would have blown down in a day on any other place on Luna. People were wearing light tan clothing that to his eye looked to be made of coarse-woven fabric, quite possibly derived from wood fibers. There were only hand-carts. There were no oxen in this part of the world. There were fish nets draped over their drying racks near the water.

The refugees from Vesta, perhaps the most industrialized place in all of humanity prior to the Plague, had been the first of the Lagrangian orbital settlers to flee their destroyed habitats. They had sent scouts to choose a place to settle and they had been cowed by the fierce winds that scoured the whole lunar globe twice a day at dawn and dusk. So they had chosen one of the most naturally protected places in the world, the massive Orientale crater, containing its own pocket sea. The inner crater walls had formed an appealing sheltered archipelago where they'd built their settlements.

Charles, in contrast to the simply dressed villagers, was a spectacle as he strolled in with his impulse rifle, a nearly featureless metal cylinder, as his walking stick. He was dressed in his fanciest sailsuit yet. It was finely-woven white cotton cloth with a fat blue stripe from his neck all the way down to his left foot. His collar and sleeves were studded with gold. Kimmer icons for his Treekiller identity and the one for Alpine were embroidered in blue on the right side of his chest. It was mostly Darkwind's design for him, impressive to Kimmer. Charles could tell that these people had never seen anything like him before.

Charles himself was impressive—tall and muscular, head shaved and wearing a trimmed beard. That didn't stop a couple of pre-teen boys from picking up rocks and throwing them at him.

It was hardly the first time Charles had been the object of poke-the-bear hijinks, but this time he had his impulse rifle at hand. With a simple wave of the wand, those rocks stopped in mid-flight and flew off. One of the boys squealed and they ran off.

A fisherman, muscular himself from a lifetime of pulling nets from the sea, stepped out from his hut and stood in the walkway.

Charles nodded. "Greetings."

The man frowned. "What did you do to those boys?"

Charles kept smiling, "Nothing. I did stop those rocks from hitting me. I suppose I could have dodged them, but it's too fine a morning to be dancing around."

The fisherman's eyes looked over his clothing. "You're not from around here."

"No. I'm traveling. I came from half-way around the world."

There was a gasp from a woman who had gotten closer to listen. A half-dozen adults were easing up closer. A teenage girl with them asked, "From the other side of the sea?"

He smiled, "No, from much, much, much farther away than that. Surrounding your sea are mountains and forests, and across them to the east is a great ocean, so huge that you would need different kind of ships to survive the winds. On the far side of that ocean, so far away that it's night here when it's daytime there, other people have settled over the years."

The fisherman nodded. "Those are your people?"

"There are many people there. So many that they wage wars between themselves to fight for land."

"We have wars." The man shook his head. "We fight for fishing rights. I fought with the Pelmarrows last year."

Charles nodded. "It is the way of people, sadly. And what do you call yourselves here in this place?"

The girl said, "We're the Shacca."

From the exasperated expression on the fisherman's face, Charles got the impression that the girl was his daughter.

He asked the man, "How many places are here in these islands?"

"Maybe a dozen."

"And are you allied together? Or does each place have its own leader?"

The fisherman sniffed and shook his head. "Hardly. In my grandfather's time, Caland," he nodded to the north, "had a say over maybe half the islands. It didn't last."

Charles considered. *How much should I tell them?*

"Do you have your histories? Legends of past times?"

The girl said, "Nanna tells us tales."

Charles smiled at her, "Tales of Vesta, perhaps?"

The girl gasped, "How do you know?"

The fisherman said, "Those are just fancy stories for children."

Charles shook his head. "No, I have seen Vesta with my own eyes. It is a giant place, a great ball of rock almost as wide as your whole sea. It is dead and silent now, covered in the ruins of the cities of your ancestors."

"That's enough tall tales for now," the fisherman grumbled. "We have to pay attention to today, not to the past, no matter how fancy it might have been."

Charles nodded, "I agree! Today is important. But the past aids wisdom. And you must still look ahead to the future."

One of the women asked, "What do you mean, the future?"

He turned her way, "I came here to tell you people of the sea that there will be change coming."

The crowd stirred uneasily. Charles kept one eye on the fisherman.

But it was time to get his message out, while he still had time. Without making too much of it, he tapped the impulse rifle with his foot. A contraption designed by him and fashioned by Shuman, the master blacksmith at Stampz, popped open at the bottom, forming a T-shape with the shaft.

Charles raised his hand. "I am a stranger here, but I'm only the first. It may be years yet, but others will come, and they have weapons much greater than yours. They are human like you, but their loyalties will lie with their masters and their own people.

"This place, this Shacca, is pleasant and well sheltered from the winds. Some day, a stranger will come and desire this place, and just might decide to take it away from you."

"He'll have to fight for it!" growled the fisherman.

"I know. But he will have ways to kill you from a distance." Charles pointed to the knife fastened at the man's waist. "Your weapons will be useless and your best warriors will be the first to die."

The woman said, "What can we do?"

Charles shrugged. "These are your lands. I came here knowing only of Vesta and tales of long ago. You people have made a life for yourselves here. I am not one to tell you how to live. But I do know this; a handful of these strangers could take over Shacca, or any of your islands.

"However, if all the islands could work together, to protect each other, then you'd have a much better chance of meeting with these strangers on stronger ground."

The fisherman said, "It'll never happen. There's been too much blood spilled among us already."

"Then it's your choice. But remember this, in unity there is strength, and you'll need it."

"Why should we listen to you? You're one of these strangers, aren't you?"

Charles smiled. "Of course you shouldn't believe me. You should find the wisest among you and make your own decisions. I've only given you this warning so that I can sleep peacefully at night."

The fisherman took a step closer. "I think you need to—"

Charles held up a hand. "Stay back. I've had my say. It's time I left."

He stepped on the iron-work T-bar clamped to his impulse rifle and tapped the control.

The crowd gasped and screamed as Charles lifted straight upward with a strong, almost knee-buckling pressor pulse to the ground.

There had been only a few times he'd launched aloft this way, but it was getting easier each time as he maintained his balance better. He tapped the controls again and there was a second pulse, lifting him higher still. He dearly wished he could have the buzzing cirrance that those spacesuit boots or the beamship itself used, but Ship confirmed that his impulse rifle didn't have that ability. He had to make do with single strong pulses.

Once he had the altitude, he secured the impulse rifle in a pouch at his side and spread his arms, letting the cape of the sailsuit catch the air, and made course for the island to the north. He hoped it was this Caland that the fisherman had mentioned. But if not, he still had to leave his message with the people of that island and then repeat the process.

He could hop across all the islands this way, arriving and making a splash, warning these people that they really should be united before the scouts from Hercules or Serenity arrived and decided that primitive fishermen really didn't deserve such nice protected lands. It was plain that the Vesta settlers had never developed the ironworking skills necessary to make muskets. The knife that fisherman had shown was hardly any better than the beaten iron knives the Kimmer made from found meteoric pebbles.

The book Charles had written, *Across the Horizon*, extolling the beauty and richness he'd discovered on his tours of the unexplored lands of Luna, had already been quite a hit, even if the copies he had paid a scribe to duplicate had to be passed around by hand.

That had been his goal. Instead of preparing for battle over a few stretches of land, he wanted the Hercs and Serenites to know that there were endless vistas of uninhabited lands, filled with game and many protected craters, not too far away. All that was needed was some brave soul to cut the first trail and mark the way for others to follow.

He had taken several trips in his beamship, the only remaining spaceship on Luna, hopping from valley to valley, sketching out a rough map for those early explorers to follow.

It was only well after he had started the project and many people had read his book that he realized he'd set in motion an expansion that would eventually lead people to this original settlement. The isolated descendants of Vesta would likely be totally unprepared for the arrival of hardy men carrying muskets.

He eyed a meadow just outside the village on the new island and circled down to a smooth landing. If anyone had seen him coming, they weren't approaching just yet. He had a moment to prepare.

It had been three years or so since Darkwind had accompanied him on that first trip around the world. It would have been nice to have him along this time, but the boy .... Charles shook his head. He needed to stop thinking of Darkwind as a boy. He was a man making his own way through life. A half dozen times, the Kimmer had left to be with his forest-dwelling people, no more sophisticated than these fishermen, and to sing his epic stories of life with the Alpine magician. Just as often, he showed up again, or more recently, signaled him with his radio that he was ready to be picked up.

Darkwind's songs were inspiring, telling the tales of traveling around the world, and even up into space where they salvaged a fortune in gold and iron. He had crafted a beautiful tale of seeing the Angel station, a golden butterfly-like structure larger than this whole island. Charles had been there with him and was still fascinated by the songs, even if Darkwind's versions were light on the science and heavy on the mythology.

Charles was reminded of his goal. Restore the Angel stations that had been lost to a comet impact, so that their real task, to slow the decay of Luna's atmosphere, might be resumed.

When he was done here at the Orientale Sea, he needed to make a pass over the Kimmer lands and listen for Darkwind again.

Charles checked the drape of his sailsuit and folded the T-bar back up onto the 'walking stick' and strode toward the town. It was time to spark a little more mythology for these people.

A couple of children saw him first and went screaming into town. He chuckled.

History repeats itself.

Return to Stampz

Ship made just one slow pass high over the Kimmer lands where Charles expected his apprentice Darkwind to be living. He could have made another, except that the sun was getting low and the darkwind was coming. He really needed to check in at Stampz before the winds got too stiff. He'd been away longer than he expected. In any case, Kimmer scouts would have seen him and word would get to Darkwind that the beamship was back in this part of the world.

On the north and east sides of the Stampz crater, he had five hiding places where the beamship could land in thick clusters of trees taller than the ship itself. There it could hide in densely forested areas no wagon could approach. Ship chose one of the sites on a random basis and landed during the early stages of darkwind when his cirrance couldn't be heard over the howl of the wind and there weren't likely any sane people out listening for him anyway.

As they settled down and Ship anchored itself, Charles asked, "Any signs?"

"No."

Ship had memorized the images of all their landing sites and took fresh images on the way down. Charles was amazed, but Ship could compare those images down to the fallen leaves on the forest floor and tell if there had been any disturbance from the time before. They had abandoned two other landing places, just to be safe, even though it was likely the changes were just caused by deer tracks.

Serenity still wanted to destroy the beamship, the wild card in the international power game, and everyone knew the rogue Alpine visited Stampz on occasion. The other major power, the Hercules Empire, had not taken any overt moves against the beamship, but Charles wasn't ready to trust them either. They could just be waiting for the opportunity.

Even though years ago the Duke of Stampz, James Neely had been happy to be shuffled off to the edge of the Hercules Empire with the understanding that he stay out of court intrigues, things were changing.

Stampz, a smallish crater with no more industry than exporting crops and acting as a way station for shipping traffic along the Gaussland Trail, was now a suddenly much more important player.

Agriculture was still its most important export, although heads had been raised when the duke, through an agent, shipped three wagons of iron to Franklin, not to mention a surprisingly large crate of raw gold. Since no one could really imagine that Charles had brought the valuable metals back with him from a trip into space, the source of the fortune was still a cause for speculation.

And merchants were quite surprised that bales of the rare Stampz blue cotton could be shipped across the mainland or down to Condorcet in a matter of a couple of days when even the fastest messengers couldn't get a simple letter delivered in that time.

James will likely have some deliveries waiting for me. He's been tolerant of my long trips, but he's too much of a businessman to appreciate my erratic ways.

Not that the duke could do anything about it, really, other than frown. Ship was loyal to Charles, no one else.

Although it was very nice to have a home base, it was only prudent that he had to sneak in and out of Stampz. He missed the days when he could land in front of the castle and the crowds of friendly people came out to greet him.

Charles took advantage of the beamship's power to recharge his impulse rifle, a convenience he always appreciated, and then went outside to get his eyes adapted to the dark.

There was just enough earthlight that the Stampz crater wall looked like an endless range of mountains with no gaps in sight. He walked quietly through the trees, practicing stealthy Kimmer skills Darkwind had taught him, until he identified his target.

Folding down the stirrups, he triggered the pulse and went flying up into the night sky. He went for extra height this time. Even with the faint glow of the earthshine spread among the clouds, it was easy to get disoriented when flying at night.

Once he caught the wind with his cape and felt the comforting tug on his ankle straps, he focused on the rim of the crater, now below him.

Over the years, a hiking trail had been worn into the rim, connecting the dozen or so guard stations. Originally stationed to protect the farmers inside from Kimmer raids, the guards these days were more on the lookout for Serenite spies.

Charles chose the closest guard station on the left and sailed down for a silent landing. It was a little risky, dressed as he was in a Kimmer sailsuit, but here at the crest of the rim, no one expected the arrival of anyone from the sky. Sailsuits were for approaching targets on the ground from a cliff above, everyone knew that.

The dwindling darkwind was still an issue and the two guards huddled behind the windbreak, taking an occasional glance over the edge down into the dark forests below.

"I took this job because I thought there'd be no trouble," one of them grumbled. "Back in Hooke, there was always some news about the Reds pushing the border and we'd be the first to be called up to help, so I thought a pleasant, out of the way place like Stampz would be better. But here, I've got to be always on the lookout for spies or something."

The other guy said, "Well, better here on the rim than riding guard for those wagon shipments. They say the Kimmer are behaving themselves since Terrance, but I can still see them watching. I know they're just waiting for an opportunity."

"Yeah, I hear you."

Charles had heard enough. He crept over to the tower where the heliograph and the thick clay fire pot were kept—the day and night signals the guards could use to alert the castle that something was wrong. He had to check the tower number.

That done, he took off again, sailing away from the guard station into the interior of the Stampz crater.

The clouds had a gap and the place lit up with earthlight. Charles smiled, even as he fussed with his cape to slide through the air a little sideways because of the wind. He was going to need several boosts from his gun if he were going to make it all the way to the castle by air.

The place had changed in the years since he'd first arrived. It was still a colorful patchwork of tilled fields, with all roads leading to the castle on the central peak, but the earthshine now reflected off canals that had been cut in the past couple of years. A clever little illustration in one of the books he'd brought back from Alexandria had inspired Shuman, the blacksmith, to craft a wind-powered water pump. When the winds were blowing, the vanes turned and caused a screw on the same shaft to lift water from the lake at the northwestern edge of the crater and fill a raised channel that flowed back toward the castle.

Shuman had made many of the pumps. Canals filled canals, until fresh water could be had at any place within the crater walls. Many of the old rain-catchers were sitting idle as people took advantage of the new system.

Last Charles had heard, Stampz was selling some of the pumps to smaller communities along the Gaussland Trail. Bigger places with their own blacksmiths were making their own.

Although Charles had nothing to do with the project, he felt a surge of pride. He'd flown across space to gather those books that formed the New Alpine Library of Stampz. His hands had picked that one book out of thousands from those ancient Alexandrian shelves, with the hope that something in those pages would make a difference in peoples' lives. And it had.

Up ahead, the castle spires were decorated with blue and white banners, fluttering in the dying winds. He wondered how much those flags could bring in the markets of the major cities, considering how much Stampz charged for its rare blue cotton. But he was sure no other place in the world had anything like it. Stampz was unique.

He saw the duke's white horse, Angela, out in her pen, exercising in the earthlight.

He moved to position his gun just right and pushed himself higher and faster. There was a balcony on a tower to the right. Its railing was wrapped with a dark cloth. He concentrated on killing his forward speed and settled down on the balcony with only a slight stumble.

Five good landings out of eight! I'm getting better at this. Much better than the first time when he had hit the wall and had to flutter to the ground like a bird with a broken wing.

The door opened and he found the cool, glass warmball in the darkness by touch, and twisted it. There was a spark and yellow light lit up the room as the ember within started burning. He sniffed. The room was a little dusty. The maids had followed orders and left his private room mostly untouched while he was gone.

He glanced at the signal rope that snaked down a tube to the kitchen level. The duke used it for more than just requesting food, and Charles was supposed to announce his arrival that way if he avoided the main entrance. *Maybe later.*

He sighed. *Sleep now, or get a snack?* It was deep-sleep, the time of day just after darkwind when most people went to sleep after a long day. Some people stayed awake the whole twenty-four hour daylight portion of the forty-eight hour day, and were likely crashed out now. Others slept parts of the day and worked through the still of the night.

Charles, living most of his life inside the beamship where he could turn the lights on and off to suit himself, often had an irregular sleep cycle. He wasn't really ready to sleep yet.

He changed into normal clothes and carefully hung his sailsuit in the wardrobe. He stashed his impulse rifle in a hidden compartment under the mattress of his bed.

The hallway was lit by evenly spaced warmballs, only a third of which were lit, here in the deep sleep of the night. He walked quickly toward the stairwell. The kitchen was down several floors.

Laughter stopped him quickly. He recognized the voices.

Leaning over the railing, he saw James Neely, Duke of Stampz, kissing Jelica Haren.

Charles cleared his throat. "Are you two still at that?"

James looked up. "Charles, you're back! I didn't get an alert." Jelica blushed, still comfortably in the duke's arm.

Why they were kissing in the stairwell wasn't hard to guess. She was still in her white healer's robe. Probably she'd just finished from a long day's work and James caught her on the way to bed.

"Yeah, I'll have a report for Jed Tylan after I get myself a snack."

Jelica wagged her finger. "Tell Patricia to give you something healthy. You've probably been eating trail bread for quads now."

He sighed. "Yes, Jelica."

"That's Duchess Jelica to you!"

"Yes, Duchess. Now would you two move on out of the way. This is a narrow staircase."

The couple laughed and retired to their chambers. When the door clicked behind them, he moved on down to the kitchen level.

The night shift in the kitchen greeted him and hurried to fix him something 'healthy'. It wasn't ten minutes later that Jed Tylan arrived, looking like he'd been woken out of bed.

He grumbled. "You didn't radio ahead."

Charles shrugged. "I thought you appreciated my attempts to get past your guards."

The plate appeared, with a salad and fruit, with the promise of fish in a few minutes. Tylan took a bread roll from his plate.

"Well, I do appreciate it, I guess. How did you get in?"

Charles related his arrival, what he'd overheard from the guards, and the number of the tower.

Jed nodded. "That was Brook. He's an experienced man, but he isn't really comfortable here yet."

Charles nodded. "I wish all the guards were born and raised in Stampz. Every time I see the ruins of Terrance, I get nervous about Serenite spies."

"I keep an eye on all the new guards we've hired. And yes, I'm more comfortable with people I've grown up with, but the duke won't hear of compelling his farmers to send their sons to stand guard, not without a more immediate threat. For now, we've got the money to pay for outside help. And I only hire people with experience against the Serenites."

Charles nodded. He wasn't about to tell Tylan how to do his job, being only a part-time Stampz resident himself.

"So, tell me, how did your trip to Orientale go?"

Charles grinned, and over the double-helping of fish, gave Tylan all the details.

Checking In

A couple of hours after midnight, the duke found Charles in the library's reading room, sitting on a comfortable chair lit by two large warmballs. He was freshly shaved and washed after the maids were alerted to bring him water.

"Good still, Charles. What are you reading?"

The duke sat in a nearby chair and reached for a book on the small shelf just at his side.

Charles put a cotton ribbon in place in his book and closed it. "It's a history of something called the Cold War."

The duke shook his head. "I've never heard of it."

"The progenitors of Manhattan and Mt. Ural had a war prior to the Star where both had weapons so powerful that they could each destroy the whole of planet Earth. Each was powerful and with weapons they could deploy in minutes. It was so horrendous that neither side dared to attack the other. Everyone would die if they did. Instead they found other ways to fight."

James frowned. "Who won?"

Charles shrugged. "I haven't gotten that far yet. At this point, their surrogates are fighting. Smaller nations. I gather that there were a lot of smaller nations at that time."

James nodded. "If more people read your Horizon book, we might get there ourselves."

Charles winced. "Don't tell me that. I tried to do something good, and now all I can see is the potential for more conflicts."

"You can't dwell on that. How many copies of your book are out there?"

"I've been told by the scribe in Zeno that twelve copies have been made. I don't know where they all went, though."

James shook his head. "There are more than that. One of my agents has seen a slimmed down version in Condorcet. Just some of the text and the maps are crude, compared to yours. Storytellers read it aloud in the marketplace, since only a few can read it themselves. Still, a lot of people are finding out about the rich, unoccupied lands on the other side of the Tranquil Sea. He reports the ferry company that traverses the Dragon Straight is looking for investors to fund a larger ferry. There's starting to be a demand for taking settlers and their wagons to the far southern lands. That's how your map shows a promising route, isn't it?"

Charles nodded. "I spent a lot of time on those maps. I hope the crude ones don't get people into trouble."

James smiled. "You and your marvelous ship have given a great gift to the people—a look at the rest of the world that they would have never known existed. You've given us a first-hand account of what's out there, along with clear pointers showing possible routes. Scouts on foot would have taken a lifetime or more to let people know the possibilities."

"Yes, but if I'm just causing a splintering of the world into many different nations, won't that be a source of even more conflict in the future?"

"Charles, it was coming anyway. Even before you were born, the southern lands were only reluctantly part of the Emperor Sheb's domain. They were only connected via ship traffic and the wagon trains on the Gaussland trail. If it wasn't for the Serenite threat, the Hercules Empire would have split in two a long time ago.

"Now with the Gaussland trail only safe to travel with large, heavily armed trains, and piracy more common in the Crisium Sea, the Southern Palace is becoming ever more comfortable governing the southern lands without any communication with the emperor.

"And that's just one example. Nobody, not Hercules nor Serenity, is attempting to maintain control of those settlers who have crossed the Peach river and have sought out new lands to the east. Settlers who are tempted by your new lands will be the same. There's no way either of the two royal houses can maintain control over such distances.

"Not unless you're willing to turn your beamship over to Sheb's army, and I know you're not thinking of that!"

Charles sighed. "The world would be a very different place if there were more beamships, wouldn't it?"

"Probably, but it's clear we don't have that technology, not even in those books on the library shelves."

Charles said, "I noticed how much more organized the shelves are now. When I went looking for a history book to read, they were even divided into historical eras. Has Lucas been working at it?"

"Yes, although Tulip was quite upset when Lucas insisted on a whole new organization scheme. Many of the books she'd carefully arranged are now scattered on different shelves." James shook his head. "I had to calm her down. When it comes to certain things, the Alpines have to take the lead."

Charles sighed. "I'm sorry Tulip is in such a situation. I'd better compliment her on something soon."

James eyed him, "Are you sure you're still in support of having a Herc as chief librarian, now that we have so many Alpines?"

Charles shook his head. "As long as the library is still officially my property, then I want it very clear that no matter what our Alpine pedigree, we're still a tiny minority and I want the books accessible to as many people as possible. I might miss the Alpine rituals, but we can't demand that a poor Herc farmer who might want to look at a book on crops must learn the chants first."

"You're starting to sound like a Herc."

Charles sniffed. "And you're *slightly* more Alpine. By the way, how many Alpines do we have now?"

"Including Heidi, Darkwind when he visits, and me?"

Charles waved his hand. "No, Alpines from Alp Island. Jelica... the duchess, *says* that you're a full-fledged Alpine now, but you still haven't gone through all that childhood cultural training that made us all so... picky about certain things."

James smiled, "So you're still not sold on my Alpine status?"

"Well, I'd hate to contradict the duchess, but I guess I don't really have any firm guidelines for what makes a person an Alpine. Something Harriman Moore said a few years back made sense to me. Humanity went through a great mixing time prior to the Plague and there's likely no *inherited* difference like hair color or the shape of my nose between Alpines and the rest of humanity. That indicates that it's cultural to me. You at least were partially educated on Alp Island, so you've gotten some of that."

James ran his fingers through his hair, grinning at Charles's bald head, "I'm not going to dispute Jelica either, but I certainly feel Alpine in some ways. She has her reasons, but you'll have to get that from her."

"I tried, but she's not very clear. But back to my question—there's Jelica, Edward Harris, Helva Wiscolm, Lucas Villia, Woodie Sparks, Dave Oran and me. That makes seven Alp-born Alpines, right?"

"Eight," Jelica said as she entered and sat down beside her husband. "We've got one more since you went off on your latest expedition—Sharra Abeth. She arrived from Franklin a couple of quads ago. She's staying with Helva at the farm, assuming they don't kill each other first."

Charles gave a long sigh. "I was a lot prouder of my Alpine heritage back before I had to deal with these guys in person. Is there a one of us who has a pleasant personality?"

Jelica said, "You're one to talk! You can't say anything without dropping into lecture mode."

James looked at his duchess and said, "Well, I've had no problems with your personality, my dear."

Jelica sighed. "Don't sweet talk me now. I was just getting ready to gripe at our wayward traveler for being gone when we need him here."

Charles shook his head. "I knew you just wanted me here to haul stuff. Just a dockhand at heart, I guess."

She shook her head. "Not only shipping, but that's important. I also need you to keep our Alpines under control."

He laughed. "Well, Duchess, how come you can't handle that? Put on a crown or something and lay down the law."

"Sorry," James said, "we're a little short on crowns around here."

"Hmm. I seem to remember something during your wedding."

"Oh, that was just something Mrs. Dustin put together for us. She insisted on crowns. I think she made them from dinnerware and wild flowers. They did look pretty impressive from a distance, but the flowers are all wilted now."

Jelica sighed. "But as far as the Alpine community, they all know I was just a teenage girl when I was stranded on the mainland. They're all older than I am, and I've never known an Alpine who was all that impressed by mainland titles."

"And I'm younger than you are, so why—"

She shrugged. "You've got the ship. You gave us back a library. As far as everyone is concerned, you're the face of the Alpines. They have to listen to you."

Charles turned to James, "So, what do you want me to ship?"

She shook her head, "No, you'll go to the farm first! We cannot have squabbles between the Alpines and the people who live here. This is the only place where Alpines are welcomed, and all it'll take is a few ill-tempered words and we could lose that. You have to fix it."

Charles could see James smiling at her. How many years had the duke been on his own, the final arbiter to every decision? He seemed to be enjoying an outspoken wife with a will of her own.

But James said, "Charles, I'll get you a list. I assume you'll wait until morning to visit the farm?"

"That might be best. It sounds like I'll need to be rested."

He didn't need to say anything more. The duke had his worries as well.

When the list showed up an hour later, Charles could see that he'd been away too long. There were three deliveries to be made, and what was more urgent to him personally, there was a message from Harriman Moore. He wanted Charles to loan him three books from the library. "Books immediately valuable to the common man."

Charles knew what was up. Moore's printing press project had made some headway. Half a year ago Harriman had shown him the first locally printed Bible. It was crudely bound, by the standards of the books in the Stampz library, but the thick book had been totally manufactured on Luna. The paper stock was made in Messala, if he recalled, made from pulped willow, which grew in great abundance around the shallow lake that took up half the interior of that crater. The design for the pulping machine had come from one of the library books as well, although the original had been water powered and the Messala version was wind powered.

As soon as Bibles started showing up in the Herc cities, there was an immediate backlash from the temples of the Way. The scribes were angry as well. There had been a lucrative business making the rare books that were used by the royal court. It took a scribe a long time to copy a book by hand. The threat of some machine being able to duplicate that effort in a fraction of the time and undercut their sales was something that they couldn't tolerate.

Moore was well aware of the issue, having faced it years ago, before the Great Burn. The Alpines on Alp Island were excited to help him with his printing press operation but not if the only book to be printed was just one lone religious text.

Machine printing would only survive if many people demanded books important to their lives. It was clear Harriman was ready to start work on expanding the range of their operations. Charles needed to offer him a good selection.

At the Farm

Charles considered what he'd need to take with him to his farm. He had purchased the land, even though the duke offered the plot for free. Charles had seen, back in his dockworker days, the traps people could fall into. Debt had to be repaid, eventually.

It certainly helped when he and Darkwind had gone into space to check on the status of Ship's great enemy, the Space City of Mt. Ural. They had seen the former asteroid in its new orbit and took advantage of the orbital positions to make a quick trip to a small mining asteroid in the Vesta cluster. Charles had only intended to use the visit to train Darkwind with space suits and how to move around in very light gravity.

Much like on his first trip into space, when they had been searching for the original library of Alexandria, they discovered more people killed by the ancient Plague. But they also returned with a cargo of pure iron and a large crate of gold. When the duke sold it for him, Charles had more money on hand than he knew what to do with. That certainly helped with purchasing the land and hiring local Stampz craftsmen to build the house and outbuildings.

I need to make a trip back into space again.

Someday, when Mt. Ural moved to a different part of the Ceres cluster, he might risk another trip to Alexandria for more books. But visiting another place in the Vesta cluster might give him more abandoned space suits. The ones they stripped from the dead on that mining asteroid had been valuable. Only a couple of them were fully functional, but even if they were damaged, the radios could still be used.

The duke had a radio in the castle, plus another at the guard station overlooking the Gate—the canyon providing the only entrance wagons could use. Others were in various hidden warehouses scattered across the mainland—places where the Stampz cargo could be offloaded, awaiting the beamship for fast transit to other places on the continent. Sadly, the radio range was limited. Only the closest warehouse could talk to the Gate. The Gate could talk to the castle.

Only the beamship, which could climb high enough to see past the curvature of the horizon could talk over longer distances to those radios.

Looking over the list that the duke had given him, Charles could see that he needed to make a number of contacts with the half-dozen or so locations that would be listening for a radio contact. *If I had a dozen more radios, we could set up a real relay system.*

Either that, or build really gigantic towers so that the radios could reach longer distances—not something he'd see in his lifetime.

And there was always the problem of limited power. When they cut away the unused part of a damaged space suit, the power cell that normally ran the air exchanger and the boots was more than enough to keep the radio running constantly for a month or so, but after that, he needed to recharge it from the beamship's power store. To extend the usefulness, they only used the radios on a schedule, listening for a signal.

Maybe I don't want more radios after all. I'd be constantly on call to keep them charged.

But the dawnwind was fading. He'd need to get moving soon. He put a schedule together and decided that coming back to the castle would be a waste of time. He packed his sailsuit into a backpack, retrieved his gun and after a quick breakfast and a visit to the library to pick up a few books, he hiked out in the direction of the Alpine farm.

...

A fan slowly turned in the dwindling breeze as he walked up to the farm. A trickle of water drained into an irrigation ditch feeding the strangest cropland he'd ever seen. There were scores of tiny plots, each with different plants, some in bloom, some not. Tall stalks in one plot shaded others with leaves barely covering the dirt.

He leaned over the edging stones and took a look at a light blue flower with many pedals.

"Charley!"

He looked up. Heidi was running his way.

He smiled. She was getting prettier every time he visited. She was about fifteen now, he guessed.

She gave him a hug. "Don't mess with my asters."

"Is that what they are?"

"Yes." She leaned over and checked to see if he had damaged her flowers. "I've got a book from the library and I'm pretty sure that this is what they are. They're pretty and the honeybees like them, but I'm not sure it's any kind of a valuable crop."

"I've never seen anything like them before. Probably one of the plants that never made it to Luna originally."

She nodded. "I've got a lot of those. If I can find someone who's interested in rare flowers, I could make a fortune."

"They're probably out there, just document everything and collect the seeds."

She gave him a tolerant look. "Like you have to tell me that! It's all I've been doing lately. And Jess Mendo can only help me a little lately. He has to concentrate on his cotton crop."

Charles nodded. "And Edward? I thought he was helping as well."

She shrugged. "He helped me find the right books in the library, but he's really not interested in gardening. He's a fish biologist, not a plant expert."

Charles frowned. "Aren't any of the other Alpines helping? I thought this would be an interesting puzzle for them."

She shook her head. "No. They were all a little interested, but since it was a Herc project, they never really paid much attention to it." She sighed. "I'm grateful you let me set up my little growing plots here, but I probably shouldn't have intruded on the Alpine farm."

He shook his head. "No. It's my farm and you have every right to be here. Consider it part of your payment for helping on that trip. I got my library and Harriman got his Bible. You deserve your seeds and the opportunity to make what you can from it. All the Alpines owe you, even if they don't realize it."

She smiled. "Thanks, but I'm not going to be able to tell them that. They're all too …."

He nodded. "Arrogant? Is that the word you're looking for?"

"Maybe something like that."

He sighed. "My people. I guess I've gotta love them."

When he left her to her tilling, he shook his head. When he'd first met the girl, she was so proud of being an Alpine apprentice, working for Jelica. Now she was comfortable talking about her botanical laboratory as a "Herc project". And it all had to be from the attitude of the other Alpines. None of them really considered an Alpine apprenticeship as a real thing. It was the Alpines and the Hercs. No middle ground was even considered.

There was a box wagon next to the main house. The ox was penned close by.

Charles waved. "Hey, Woodie!"

The gray-haired man looked up from his book and waved back.

"What are you reading?" Charles asked as he got closer.

Woodie Sparks shook his head. "It's a fiction novel, I think. A murder mystery in some city on Earth. I spend more time trying to make sense of that strange culture than I do trying to figure out who killed the dancer."

"What's the city?"

"Boston, it's called. The author mentions a lot of local landmarks, but I can't make sense of it."

"What era?"

Woodie shook his head. "People drive around in 'cars', some kind of motorized vehicle, and half the people carry guns in their pockets. There's a communication device called a phone. The main detective limps because of some injury he received in a war."

Charles shrugged. "Doesn't narrow it down for me, but I haven't read much fiction." He looked at the wagon, secured in place with stakes in the ground. "Are you sleeping out here?"

Woodie nodded. "Too much noise in the house. Besides, I'm comfortable here in my wagon. I've slept on the trail for nearly a decade now. I'm thinking of taking up the duke's offer and go back to being a driver."

Charles smiled, "Giving up on being an Alpine again?"

"Never that. And I'll certainly come back, but I'm used to working." He grinned. "And you're hardly the guy to say that staying at the farm makes you a better Alpine."

They laughed. Charles nodded. "Yes, I can certainly understand the appeal of being out on the trail. But, whether you go or stay, I've got a question. Which book in the library should be widely available to anybody in the world?"

"Your preacher's got his printing press running?"

"Yes, and it looks like they're starting to branch out. Got any book suggestions?"

Woodie frowned thoughtfully, then shook his head. "Nothing I can think of right now, especially for Hercs."

When Charles went into the main house, there were no raised voices, but for some reason it didn't feel as comfortable as the last time he visited.

The sight of a man in a scribe's black robes sitting at the kitchen table startled him for an instant.

"Lucas. I didn't realize you were here. Are you staying out at the farm now?"

The man was in his sixties and was nearly as bald as Charles was.

"No, just visiting Helva. Edward and Woodie live here. And that new-comer, Sharra Abeth." He sniffed. "She and Helva don't get along."

Charles sat down, trying to ignore the scribal robes. Lucas Villia had worked as a scribe since the Burn. He'd been some kind of assistant to the Alpine Ambassador before that.

"I'm glad you're here," Charles said. He asked his opinion on which books should be copied for the masses.

Lucas shook his head. "If this were Earth, then I'd suggest an almanac, but we don't have seasons like they did. Knowing when to plant and harvest your crops was a handy thing to know back in ancient times. Maybe one of the books I gave that Herc girl might be useful."

"Heidi? She said she had a plant identification book."

"More than one. Perhaps one of the simple ones. I doubt any locally-built printing press could print good pictures of the plants."

"I'll take a look."

Helva Wiscolm entered, "Charles, you're back!"

He got to his feet and helped her hobble to the table. When she sat, she straightened her shoulders and beamed. "I'm so glad you're back. How long will you get to stay this time?"

He chuckled. "Not long. The duke gave me a big list of things to be delivered."

"Well, he shouldn't do that! You need a rest."

"According to the duke, that's all I've been doing. Traveling around the world for my own amusement." He laughed. "And maybe I have. Let me tell you about the people from Vesta."

He gave them an entertaining version of his visit.

"But maybe I should tell everyone? Where are the others?"

Helva frowned. "Edward is sleeping late. He's been reading a lot."

Lucas said, "Well, we all have."

Charles nodded. "I saw Woodie when I arrived. He was deep in a murder mystery."

Lucas said, "I'm staying at the castle, since I spend all my time in the library anyway. And Dave Oran is too, but that's the duke's call."

"Oh? Why is that?"

Lucas grinned. "Well, officially it's so Dave and the duke can work out the new business—making cotton-based rope to sell—but I'm pretty sure it's because Dave has been living in Serenite territory for all this time. I can't imagine any Alpine would be working as a Serenite spy, but the duke is just being cautious, keeping Dave as a guest at the castle rather than letting him roam around on his own."

Charles nodded. "It's sad to be so suspicious, but I've seen what happened to Terrance. Maybe I'll get to see him soon. I'd love to get a better feeling for what it's like to live under the Red Court's rule."

Helva sighed. "And then there's the new one."

"Where is she?"

"She took off for a hike. We had words this morning."

Lucas asked, "What is it this time?"

"Same old thing. I was a sell-out for teaching Herc children how to read."

Lucas shook his head. "Charles, you should talk to her and set her straight."

"Me? I'd think she'd pay more attention to you than me. I'm the youngster here!"

Helva patted his hand. "Charles, so is she. She's a girl. Maybe your age. She *doesn't* trust us old people."

Lucas grinned at his expression. "Helva, nobody told him."

Helva giggled. "Yes, Charles, why don't you go track her down. Maybe she'll listen to a good-looking guy like you."

Fishing

Charles had no inclination to go chasing after a girl. Not even a supposedly unattached Alpine girl his age. He'd been interested in Jelica back when she was the enslaved healer at Terrance, but although he took her rejection tamely, it had left its impression. He was involved in something a lot more important than falling in love and making new little Alpine babies. He was content with that.

Since his childhood, he had been taught that Alpines were responsible for bringing back the *oldman* technology, to revive humanity from the depths it had fallen. But when he had come into possession of a talkative beamship that knew a lot more about that technology than he did, he had discovered the hard truth.

Unless the Alpines were successful and rebuilt the old technology, Luna's atmosphere would gradually dwindle away and everyone would die. It would be thousands of years yet, but unless the Alpines took their duty seriously, then the bright green world, full of life, would freeze and dry out, becoming as sterile as it had been originally.

Charles had no idea how to bootstrap an iron age culture, where nearly everyone was illiterate, into a space-traveling one like it had been before the Plague, but he had to take every little step he could.

But if encouraging all the Alpines to stay the course with him was part of his job, then he had to do that as well.

Still, he was seriously grateful when Edward Harris came out of his room carrying a net.

"Charles, you're back?"

"For a little while. Are you going fishing?"

He grinned. "Any excuse to go fishing is a good one. I'm going to sample the canals. Want to come along?"

Edward had been the first of the scattered Alpines to show up once the story of a duke of the realm marrying an Alpine commoner spread far and wide across the empire.

He didn't have all that far to travel. The marine biologist had been studying the fish in the inland Humboldt Sea when the Great Burn had destroyed Alp Island and forced him to become a simple fisherman to survive. He'd been hauling nets for just about as long as Charles had been loading ships on Port Gartner's docks, and they got along well.

Edward led him to the closest canal. "Nobody is stocking these canals deliberately, so it's a great opportunity to see what varieties show up on their own."

Charles helped with the net, talking about the isolated Orientale Sea. "Fishing appeared to be their primary industry there, and it obviously supported a dozen small communities."

"You didn't find out which varieties?"

"Sorry, I didn't think about it at the time. There were some fish, filleted and drying on racks, but I'm afraid I don't know the species by sight."

"How big were they?"

"The largest were as big as my forearm. The smallest were hand-sized. I wasn't really paying attention. I was a stranger there, concentrating on the crowd."

Edward frowned. "The Vestans could have made an effort to stock their sea, back when they first settled and had a ship. I'd really like to nail down whether the primary fish migration happens through connecting rivers, or via waterfowl carrying fish eggs on their legs."

Charles told him about Jack Lake in Gaussland. "It's totally isolated. There are no rivers connecting it with the Peach River."

"But you don't know what fish they had?"

"Sorry. It didn't occur to me to ask. Still, many of the merchants that visit Stampz also stop in Gaussland. You could ask them what fish are available there."

Edward nodded, with a grumble. "Hercs. I'm not really comfortable around them. I was pretty much a loner back at Humboldt. I only dealt with a couple of merchants back there."

Charles nodded. "Heidi told me you helped her with the plant identification books."

The fisherman shrugged. "She says she's an Alpine apprentice, but what does that even mean? She was obviously born a Herc."

Charles wasn't comfortable chiding his elders into accepting the Hercs, especially when he wasn't very accepting himself. He dropped the subject and helped Edward count the minnows and crayfish they caught in the net.

Edward was content with what he found. "The water screws limit the size of fish that may be transported in from the lake and the river, I don't expect to see any larger fish until they have a chance to grow on their own."

"Would it be worthwhile to stock the canals?"

Edward grinned. "It might make me happy, and some of the farmers too, but I doubt there'll be an economically significant number of fish that can be supported in these waterways."

Charles noticed a man watching them from a distance. "Somebody seems interested in what we're catching."

Edward chuckled. "That's the new girl."

"What?"

"Yes. She dresses like a man. Pretty unpleasant, if you ask me. Sharp-tongued. I've never attempted a conversation with her, but she's not like any Alpine women I've ever known." He shook his head.

Charles sighed. "I guess that's my next order of business. I need to meet her, and then be on my way with deliveries for the duke." He smiled. "And I'll have my eyes open for fish when I travel from now on."

. . .

Charles strolled up the path to where she was standing. He noticed the knife at her belt. From the scabbard, it looked well-used. Her hair was cropped short, making her look even more like a man, at least at first glance.

"Hello, there. Are you Sharra Abeth?"

She looked past him. "Are there fish in these canals?"

"Um, not many. Just minnows, insects and such. Edward says that the fish haven't had time to grow larger yet."

"Any bass?"

"That's what Edward is trying to do, identify the species. It's too early yet. The canals are new."

She frowned. "And who is Edward?"

"Edward Harris, Alpine. He was a marine biologist. He's been a fisherman up north at the Humboldt Sea since the Burn."

She nodded, and then turned to walk away. Charles followed, a few paces behind her.

"Are you interested in fish?" he asked.

"I've had experience." Her hand crept to the knife at her belt, then dropped.

Charles said, "I've just heard of your arrival. I'm Charles Fasail, also an Alpine."

She nodded, not looking back at him. "I've heard. You've got the beamship."

"Yes, although sometimes it feels like the ship has me. I'm tethered to it most of the time. It's not something I can leave on its own for long."

She paused and looked at him. "You're bald."

He chuckled, rubbing his hand over his dome. "Well, it's a personal choice."

She shook her head. "The stories never mentioned that."

"What stories?"

She shrugged. "People talk."

He said, "I need to go the other way. It's been nice meeting you."

He'd barely taken a step when she asked, "Where are you going?"

He shrugged. "I've got deliveries to make. Like I said, I can't leave the ship for long."

She frowned, "For the Hercs?"

"For the Duke of Stampz, who is Alpine, the last I heard."

She wrinkled her nose. "I've met him. You follow his orders?"

Charles sighed. "Alpines have a refuge here, a place to live among their own kind, and that's all due to the foresight of the duke."

"You bought that land with a fortune in gold, from what I heard."

He fixed his eyes on her. "And do you think that would have happened in any other place in this Empire? The duke has been supportive of me from well before I had the beamship, and before I had any gold of my own. We work together."

"It looks like he's got a tame Alpine running errands for him."

Charles clamped his teeth together. If a man had insulted him, his old dockworker instincts would have urged him to answer with his fists. As it was, in spite of her knife and her attitude, he couldn't beat up on a little girl.

Nor was his tongue as quick as hers was. It was best to just keep on walking. He didn't need to prove anything to her.

She followed after a moment.

Heidi was still working her garden plots. Charles ignored the girl following him and called out.

"Hey there! I need to talk."

Heidi got to her feet and brushed her hands together. Her eyes flickered at the other figure still keeping her distance. "What do you need?"

Charles talked about her plant identification books, and the possibility of getting one of them duplicated on the new printing press.

Heidi frowned. "Yes, there's one that's pretty light on illustrations. It might be a good choice."

"I don't want to take the ones you really need."

She nodded. "I understand. This one was useful at first, but I really don't use it any more. I'll go get it." She dashed over to her hut and came back with it.

Charles thumbed through the pages, reading the descriptions. It was a good choice. Plants were identified. There was a paragraph for each listing the uses; food, dyes, or medicines. It also had planting guidelines.

"This will be ideal. Many of the plants aren't available on Luna, but it will fire people's imaginations. Some people will want to be able to read, just to take advantage of a book like this."

Heidi smiled. "I could read, but when I started this project, I needed to go ask Jelica what some of the words meant."

He nodded. "That's always the sign of a good book—stretches your mind."

Heidi whispered, "Are you sure that girl is an Alpine? She's nothing at all like Jelica."

Charles gave a tight smile. "So I've been told. Don't worry about her. She's not very friendly."

Heidi winced. "I know." She gave Charles a last smile and went back to work.

He gave the book another look and started back toward the main farm house.

Sharra came up closer. "So you like the young ones?"

"What?"

"You like young girls." She sniffed.

He chuckled. "You just can't help yourself, can you?"

"What?"

"You can't open your mouth without insulting someone. If you really want to know, Heidi was wondering if you really were an Alpine, and I couldn't really give her a good answer. I've seen no signs of it. At least Heidi has been well trained."

Sharra sniffed and hurried off at a quick pace.

Charles packed the book safely in his pack and strolled on.

Up the Slope

"Lucas," Charles asked, "could you inform the duke that I've gone off to make his deliveries." He'd come back to the main farm house to check in again before leaving.

The man in the black robes nodded. "Certainly, I was just heading out myself."

Helva frowned, "You won't stay to eat?"

Charles smiled at her. "I'll be back in a couple of days. No more long trips for a little while yet. I'm still looking forward to more time in the library with a good book with nobody trying to shoot at me."

They laughed. He'd told all the Alpines dinnertime tales of being shot at from time to time. Probably they believed him.

"Well, take some of my tea cakes with you, won't you? I just baked a fresh batch."

He chuckled. "I'll never turn that down."

Lucas waved her down. "I'll go get them for him, Helva. You stay put." He hurried off to the kitchen.

Charles smiled at her. "Do you bake all the time, or just when I'm around? It seems you always have something just out of the oven."

She blushed. "I frequently made treats for my students. It's a little different with no one around but gray-haired Alpines."

"Have you considered teaching the Stampz children?"

She sighed. "The duke asked that, and I've been considering it, but it's such a long hike to the castle, and now with the new girl...." She shook her head.

Charles nodded, "I'm sure that we could make—"

Sharra pushed open the bedroom door and came out. "Hold on! I'm coming with you." She had a cloak over her shirt and carried a bag in her hand.

"What?" Charles frowned. He hadn't realized she had been listening.

Lucas came out of the kitchen carrying the pastries. "What's going on?"

Helva said to Sharra, "Dear, it's not proper for a young lady to go off on a trip with a young man like that."

Sharra sniffed. "Well, he took that little Herc girl all the way up into space, if the stories you've told are correct! And I'm certainly able to take care of myself. I've been on my own for years now."

Lucas said, "Charles, maybe it's not the wisest choice to take her along."

"Hey, it's all news to me. This is the first I've heard about it."

Charles was very aware of Heidi's earlier words. Everyone said Sharra was Alpine, but other than her obvious hatred of the Hercs, she'd shown no evidence of being Alpine to him. Just how wise was it to take an unknown person along aboard the beamship?

None of the other Alpines had ever asked to come along. Jelica was the only one who had traveled with him, and only because she was escaping captivity from Terrance at the time. He'd just assumed it was because they were all older and maybe they really did believe his tales of being shot at with laser cannon.

Or maybe because they thought it was just too long of a hike to get to the ship.

Charles looked at Sharra, "It's a journey to get to the beamship. Are you up to it?"

She just gave him a tolerant look. "I've hiked all over the empire on my own. I walked into the Gate by myself. Walking doesn't bother me."

He glanced at Lucas, then said to Sharra, "I'll let you come with me to the ship. If I'm not satisfied you really are Alpine by the time we get there, then you'll be hiking back on your own. Can you live with that?"

She nodded, her face not giving him any clue whether or not she was insulted by his distrust.

He sampled a tea cake and complimented Helva on her cooking, and then headed out, Sharra following. He waved at Woodie on the way toward the northern crater wall. The man frowned and went into the house, probably to find out what was going on.

For the first few minutes, Charles walked in silence, paying attention to how well she was coping. He had actually intended to put on the sailsuit and fly back to Ship, but that was out of the question with a hiking companion.

She was keeping pace with him and showed no signs of fatigue. He'd check again later, but at first glance it appeared she was used to hikes, just as she'd claimed.

He even caught a glimpse of a smile, before she realized it and returned to her solemn face. Maybe she was happier hiking. She obviously wasn't happy being around people.

One question nagged at him. "Were you married to a Herc?"

"What?" She was furious. "What makes you think that?"

"Well, you hate the Hercs, and a bad marriage might do that to a person. And then there's your name, Abeth. I can't know for sure, because I didn't know everyone on Alp Island, but it's not a familiar name among the Alpines. I can match nearly all the names of the others to someone in Alpine or Alexandrian history. For example, Helva was the name of one of the important elders back at the time of the Plague. We're a big family, in some ways. I can remember a Sharra or two in the histories, but I've never heard of an Abeth."

"No! I was never married, to anyone!"

He nodded. "It's just you are probably my age, within a year or two, and all the children of Aristoteles were in school together. Now I can't say I made friends with everyone, because I didn't. It's just that I don't remember the name."

She grumbled. "Not everyone lived in Aristoteles."

He nodded. "There is that." He waved at a farmer, working off in the field.

She said, "You're friendly with all these people."

He nodded. "Not everyone. But I've worked with the people of Stampz, and we've been through trials together."

She said, "You rescued them from a flood."

"Yes, but I caused the flood in the first place. If they had lost their farms and families because of my mistake, then it would have been all on my head. Every time I see one of these farmers making a good life, if relieves some of the guilt."

"How could you have caused a flood?"

He weighed the promise of secrecy against the years that had passed.

"Keep this secret, okay. But during a Kimmer attack, I triggered the destruction of a laser cannon to keep them from using it to burn Stampz. That explosion in the Gate caused an avalanche that blocked the river, damming the water. It was backing up into the farmlands, flooding the crater floor. I was only able to clear the blockage using the beamship's firepower."

She nodded. "I saw the huge stone slab that nearly blocked the canyon, the Gate, when I walked in. It looked recent. You cracked it with the beamship?"

He nodded, and told her of seeing the floodwaters that had scoured the Gate and sent a flood surge down the Spanish River.

"I've made so many mistakes, and a mistake using the *oldman* technology has the potential to be a very bad one." He brushed his hand over his shaven head. "I never want to cause any more death and destruction. I'll never outlive my guilt."

He forced a smile, not looking at her. He waved at the fields around him. "But the floodwaters receded and the farmers reclaimed their fields. How can I not rejoice at their successes?"

They walked on, crossing a little wooden bridge. He smiled down at the canal water.

He pointed ahead. "You can see the path up the crater wall. We'll check in with the guards posted at the top, and then find a way back down on the other side."

She nodded. "Your beamship is outside the crater?"

He smiled, but said nothing. He would need to take a good look at the forest outside from the rim. Finding Ship's hiding place from the air was a lot easier than winding through the trees on the ground.

"Well, I've confessed one incident from my dark past. I know nothing of your history. It's time to tell me more. I can't lead a potential Serenite spy to my ship."

She sniffed. "I'm no more Serenite than a Herc."

He said, gently. "You need to convince me of that."

She walked in silence for a while. When the trail climbed and they began winding a switchback trail up the slope, she said, "I don't like to talk about my past."

"There are parts of my past that I'd like to forget entirely," he said. "But you can't have trust based on silent glares."

"I've never had much use for trust."

"We can't get to the other side without it."

She slowed down a little. Charles kept up his pace, letting her fall back. If she wasn't ready to talk, then it wasn't time for him to let her see the ship.

Is that really fair? She might have good reasons for keeping quiet.

But the beamship wasn't his personal toy. It really was life or death for many people, depending on who was giving Ship the orders. He had to be the gatekeeper, even if it offended people.

About two thirds of the way up to the top, she caught up with him.

"Charles, wait a minute."

They paused, sitting on convenient rocks. He pulled out a bag and took a sip of water. She did the same.

Not meeting his eye, she held her bag and said, "My mother didn't survive two days after the Burn. The local guide who was hired to take care of us on our trip through the Franklin markets and keep us safe realized at once that we were now truly powerless. He took Mom's money, but he wasn't content with that. Bound and gagged, we were carted to Hooke and even farther, I lost track."

Charles didn't say anything. He was sold into slavery as well, but he supposed it could be much worse as a girl.

She put her hand across her eyes. "I knew he was going to sell us. That's why he had to get us far away from Franklin—too many people knew my mother."

Her voice caught. "My ... my mother was a very beautiful woman. I was trussed up like a farm animal and stuffed in a bag, but I heard ... I heard my mother's screams."

She breathed heavily for a bit. Then she said, "I was sold, and after a long time, I escaped. I wore a man's clothes for safety and kept off the main trails. I never felt safe."

She glared at him. "Is that a good enough explanation of why I dress the way I do and why I hate the Hercs?"

He nodded. It was a very believable tale. Jelica Haren was also sold as a slave, although she managed to survive with a relatively honorable master who only needed a housemaid.

Every one of the Alpines had harrowing tales of their life after the Burn.

Is this just human nature to take advantage of powerless refugees, or were we Alpines so arrogant that everyone secretly hated all of us and turned against us in a flash?

He got to his feet and said, "We need to keep moving. We still have a ways to go."

He mused as he walked. *I haven't made it any better. The instant I had the power of the beamship, I made high and mighty proclamations and backed them up with Ship's laser. Maybe the duke's people like me, but everyone else just fears me and will turn against me the instant I'm powerless.*

They walked up to the crest and Charles called out to the guards.

The voice of the man who responded sounded familiar. It was Brook, the guard who had been griping about duties when Charles had arrived.

To Juniper

Brook frowned at him, giving nothing more than a glance at Sharra. "You're the guy."

Charles smiled. "Tylan said you were experienced. How did you identify me?"

The burly guard, with a beard that looked like it had been recently trimmed with a hunting knife, grumbled. "We've been told. A young guy, big, and with a shaved head. You have free passage, but we're supposed to give a flash back to the castle when you leave."

He glanced at Sharra. "He's with you?"

Charles nodded, still smiling. "Have you seen any activity below? Kimmer... Reds... bear?"

Brook shook his head. "Flocks of birds. That's about it. We've been watching."

"Good enough. We'll be going then."

Brook asked, "Do you know the trail?"

"I've been through here before."

They passed on. Brook watched them until they were obscured by the trees.

Sharra said, "He had his suspicions."

"About you or me?"

"Me. He kept looking at my hips."

"How many people are tricked by your costume?"

"It's good at a distance. I can also run, in a pinch. I don't carry much with me."

He glanced at her small bag. "Is that all of it?"

She nodded. "I've been intending to leave for the past couple of days. I don't get along with the rest of them. They were happy to see me go."

He had mixed feelings. *"The more Alpines the better,"* one part of him said. *"The farm would be more peaceful without her,"* said another.

He made sure he led the way, stopping from time to time to keep his landmarks clear in his head.

"We go this way." He cut off from the main trail, one that eventually led to the northern branch of the Spanish River and on toward Humboldt.

Sharra didn't question him. He wondered if opening up about her past had brought back memories she'd rather have forgotten. He had many of those himself.

But finally, when he'd stopped and backtracked a few dozen meters to avoid a minor crater wall, she asked, "Are you lost?" She brushed aside a branch that snagged her short-cropped hair.

He grinned. "If you want to hide a beamship, you have to make sure no trails are nearby."

She shook her head, "But are you lost?"

He was, but he didn't want to say it. Instead he pushed on until they had to climb another minor ridge. He went to the clearest spot and shouted, "Thunder and lightning, one, two, three!"

She was about to ask him what he was doing when there was a crack like a nearby lightning strike. He tilted his head slightly to make sure he had the right angle. Echoes began rumbling from all around.

"What was that?" she asked. "Did you call for lightning?"

He chuckled. "Just the thunder part. It's this way." He pushed through the underbrush until he found a game trail just wide enough to squeeze through.

She was fighting the underbrush as well. "I'm never following you through the forest again. Men never admit it when they're lost."

He said, "Aren't you pretending to be a man?"

"Shut up."

It wasn't too much later that he recognized his final landmark.

"Slow down."

"What?"

"I said, slow down, don't go ahead of me."

He was creeping ahead step by step.

"What are you doing?"

And then there was a loud voice and birds took to the air all around.

"HALT AND STATE THE PASSWORD!"

Sharra gasped.

Charles pointed. She looked, and saw the metal through the trees.

"Is that the ship?" she whispered.

"Yes. Now be quiet."

He reached out his hand.

"HALT AND STATE THE PASSWORD!"

He shouted, "Ship, it's me."

"COUNTER."

"Castor canadensis."

"ACCEPTED."

Sharra looked puzzled. "Beaver?"

He smiled, pleased she even recognized the genus and species term.

"We can enter now. Without the right password sequence, you'd be shoved back with a pressor beam. It's dangerous."

They wound closer through the trees. Her mouth was open in awe as she stared up at the cylindrical tower among the trees.

"Can I touch it?"

"Sure. It's metal, mostly."

She reached out and placed her palm on the surface. "I have a memory of seeing a ship, two ships, at a distance. They looked like this."

Charles nodded. "Side by side, parked about half a klom north of the main Library entrance at Aristoteles."

She blinked. "I guess. It was so long ago." She sighed.

"Ship, open the outer hatch."

The entrance appeared and Charles went in. After a moment, he said, "Are you coming?"

"Right." She entered, cautiously looking around at the small room.

"This is an airlock. Two doors to isolate the inside air from whatever is outside. Only one door opens at a time."

He raised his voice slightly. "Ship, this Sharra Abeth, a guest for the next trip."

Ship's voice, at conversational level, said, "Welcome, Sharra Abeth."

"The ship is male?"

"The voice is. Ship is an it. However, you are authorized to converse with it."

Charles tapped a green glowing panel beside the inner door. The outer door closed and immediately the inner door opened, giving them access to the cargo area.

He'd set up a number of codes once he started dealing with more outsiders, like the warehouse people. If he introduced someone as a "guest," then Ship knew it could interact with that person. If someone was a "passenger," then that person was restricted to the cargo level unless specifically invited up the ladder. If Charles omitted the introduction, then that person was potentially hostile and Ship was to monitor them closely.

"It's a bit cluttered. I haven't cleaned up after my last journey." There were a number of empty crates stacked up against the wall, as well as another crate overflowing with bones and scraps from so many meals he'd lost count. "I really need to clean this place up. I guess I'll be doing that soon enough."

She nodded, staying close to the hatch. "You'll carry the duke's deliveries in here?"

"Yes. This was designed as a cargo ship. It was rebuilt with some additions such as the laser cannon when the Space Cities went to war with each other, but this cargo bay and another just like it up at the top are the main design features. I never really use the upper cargo bay, it's useless for ground deliveries. Back when ships like these transferred cargo between weightless stations in space, both cargo decks were used."

He walked over to the ladder. "Command deck is this way." He climbed. She followed.

He sat down in the command chair and asked, "Ship, were there any intrusions?"

"No. Assorted animals and birds."

Sharra, still standing, asked. "Animals?"

Ship replied. "Only rabbits and mice. I was not able to identify the species. It was dark."

"How could you tell the rabbits and mice in the dark?"

"I was listening. I could hear the noise of their passage through the vegetation, and the rabbits make a distinctive rhythm as they move. If there were animals such as lizards and insects that made no noise, I was unaware of them."

Sharra turned to Charles. "It really can talk, can't it?"

He nodded. "Ship, turn on the display. We'll be leaving as soon as you do another security sweep."

Sharra was fascinated by the images. Charles tried to stay on task, rather than showing off for his guest. The list that the duke had given him showed a couple of deliveries that were delayed past their original promised dates. It wasn't his fault that the dates were too aggressive, but still, it was his job to make it right.

He pointed to the other chair, but kept his eyes on the display. There was nothing that Ship had noticed. Concealed by the trees, all it could do was listen for anything suspicious.

Sharra noticed the line that gave a time and the words, "Call for thunder noise. Charles Fasail voice identified."

"Ship heard you. From that distance?"

Charles nodded. "It can hear very well, and speak very loudly."

"But it wouldn't have made the noise for me?"

"No, it's in hiding. My unique voice and the correct words are both necessary."

But he didn't want to get too deeply into his security precautions. Some things he kept to himself. Not even Darkwind knew of them all.

"Ship, take us up. We're headed for the Juniper warehouse first. Your preferred path."

"Lifting in three, two, one."

Sharra gripped the the armrest of her chair, and then gasped as the display showed the ground dropping away rapidly.

Charles said, "Ship has a preference for what it calls a ballistic path— almost like a ball fired from a cannon. Only we go much higher than any cannonball can reach. I tend to prefer a slower path."

There was a noise that shook the place. "What was that?" she asked.

"We've gone faster than the speed of sound through the air. It's like we broke the air going through it so fast. It's like thunder. Now, be quiet for a moment, I need to make contact with the warehouse."

She nodded.

"Ship, radio on."

There was a brief tone, like from a little whistle, signalling that the radio was active.

"Calling Juniper. Calling Juniper. Please respond."

About half a minute later, a man's voice said, "This is Juniper."

Charles read from the duke's list. "Pickup number 833. Repeating, pickup number 833."

"Confirmation number 322221. Number 322221."

Charles said, "Confirmed. Message end." The whistle tone repeated.

Sharra was frowning. He nodded, "You can talk now."

"You have radio?"

"Yes, on my last trip into space, Darkwind and I collected a number of spacesuits, many of them damaged. But even if they couldn't work as suits anymore, the radio portion could be salvaged."

She frowned. "Were those spacesuits...?"

He nodded. "Yes, there were many dead bodies on that mining asteroid. It appeared the miners went crazy during the Plague. They fought and killed each other. It wasn't pleasant, removing the suits from those dried out husks, but distant communication is too valuable. All we could do was to pile the bodies together. It wasn't a place where we could dig a grave."

"Radio would be so valuable. How many do you have? Has the Emperor found out about it?" She seemed concerned.

He shook his head. "Empire-wide communication is a nice daydream, but it doesn't work that way. These are line-of-sight only. On flat land, the horizon is what? Two to three kloms? Two people standing might communicate five kloms away. It's better from a height. The guards watching the Gate from the crater rim can radio the castle. But still the duke can't communicate with these distant warehouses."

"But—"

"But I can," he nodded, "because I'm many kloms high in the sky. But that's only a brief moment in time."

She glanced at the display, but all that could be seen at their height was a hazy swirl of clouds. She glanced down at the text. "We're thirty kloms high!"

"And dropping. Yes. Ship likes to go up very high, very quickly, making it hard for any laser cannon to aim at us. Lasers are also line-of-sight. But sometimes it's safer sneaking into a place flying sideways just above the trees."

"You've been shot at."

He nodded. "Too many times. Bullets and cannonballs can be safely ignored, but you can't really dodge laser fire. You just have to make sure they can't aim at you."

She frowned. "Are you sure those warehouses are hidden?"

He grinned, "They are until they're not. Those codes I exchanged with the people in the warehouse give me a little confidence that they haven't been taken over by Serenite spies nor seen any sign that the location has been identified, but I guess we'll know for sure when we get there."

She looked at the numbers on the display again. "Where are we?"

He shrugged, "Somewhere north of Zeno. Ship knows. I'd have a hard time locating it on foot."

Ship spoke. "Prepare for approach."

Charles turned to focus on the display. The clouds parted slightly and green showed as trees whipped by at high speed.

Getting Stock

The ground dropped away as the beamship approached the rill.

Charles said, "It's a collapsed lava tube."

She nodded. "I'm familiar."

Still oriented vertically, the ship dropped into the canyon and moved sideways through the half-klom-wide channel, slowing down to a crawl as it approached the entrance to the un-collapsed portion. There were the ruts of a wagon trail down at the bottom, and that's where the ship landed.

Ship said, "My laser is aimed." Charles nodded. There was a flicker of green light, much less that the laser's deadly maximum.

Ship continued, "I see no signs of attacking forces." In that fraction of a second, the cameras had a good look at the dark interior.

In the cavernous entrance, there was a ox-drawn flat-bed wagon piled with cotton bales and assorted crates. There was no covering that could conceal a weapon.

Charles let out a sigh. "It's probably safe. You can stay here and watch with the display or climb down to the cargo level. But stay out of the way."

"Okay."

He went down the ladder in a hurry and spoke, "Ship, open the cargo entrance."

There was a metallic rumble and the wall of the cargo level began to slide to the side.

On the trip to the mining asteroid, when they discovered an abandoned fortune in gold and iron, Charles had griped out loud about how difficult it would be to haul all of that back in through the airlock.

Ship told him there was another way. If the interior of the ship was reduced to vacuum, with Charles and Darkwind remaining in their spacesuits, the wide cargo door could be opened and large items could be loaded directly.

And that's what they did. Unfortunately, no one thought to protect their food and water stores. They were eating hard, dried food with limited water rations on their way back home.

At least now, they didn't have to worry about vacuum.

Charles watched from the shadows as the driver urged his ox up closer to the ship. There was a strange blackened mark on the trail, scoured by the ship's laser on a previous trip. The driver brought the wagon up to the mark and stopped, throwing the brake to keep the wheel from turning.

He yelled out, "Hey, any gossip from home?"

It was a legitimate question for the men posted at the warehouse, but if the driver hadn't spoken those words, then Ship would blast for the clouds without warning.

The duke had written down the answer in his notes.

"Tell Quen that his sister has a new baby boy, named Will." Charles had a message from home for each of them. By the way the driver reacted, he was overjoyed with the news that his mother was recovered from her illness and had chosen to start work at the Blue Weavers, a group that made custom cotton tapestries from the blue and white cotton grown at Stampz.

The driver got down from the wagon and bounced his way back to the lava tube entrance, which gave Charles the signal to start loading.

It's pretty convenient for everybody else that the beamship pilot spent his growing up years as a dockworker.

He patted the ox on the flank and then began carrying the cotton bales and cargo crates from the wagon into the ship. The warehouse's radio, a bow-shaped device that had been extracted from the shoulder of a spacesuit, was also included.

Everything had a number on it, and Charles stacked the goods in separate piles by destination. He saw Sharra come down the ladder and watch him work, but she made no effort to help.

When he was done emptying the wagon, he left a freshly-charged replacement radio, the sheet listing the gossip from home and a few of Helva's tea cakes as a bonus. There was no guarantee that all the warehouse people could read, but the duke had instituted a system that only people who could read could be promoted to leadership positions. It was especially critical for the warehouse people.

As the cargo door began to close, the driver raced out to move the ox and wagon. Ship lifted as soon as everyone was clear. The buzzing noise of the beamship's tractor beams, grabbing at the air for a fraction of a second each time, shifted in pitch lower as they rose higher into the air.

Charles settled into the command chair, sipping water from his flask.

Sharra asked, "We're not going as high this time?"

"I guess not."

"You just guess?"

He shrugged, with a grin on his face. "Ask Ship."

She frowned then asked, "Um. Ship? Why are we flying this way, low to the ground this time?"

"Item 1: While an abrupt ballistic launch makes it unlikely I could be targeted with a laser cannon, it is also visible from multiple tens of kloms. An adversary who documented the angle from which I was seen more than once could triangulate those observations to identify the location of origin. Warehouses are hidden locations and should remain so for as long as possible.

"Item 2: Charles prefers travel close to the ground enabling him to identify landmarks and acquire information about where and how people live. Danger of attack is minimized by staying low, thus being visible for only a brief moment.

"Item 3: All previous attacks were made possible by predicting where I would be and having laser cannon in place, ready to fire. Humans are creatures of habit and should all course decisions be made by Charles, adversaries might predict where we would be. Charles has ordered that I choose random paths."

She frowned. "Do you know where to go?"

"Charles has told me the destinations. I have a map of human settlements and existing wagon routes. I chose varying paths minimizing times when I will be visible."

Charles gestured to the display. "Since we're taking the scenic route this time, you might as well take a look at the scenery. We'll be climbing to a higher altitude in a little bit to increase our radio range."

She looked at the crater wall passing in the distance. "Where are we headed?"

"A warehouse location near Franklin. Again, I don't know the exact location."

She sighed. "I can't get over how fast we're traveling. Since... since the time I started traveling, I've been walking. You don't know how long it takes to travel that way."

He chuckled. "Don't I? I have my own tales of sore feet. Want to compare travel stories? I bet I've walked more kloms than you have."

She shook her head. "I've steered clear of cities. I have no way of proving how far I've walked, and I'm not interested in playing that game."

A little later, she asked, "Are all your warehouses hidden like that? How did you find that lava tube? It's pretty far from most trade routes, isn't it?"

He nodded. "It's deep in Kimmer territory."

"Kimmer? And they let you stay there?"

He nodded. "We have an arrangement. Darkwind, my apprentice, knew of it. Kimmer have a deep distrust of constructed buildings, but in times past, they took advantage of natural shelters like that. They moved to a different shelter, closer to better hunting grounds and farther away from the encroaching sky beasts, that's the Hercs."

She frowned, "And they sold it to you?"

"More like rented it. We pay a regular tribute; they let us use the location; and they refrain from attacking the supply wagons. Hopefully, some day, we won't have to hide the beamship and use these out-of-the way warehouses. Either side can call an end to the arrangement."

She frowned. "I knew you traveled with a Kimmer boy. I didn't know he was your apprentice?"

He smiled. "Yes, Darkwind is an apprentice Alpine, and he lets his people know that. Although he calls what he learns 'Alpine magic.'"

She sniffed. "There's no such thing as an Alpine apprentice, no matter what your Kimmer or that Herc girl are doing."

Charles sighed. "Alpines seem to be the most intolerant people I know. Alpine apprentice is what they are, regardless of what you people think."

He realized that he'd lost all doubt about her claim to be Alpine. From her knowledge of some technology, to the way she read the ship display like someone who had been reading since she was a child, and yes, to her hatred of the Hercs. It all screamed that she was Alpine.

She was quiet for a bit, then asked. "What do you give the Kimmer? Your tribute."

He sighed. "They wanted muskets and powder, like they had gotten from the Serenites, but nobody on our side wanted that deal. Instead, they got a number of nice Franklin Metal Works hunting knives as the initial payment and some sturdy cotton cloth on a regular basis. I'm not sure how long they'll be content with that."

She nodded. "I can see the knives, but why the cloth?"

"Sailsuits. When Darkwind showed off his sailsuit made of cotton, it impressed them. The originals are made of bleached deerskin and while they work great, sometimes the seams give way, and believe me, you never want a seam to give out on you when you're riding the winds!"

She frowned. "Why bleached?"

He sighed. "I don't know exactly. I gather it's part of their process to make the deerskin thin and flexible, but I suspect it's now tradition to bleach them as white as possible."

He shook his head. "I have an old sailsuit made of deerskin, but I doubt I'll ever use it again. I trust the cotton one much more."

She asked, "You've flown with a sailsuit?"

He smiled, glancing out the display at the clouds. "I love it. Do you want to see it?"

She nodded.

He went down the ladder and brought up his backpack. Not quite willing to dress in front of her, he unfolded the suit and held it out so she could feel it.

"It's quite gaudy, isn't it?" She fingered the gold studs.

He chuckled. "That's Darkwind's design for me. It's meant to impress the Kimmer."

"They don't feel offended that you wear it?"

He shrugged and said, "I haven't seen signs of it. Darkwind has been pushing the idea that Alpines are an isolated branch of the Kimmer."

She laughed.

"There's a basis for it," he said. "The Kimmer are descended from the bioengineers that were here on Luna when the Plague destroyed everything. There's evidence in their songs. It's not too big a stretch to relate the science-loving Alpines and the descendants of the scientists who populated the freshly-terraformed world with its plants and animals."

She shook her head. "I've never heard that before."

He shrugged. "Nobody would believe it, even if I told them. Nobody would *want* to believe it, especially the Hercs who are more comfortable with shooting the Kimmer than talking to them."

There was the radio whistle tone. Charles glanced immediately to the display. Ship had started its climb.

But the voice coming from the radio was familiar. It sounded like Harriman Moore.

"… if you have a chance, I really need to speak."

"Harriman? Is that you?"

There was no reply. "Ship is there any response?"

"No, the signal dropped away. It was just a weak signal."

Sharra asked, "Could it have been someone else?"

Charles frowned. "Not likely, only the warehouses and Harriman have my radios, and it sounded like him."

"Do the Empire or the Serenites have radios?"

He sighed. "It sounded like Harriman and all of my radios have the same encryption. If there are other radios out there, Ship wouldn't have been able to decode the words. It has to be him."

He looked at the display. "Ship, change course for Messala."

Off to Messala

Sharra asked, "Why are you so concerned about this preacher? This is the same Herc, right? His message didn't seem all that urgent to me."

Charles didn't have a good feeling about it at all. "I had to convince Harriman to take the radio in the first place. I wanted a convenient way to make arrangements when we needed to meet. He travels, and I wanted to keep our meetings as secret as possible."

"Why?"

Charles looked at her. "I'm too dangerous. Anyone who is my friend is in danger. To the Serenites, any friend of mine is just another tool to be used to kill me."

He turned back to the display, "Ship, can you move over the position of our last visit and still be able to hide in the clouds?"

"I will attempt it."

The girl seemed frustrated, but said nothing.

Ship arrived over the wide but shallow lake that covered much of the western portion of Messala's crater. The display was erratic, showing the ground only momentarily when the clouds thinned.

Charles sighed. "They'll see us this low. Go up a little higher."

Sharra asked, "Can't they hear the buzzing noise of the ship's engines?"

"If they know what it means. That's what I'm hoping for. Harriman will recognize the sound and make contact. If we go too high, it can't be heard from the ground."

They made two passes over the settlement of Russleton on the eastern side of the lake and then Charles had Ship land on an island they had used before. It was within radio range, but hidden among the trees where no laser cannon could reach.

Sharra looked at the scene on the display. "Are we going outside?"

"I will a bit later. I need to stay by the radio for now."

It wasn't long. The radio whistle sounded.

"Charles, is that you?" Muffled, in the background, were other voices. The preacher was talking quietly in the back of his covered wagon.

"Yes, Harriman, I'm at the old location. I've got your books. What did you need to talk about?"

There was a long sigh. "I'd rather see you in person, if possible. I'm used to talking to people face to face, not to a little gadget around my neck. At least for important things. I suppose I could borrow a boat."

"I could hop over to your side."

"In the ship? That wouldn't be wise."

"No, I can fly over, just me, like a Kimmer. I've learned a few things."

"Hmm. That sounds like you. Can you reach the lumber yard I showed you a while back, perhaps in an hour or so? It should be deserted this time of day."

"I can do that."

"Good. See you then."

Charles said, "Message end." The radio went silent.

Sharra stared at Charles for a moment. He seemed to be lost in the display, but there was nothing showing but a maze of tree branches.

"Well, what are you going to do now, wait for a breeze to catch your sailsuit?"

He looked up as if he had forgotten she was there. "Oh, no, that won't work. You usually have to sail from high ground to a lower level. But I have a way around it."

She frowned. "You're worried about him."

He nodded. "He's not himself. Something is weighing on his mind."

"He sounded okay to me."

He shook his head and got to his feet. She did, too. He stepped to go around her, but he brushed up against her arm.

Whack! It happened too quickly. He put his hand to his face, where it stung.

Just a little dazed, he realized Sharra's eyes were wide. She was breathing hard and she had her knife in her hand.

He stepped back. "What?"

She blinked and shook her head, sheathing her knife. "Sorry. It was just instinct."

He nodded. "I need to get to the ladder."

She stepped back out of his way.

He was grateful to go down to the cargo level, backpack in hand.

Well she certainly isn't a spy sent to seduce me. What is her problem?

Whatever the issue, he wasn't going to make the mistake of getting any closer to her than was necessary.

It was a few minutes later when she came down.

He was shaking the folds of his sailsuit, making sure that the straps were fixed correctly. The books for Harriman were secured in a small pack low on his back under the sail.

She said, "You're really going to fly over to the other side of the lake in that?"

"Yes."

"How?"

He held his impulse rifle. "It looks like a simple metal rod, but it's really a tractor-pressor beam projector. If I fold these flaps down, I can stand on it and shoot myself up into the sky. Once I have altitude, I can ride the winds to get across the water."

"You're crazy."

"I've done it many times." He managed a smile. "It's easier than hiking through the forest when you've forgotten the path."

She almost managed a smile in return. "So you *did* get lost!"

He shrugged.

She frowned again. "This could be a trap. Aren't we pretty close to the Serenite border?"

He sighed. "You're right. It could be." He reached for the radio at his collar. "That's why I'm wearing this. If I get in trouble, Ship is ordered to take off on its own and fly directly back to Stampz. I'm not going to let anyone capture it, or worse, destroy it. If you want to go outside to look around, you should do it now. If there is trouble, it just might take off without you."

She shook her head. "I don't know why you take this risk. The deliveries for Stampz, I can understand. It's payment for a safe place for the Alpines. I don't see any advantage in helping a Herc with his holy crusade or whatever it is."

He shook his head and went to the airlock.

"You're leaving now?"

He nodded. "Better to be there early. I can scout for trouble."

And he didn't like the way she talked about Harriman, but he didn't want to fight with her about that either.

They went outside. She swatted at something buzzing near her ear.

He said, "You can listen in on the radio if you want. Ship will tell you how to turn the radio on."

She frowned. "Serenites might have radios, too."

He shook his head. "Ancient ones, probably, but unless they're recharged, they're useless. And like I said before everything is encrypted. Without my code they couldn't understand anything we say." He kept his own reservations quiet.

She looked ready to make some other argument, but he stepped on the fold-out steps and launched skyward.

He sighed. It was refreshing to feel the wind on his face.

He tilted his chin. "Ship, are you there?"

Seemingly from all around him, the voice replied. "Yes, I hear you."

"Notify me when Sharra is back inside the ship."

"Acknowledged."

The cloud layer was low today. He concentrated on locating the lumber yard. From what Harriman had shown him before, workers cut down appropriate sized willow trees and bundled the major limbs into rafts and sailed those to the lumber yard. The trees were stripped and pulped and made into a paper. In addition to the initial demand for paper to make the church's books, the Russleton people had discovered that there was a market for paper from other cities as well. They were attempting to scale up paper production to see if they could turn a profit.

Those rafts could only sail up to the eastern shore using the darkwind's west to east flow, so in mid-day there wouldn't be much activity.

"Sharra Abeth has returned to the interior. The airlock has been sealed."

"Good. Thank you."

It wasn't long before her voice came on. "Charles? Are you there?"

"Yes, I can hear you. You don't have to shout."

"There's wind noise. You're still flying?"

"Yes. I'm making a circling pass, looking for anyone who might be alerted to my presence. Thus far, no one has noticed me. I don't buzz like the beamship, and no one has looked up."

"You be careful."

"I'll talk later."

"Okay."

While the white sailsuit might be difficult to see against a background of white clouds, it was still likely to stand out once he was on the ground.

Maybe I can get someone to make me a sailsuit in different colors—something that would look like a farmer's work clothes at a distance. Darkwind would be scandalized, though.

He settled down behind a tall pile of brush, and waited in silence in case someone had seen him and came to investigate.

"Ship, I'm safely down," he whispered into the radio. "I'll be moving to a better location. I'll check in every ten minutes or so."

"Understood."

Sharra said, "What are you doing?"

"I landed in a hidden location. I now have to walk to a place where Harriman can find me."

"Be careful."

He shook his head. She was a nag. Was she really worried about his safety, or did she realize she was trapped inside the beamship, but unable to give Ship any important orders?

Over time, he'd locked down many of Ship's functions. He could still order the laser cannon to fire at an enemy, but no one else, not even Darkwind, had that capability, and Charles's apprentice was the only other person trained to fly the beamship.

He brushed his hand over his skull. There was a little fuzz. He'd need to shave it again soon. He'd been bald for years now—a constant reminder of his guilt—all the people he'd killed and the mistakes he'd made.

He'd never leave the beamship where someone else could make those same mistakes.

The pulping machine had a large, four-sailed fan that caught the dark-wind and dawnwind gales for power. The sails had to be furled and unfurled to handle the uneven force of the winds, but by carefully trimming those sails, they could run the pulping machines for several hours each day.

He and Harriman had met by that place before. He kept to the shadows as he approached.

Charles found the abandoned millstone that had been used in previous years at that location and sat down. Russleton had failed to become a grain producer and the mill had been abandoned before the church took it over to make their paper.

Sharra spoke, "Hasn't it been over an hour now? Maybe he isn't coming."

"Sharra, you can listen, but don't make any noise for now. I'm out of sight, but someone might be able to hear your voice."

She whispered, "Okay, sorry."

It had seemed to be over an hour. He remembered a merchant back when he was a teenage dockhand at Port Gartner. That well-dressed man had constantly griped about the time. There was a bell-ringer in town, but the merchant was convinced that the chime was always late.

In one of the books Charles had read, it spoke of a wristwatch, just in passing, as if everyone in the world had a clock on their wrist. There were times when he wished he had something like that.

Normally, when he needed exact time, he just asked Ship. But not now, not when he had to keep quiet.

There was sound of footsteps. Harriman turned the corner. He smiled, then gestured Charles to follow him.

Hurriedly, they entered a doorway and found an empty room.

Harriman sighed. "I'm so glad to see you one last time."

Charles frowned, "What do you mean, 'one last time?'"

The old preacher showed his years as he sat on an old wooden crate and set his bag down beside him. "I'm afraid that I've made too much noise in the world. Some of the others have been captured, and I'm sure they're coming for me."

Unsettling News

"Who is after you?" Charles sat next to him. He listened, but other than the creak of an old wooden building, he couldn't hear any activity.

Harriman Moore, itinerant preacher and more recently the leader of a movement to print books, looked more worn out than Charles had ever seen him.

"It's been building over time, but recently the scribes have joined forces with the priests of the Way of the Earth, and have been making a lot of noise in the imperial court." He sighed. "Both of them are very entrenched into the politics of court life.

"The Way has always been annoyed with the idea of any other religions, but we were too small, and more active out on the fringes of the empire, so they didn't make too much of it—at least not until recently."

He smiled, and Charles saw more of the old Harriman in his eyes. "Putting Bibles into people's hands where they can read for themselves has inspired many. I had thought the idea of printing more might just be a dream, always just out of my reach, but so much has changed.

"The number of people who can read has blossomed. People are teaching each other how to read and there are many I've never met, just waiting for the opportunity to hold the book in their own hands."

Charles nodded. He pulled out a stack of five books and handed them over.

Harriman looked at the titles. "These will be helpful. It took two years to find and train the people who could accurately read pages from the original Bibles and produce plates for the printing press. They have done a wonderful job, but they ache to do more. If we can prove the value of printing to people who have no interest in the Bible, perhaps we can survive."

Charles nodded. "The scribes are making noise?"

"Oh, yes, and they have the ear of the emperor, day in and day out. To them, this surge of people who can read and write for themselves is a clear threat. And the idea of a machine which can make a whole book is a cause for panic.

"They have made the case to the court that we are bandits, stealing away the scribe's money, and the emperor's tax on those fees. It has been enough that guards have appeared, questioning us and threatening our operation. Some of us have disappeared mysteriously. Some have gone into hiding."

Charles frowned. "And how about you? I could relocate you to some safe location."

Harriman shook his head. "My life is getting up in front of people and telling people the story. I could never hide away in a cave somewhere. I do admit to peeking around the corner before walking out onto the street, but I still have my job to do."

"They'll come for you. You're the leader."

Harriman nodded. "Then they will come. And that's why I wanted to meet with you."

He opened his bag and pulled out a thick book and handed it to Charles.

"If I may be so bold, I wish to donate this to your library."

Charles carefully opened the black book, larger than most of the ones he had. It had stiff covers, thin wooden slabs covered in cloth. The binding was sewn and covered as well.

He had seen the earlier copy and this one was a much better crafted version. He opened the pages and read a few lines. "Of course this needs to be in the library. I will make sure of it."

Harriman nodded solemnly. "It is my dream to have a copy in every community. I never again want that situation where God's word was lost from the world." He smiled. "In spite of everything, copies are being distributed. I had hoped that they would be met with celebration, but even if they have to be smuggled in secret, the word is spread."

There was a knock on the door. Charles jerked, startled at the noise.

A voice called, "Harriman, it's time to go."

The preacher put his hand on Charles's wrist. "It's okay. There are people looking out for me."

Charles carefully secured the Bible into his small pack and Harriman collected the secular texts into his.

The man at the door—Harriman introduced him as James Sull—was perhaps in his thirties. Sull seemed startled at the sailsuit Charles wore, but took Harriman's bag and with the briefest of greetings, hurried Harriman off toward the trees.

Charles nodded to himself. Harriman wasn't alone. He'd built quite a collection of people who shared his dream and wanted to take care of him.

But if there were guards about, looking for the people who printed books, then perhaps he'd better get back to the beamship.

"Ship, I'm heading back."

"Acknowledged."

He was barely in the air, out over the lake, when Sharra asked, "Are you flying?"

"Yes. You can talk."

"What in the world are you getting yourself into? It's not enough that all the Serenites want you killed? You have to get involved in a criminal organization and have the Herc guards after you as well. You're crazy."

Charles grit his teeth and concentrated on getting a little more altitude before responding.

"Since when do you have such respect for Herc laws? And you believe the scribes when they brand their competitors as bandits? That makes all Alpines bandits!

"Harriman Moore is my friend. He was the only friend I had at times, and the only source of wisdom I had in a world sadly lacking in it."

"But he—"

"Who do you think helped me bring the library back from Alexandria? It wasn't any Alpines. It was a little twelve year old Herc girl and Harriman Moore.

"My father said, 'An Alpine should be judged by the help he gives the world.'"

"Well, yes, but—"

"That library is the most important thing that's been done for the world in my lifetime, and there wasn't a single Alpine who helped me.

"So if that traveling preacher needs my help, he's going to get it! No matter what the emperor says."

She sighed. "On your own head. I just think you don't need any more enemies."

He agreed with her on that. He flew on in silence.

The tall beamship standing among the willows was easy to find.

"Ship, I'll be landing in a moment. Prepare your route to the Mulberry warehouse."

"Acknowledged."

· · ·

The warehouse codenamed Mulberry looked from the outside to be a simple farm with a hectare planted in corn, all wrapped up inside a small crater. There was a wagon trail that wound up the crater wall in a spiral. The beamship's landing site was in a small cove of trees near the buildings. Charles was in and out within an hour. Half of their blue cotton bales were unloaded and various crates of goods purchased from Franklin merchants were loaded into the ship.

Sharra was silent the whole time. Charles worked off his frustration loading the cargo.

It's not going to work out between us. There had been moments when they seemed to be cheerful together, but it didn't last. They had too many differences. And likely, someone had soured her on men anyway. *Probably when she was a slave.*

He couldn't blame her for that, but it wasn't something he could do anything about.

Jelica had a little of the same anger when she was captive at Terrance. She was much happier now, and so was the duke.

He suspected Sharra had suffered a worse time than Jelica.

I had a hard time being a dock worker, but it made me strong, and it helped me develop some skills as well, working with others. It would be sad to have part of your life so bad that you don't want anyone to know about it.

He wasn't ever going to ask her, and she didn't seem to want to tell him anything about her past. That was her choice.

On the flight from Mulberry to Apple, off in the trees about twenty kloms west of Condorcet, Sharra went down to the cargo level to take a nap.

Ship flashed text on the display, "There are currently unknown radio signals. Limited triangulation places the origin of the first party near Beltis Island. Unable to identify location of the other party."

Charles spoke quietly. "I understand."

The text vanished from the display. This wasn't the first time this had happened, and it was very worrying. Since the time he and the duke had acquired the radios, they had been thinking of radio as their own private magic. This recent discovery that Serenity was using radio as well was something he only discussed with the duke behind locked, soundproofed doors.

The duke was frustrated that Ship couldn't listen in on the signals. Former Grand Admiral Bardin had recently succeeded to the Red Throne and the limited news from the Serenite capital was disturbing to James for a number of reasons.

For one, the previous royal family of the Serenite Landrule, the Neelys, were his family members. He had fled from Posidonius as a child to escape a previous purge, and his mother hadn't survived, but there were cousins he knew, if they managed to survive King Bardin.

In addition, Bardin's consolidation of power increased the likelihood of a new invasion. The empire's hold on the lands south of Stampz down to Hubble and Condorcet were the most weakly defended. Even Stampz might be vulnerable to a major push.

Charles was content with the encryption. He didn't want Bardin's forces to be listening in to him either. The same with Ship's limited ability to triangulate the origin of the radio signals. Ship couldn't narrow the source down any tighter than a hundred kloms. That was enough to make Serenite's fortress on Beltis Island an easy guess, but if Serenity had the same capabilities, then the secret warehouses were still hidden.

Not that Charles was sure that Serenity was even aware of their radio messages. None of the small radios salvaged from the spacesuits could even report the existence of radio messages not encrypted to their same code. Long distance detection would depend on altitude, and thus, another beamship.

Charles could only hope Serenity's radios were salvaged museum pieces brought back to life somehow.

The more likely possibility was that Mt. Ural had sent their lone beamship down to contact their long-abandoned colony on Luna. The Serenites were descendants of the Uralites, just as the Hercs were immigrants from the abandoned space city Manhattan.

If the Uralites were now directly supporting King Bardin with *oldman* technology like radios and more laser cannon, or even their beamship, then things could get much worse.

Charles had faced the Uralite beamship before and never wanted to see it again.

...

At Apple, Charles unloaded all but one bale of blue cotton and took on a few more crates from Condorcet. He worked hard, not trusting the trees to hide Ship well this close to Serenite lands.

They lifted off, heading for warehouse Maple near Hahn.

Maple looked like a burned out farm, destroyed by the Kimmer back before the Terrance invasion. That warehouse got the last bale of cotton and Charles was back in the air, heading toward Stampz.

"Sharra!"

She came up the ladder. "What is it?"

"Are you staying at Stampz? You had mentioned leaving."

"Why do you ask?"

He hesitated. "I need to talk to the duke about an urgent matter."

"What?"

He shook his head. "State secret stuff. I can't say. But if you are staying at Stampz, then I'll land the beamship near the castle and you can hike back to the farm easily.

"If you're leaving, then I'll land the ship in one of the many hiding spots like it was before, and then fly using my sailsuit back to the castle, leaving you to find your own way from there."

She asked, "Do you want me to stay?"

He sighed. "Yes. Stampz is the safest place for Alpines right now. I'm sure you can handle yourself, but even it it's unpleasant here, stay a little longer."

She nodded.

Planning for the Worst

The beamship landed in a cloud of dust in the shadow of the castle.

Charles had the cargo door already open and was carrying the first crate out when Jed Tylan came running up.

"What's going on?"

Charles nodded to him. "Great, you're here. Tell the appropriate people that these crates are from the warehouse and tell the duke that I need an urgent discussion with him."

Tylan's frown went deeper. "On it."

The head of the Stampz guards turned and yelled at the gathering crowd. "Please stay back out of the Alpine's way."

Sharra slipped out without a word, carrying her bag and took the road toward the Alpine farm.

Charles had started a pile when some workmen came out with a cart to load them all up.

Charles smiled and waved to the crowd. When he unloaded the last crate he closed up the cargo door and went back inside to stow some last minute items and get any more detailed information about the radio messages.

It took a few minutes, but shortly he sealed everything up and went into the castle to talk to the duke.

...

Duke James closed the soundproofed door of his little privacy room and started another warmball for light. "Bad news?" he asked.

Charles said, "Ship got better readings on the Serenite's radio signals. One is definitely coming from Beltis Island, but we knew that already. It's the other one that's bad news."

"Did you locate it?"

"No, the triangulation failed again, but Ship examined the radio signal, and its strength followed a predictable rise and fall over time. According to Ship, the other side of the conversation was coming from an object in a high orbit around Luna, far above the atmosphere."

The duke sighed, "Mt. Ural."

"Probably. Either their beamship, or Mt. Ural itself, has moved into an orbit around Luna. Ship predicts that for a one-hour window every four or five hours, the Uralites can converse with the Serenites. They've been doing that for some time now."

The duke seemed lost in thought. Then he said, "The Uralite beamship has landed and left the Serenites with radios. The question is whether they are actively aiding the Serenite military, or just in negotiations. What do the Uralites want?"

Charles leaned back in his chair. "From Ship's observations back when we went into space, for hundreds of years Mt. Ural has been moving among the mostly uninhabited space cities, finding surviving remnants with their own farming capabilities. They take resources from the habits they conquer, and then move on. Their targets have been dwindling. They completely depleted the Vesta cluster and who knows how many farming habitats are left in the Ceres cluster.

"Long term, Mt. Ural needs food for its population. Either they want their beamship to lift food supplies from Luna, or else send their excess population down to live on Luna.

"I don't see them giving the Serenites anything for free."

James nodded. "King Bardin would love to have an influx of *oldman* technology, but just how many Uralites are we talking about?"

Charles shrugged. "I don't know. But if the original asteroid has been tunneled throughout, then there could be millions. Still, they've been importing their food for a long time, I suspect it's a lot less."

"Bardin wouldn't welcome that many. He wants the weapons, not the people. The Landrule of Serenity has been feeling its own population pressure, bounded on all sides as it is by empire lands."

Charles shook his head. "The Uralite beamship is a brother to my own ship. Very similar in cargo space. With special fittings, they might be able to bring down two or three hundred people at a time, at a guess. It's not like a million people marching off the beamship all at once. I bet they could take a few at a time. People come down, food goes back up for the remaining population."

The duke drummed his fingers on the armrest of his chair. "The people arriving would need to be fed and supported before they integrated into a Lunar lifestyle. They'd have no experience with a forty-eight hour day and the sunwinds. Their food would be different. The air would be different. Many would come down sick. They might even bring new diseases that are common on Mt. Ural but unknown here."

Charles was impressed. The duke had taken classes on Alp Island before the Burn and learned much about ecology from Charles's own father and the other Alpine instructors. James was looking at the problem as if he were going to have to host the immigrants. Would King Bardin see the issues as well?

"Bardin will use this to push the boundaries." The duke nodded. "If he can manage to take over empire lands, then he can settle Uralites there and use the conquered farmland to supply food to his new allies.

"He won't want the Uralites walking around in Serenite cities."

"Why is that?"

James gave him a sad smile. "People always suspect others of using the same strategy that they use themselves. Serenity has become very adept at sending spies into empire territory that then act without warning. Bardin will suspect the Uralites of using the same technique against him. His throne is too new to risk that."

He shifted in his chair. "How many people know this?"

Charles shook his head. "You and me. Ship knows how to keep secrets. It notified me with a written message when Sharra Abeth was not in sight."

The duke smiled. "How did your trip with her go?"

"Not well. There were insults, yelling, and she hit me once. We ended in silence, but at least she hasn't left Stampz yet."

James shrugged without commentary.

"Back to the issue at hand. I need to notify the imperial court about this new development as soon as possible. The Serenites could already be preparing a major new invasion, with more weapons than before."

"Sorry, but I decline to land in Hercules and give them the message."

James chuckled, "Yes, probably not a good idea."

The empire hadn't adopted a shoot-on-sight policy against the beamship like Serenity, but that didn't mean they wouldn't try if the opportunity arose and they felt threatened.

The duke asked, "You've seen Mt. Ural? How big is it?"

"Only from a very great distance. I don't know the exact size. Ship might know. But it's a large rock, tunneled within and built up on the outside. Its beamship just appeared as a dot beside it. Why? Is it important?"

"Probably not. I just wonder if it could be seen from the ground."

"Possibly, but it would be a rare sighting, like the Angel stations."

James nodded, remembering the reports Charles had given him. "The butterflies in space. I've never seen one."

Charles just nodded. It was a disadvantage of living on a cloudy planet. Seeing the stations, or even a sky full of stars was something only a handful of people had experienced.

James took a deep breath. "Charles, you rarely allow anyone on your ship, but I was watching you unload cargo through that large side door. I have a very unusual request to make."

...

Duchess Jelica listened, her eyes wide. "You want *me* to go?"

Her husband nodded. "The Sheb estate in Franklin has the largest herd of horses in the world, maybe as many as twenty. It may be the only other place in the world where Angela could be bred. We've discussed it before."

She nodded. "Well yes, you talked about a trip."

"And you always said you were too busy to leave your healer duties. But isn't it true that you could take a few days to make this state visit for me?"

She glanced at Charles, listening. "Just me and the horse in the beamship?"

"No, more than that. Paul Trask would go along to attend to Angela and keep her calm. You'll have a driver for the carriage. You'd be dressed up in your finest to meet with my father's family. Charles tells me that he can make room for a traveling carriage and an ox, so you could bring your clothes and such. He'll land outside of Franklin and you'll arrive at the estate just as if you'd ridden in the carriage the whole way.

"If everything goes smoothly, then you can return the same way, making contact with the ship via radio to come pick you up. If there are problems, then you can always ride the carriage back. Retrieving the mare and her foal will be a problem for the future."

Charles imagined how much cleanup he'd need to do, carrying livestock in the cargo hold. As a dockworker, he'd seen what it was like when animals were transported on ocean-going vessels. He'd definitely need to make sure Ship kept the beam gravity on the cargo level as close to normal as possible.

Jelica asked, "And you can't come along?"

James shook his head. "Things are too risky right now. I wouldn't send you if I wasn't confident that you can handle this."

. . .

Charles was getting itchy the second day the beamship was sitting out there in plain sight. The word had gotten out and people from all over Stampz were taking time out of their day to come look at it. He smiled and waved at a mother showing her children the strange metal thing that had come to visit.

But if the word was out, then surely there were unfriendly eyes watching. He wanted to lift off and get somewhere unpredictable as soon as possible.

But Jelica had preparations to make.

Heidi was called in and promised to spend the noon hours each day to help the two nurses Jelica had been training. Unless Jelica could be confident that the health of the Stampz people was being taken care of, she couldn't concentrate on the state visit.

Jelica's biggest worry was the impression she had to make at the Sheb estate. She was taking intense training with a couple of older servants that had been with James since he was a teenager—teaching him to survive the political pressure when he was a Serenity-born outsider in the court at Hercules. Jelica had to be familiar with the manners and protocols she would face.

From her arrival, James had ordered the best dresses his seamstresses could create as gifts for Jelica. The latest version was being rushed to completion. A couple of her previous dresses were also back being enhanced with extra trim to catch the eyes of other court ladies.

Her hair was was being trimmed and styled. James caught a glance of her in the hallway with her face layered in some kind of cream.

The duke called him in for another secret meeting.

"Charles, how much space is left on your cargo floor?"

Charles sighed and shook his head.

On the third day, it was a spectacle as the crowd gathered to watch the laden carriage being backed into beamship's cargo door with four workers pushing. They secured the carriage in place with large flat stones and then the ox was led in to a small makeshift pen on the right side. The driver climbed up to set the brake.

Then came the duke himself, leading Angela the horse inside, leaving her in the care of Trask on the left side of the carriage.

Jelica came in through the airlock hatch in a white and blue trimmed traveling dress, complete with a matching bonnet over her carefully styled hair.

Last came two men with a bale of blue cotton and several crates. They were last-minute replacement workers for the Mulberry warehouse.

Charles sealed all the doors and looked over his cargo floor. He didn't trust the two animals. The carriage might shift if Ship had to maneuver, and other than Jelica, he barely knew Trask and didn't know the other two men at all.

Unusual Cargo

Jelica appeared calm, sitting in a chair against the hull—there was no way she could climb the ladder in her fancy dress. Still Charles could sense her nervousness. The state visit was much more than a visit with James's relatives and an opportunity to breed horses.

Charles hadn't been told, but he suspected that Jelica carried urgent messages for the emperor. Probably in that large, beaded tapestry bag she held tightly in her gloved hands, was a detailed analysis of King Bardin's communications with the Uralites and the possibility of a new Serenite invasion.

It would be up to Duchess Jelica of Stampz, the Healer of Terrance, to make the right contacts at the Sheb estate and pass that analysis to the person who could get it rapidly to the imperial capital. Charles had memories of that time years ago when he was sent as an ambassador from Stampz to plead for gunpowder from the Southern Court. He hoped Jelica was more successful than he had been.

Charles raised his voice. "We will be lifting off in a couple of minutes. Those of you managing the animals, be prepared. It will feel like the ground is shifting under your feet, like a quake. Expect the animals to be startled."

Trask, by the horse, nodded. The other two moved closer to the ox.

Jelica gave him a slight smile as he reached for the ladder.

Up at the command deck, he sat in the chair and whispered to the Ship. "Have you seen any suspicious activity?"

Ship's replies were all in text on the display. "No."

"Are you prepared to lift?" They had discussed the problem with the animals previously. *I'm more worried about it than Ship.*

"Prepared."

"Lift."

Outside, the crowd moved back as the dust began to blow. Then, they lifted, at a painfully slow pace. But then it picked up. Charles didn't relax until the clouds covered them.

"Ship, give me a divided image. Inside and out."

On the right-hand side, he could see people trying to keep the animals gentled. The buzzing noise of the cirrance couldn't be helped. Perhaps they would get used to it.

The trip to Mulberry warehouse was likely to take four hours, but traveling high above the ground, there should be no difficulty en route.

An hour into the trip, he climbed down the ladder.

The animals were content with their feed bags, and it hadn't gotten too stinky yet.

He sat down beside Jelica. "How are you doing?"

She smiled. "I'm looking forward to the couch in the carriage. This chair is not terribly comfortable."

He shrugged. "I'll keep that in mind for next time."

"Next time?"

He sighed. "That's the way it goes. Your husband asks me to try something new and unusual, and it turns out that I end up doing it on a regular basis. I realize that this is a cargo ship, but I didn't really think about it in those terms until the duke started shipping cotton this way."

She smiled. "He does that. You don't really see what he's thinking about behind that smile until he's suddenly explaining some grand detailed plan that he's been working on."

"You probably see more smiles than I do. He always complains that I bring him bad news."

She nodded. "I expect nothing less from you."

He shrugged. They were just killing time. He glanced over at Trask. The man was whispering in the horse's ear.

When Charles first came to Stampz, Angela was the duke's pet and none of the other caregivers were as close to the horse as he was. Over time, the man's duties and now Jelica had taken much more of his time. Paul Trask had been one of the boys that fed the horse. Now he was probably closer to the animal than the duke.

Charles hadn't heard, but now he wondered if Trask would be staying with the horse or returning to Stampz with Jelica.

He turned to Jelica. "Would you like a book? I have several up on the command level."

She smiled. "Yes, that would be good."

"Any topic?"

She shook her head. "Just something to get my mind off of things."

He went back up the ladder and checked the shelf he'd built about a year earlier. It was wide enough for thirty books or so, with a cotton band that kept the books secure even if there was some disturbance.

He had turned Harriman's Bible over to Lucas and seen that it was properly shelved. The books that he'd read on his trip to Orientale were returned to the library as well and he had picked up a number of others to replace them.

He was thumbing through the spines, looking for something that might appeal to her when he noticed a white item sticking out below the shelf. He tugged it clear with his fingernail.

It was a white feather. He couldn't identify the bird species at first glance, but perhaps it was a gull. He hadn't seen a gull in a long time. It looked a little flattened, like perhaps it had been weighed down under something.

Or maybe used as a bookmark? Had it fallen out of one of the books?

He set it aside and chose a biography of Lucretia Borgia. He hadn't a clue who that was, but it sounded like a female name.

When he handed it over to Jelica, she puzzled over the title. She asked, "I was told you and Sharra didn't get along."

"We had some good moments, but we argued a lot. I know everybody assumed we'd hit it off, but really, we're very different people."

"That kind of thing is hard to predict. Still if you had gotten along...."

He sighed. "I know. We're both unattached Alpines nearly the same age. I understand. But don't hold your breath."

She nodded, opened her book and waved him off.

Charles went back up.

...

The corn stalks waved as the beamship landed near the trees. The warehouse crew was already hurrying toward them, probably puzzled by the unscheduled landing. Charles hadn't even radioed ahead to warn them this time.

It was hardly clockwork as they unloaded. The cotton bale had to be unloaded first, before they could even move the ox into place between the traces.

Trask kept the horse out of the way until the carriage was unloaded.

Charles didn't even try to help with it all. He spoke to the warehouse people, giving the commander the instructions from the duke. There was a sheet of paper that detailed the new items unloaded for the warehouse and the information on the replacement workers.

Charles helped Jelica up into the carriage. She smiled. "I'll have to finish this book. It's intriguing."

He shrugged. "That's okay. I have others."

As soon as the carriage was on its way, with Angela the horse following behind, Charles was tempted to borrow a broom and sweep out the dung, but he really didn't like being out in the open, even in this relatively secluded crater.

"Ship, is everyone out?"

"Yes."

"Then seal the doors and lift off. I want to go back to one of our hidden sites near Stampz."

"Acknowledged."

He climbed the ladder and the beamship lifted off, accelerating rapidly. It was a contrast to how they had left Stampz.

"I hope it doesn't get stinky in here before I get everything cleaned out."

"I could circulate external air if you need it."

"I'll be okay. At least you won't be bothered."

"I monitor the air for contaminants."

Charles shrugged. How could he possibly explain the visceral aspects of stink to a machine?

There were times when he thought Ship and he were buddies. They could talk about many different things and it was very nice to have a non-judgmental friend to discuss things with.

"Ship, what did you think about Sharra Abeth?"

"She was female. My baseline for assessing female humans is limited."

He chuckled. "Yes, I guess so, just Judith and Heidi, right?"

"There was also Nan Piper, a member of an earlier crew."

"Oh, a Manhattanite? What did she do?"

"Cargo management and piloting approach."

"What's piloting approach? Although I could use a cargo management expert as well."

"There is navigation, which is choosing the path to travel between one celestial location and another, but there is also the need for high precision, short range piloting when entering the docking facility of a zero gravity station. This was called piloting approach."

Charles remembered Ship's reluctance to tackle certain docking situations during their trip to locate Alexandria and bring back the books. There had been a few minor bumps and scrapes, if he remembered correctly. Would a human piloting approach expert have done that better?

I've never really learned how to pilot this ship as well as I should. Once I discovered that all I had to do is talk to Ship directly and order it to fly, I never really learned all the details of the manual controls. Are they better? More precise?

He was conscious of the old bloodstain on his chair. Ship had been the last ship surviving the second Manhattan immigration, when several thousand were brought to the York peninsula to start a second settlement there. York had been conquered by the Serenite navy and the beamship was captured. The new owners attempted to use the ship as high speed communication between ports in the Crisium Sea, but they never learned to pilot it themselves.

A nameless York pilot had hidden Ship's ability to talk as well as its laser cannon. That pilot had disobeyed his Serenite master's orders and had been killed for it. The Serenites had barely made it to the ground safely using the manual controls, and quickly lost their lives to a Kimmer hunter. And there, Ship rested for nearly a century, until Charles decoded the security password and became Ship's new master.

"Alert: I detect smoke."

Charles jerked upright. "What? Something is burning?"

"It is faint."

"On the cargo deck?"

"Possibly. Comparing images from earlier today, there is a crate next to the cargo door that wasn't there prior to loading."

Charles grabbed for the ladder and dropped the whole distance to the cargo floor with a thud.

"Where is it?"

"Against the wall, near the ox excrement."

Charles jumped the distance in one bound.

It was a simple wooden shipping crate with an identifying number, just like all the others he had been transporting between the warehouses.

He tugged at the lid, but it was stiff. He tugged harder, and it opened up.

For an instant he couldn't understand what he was seeing. And then he did.

The crate was two-thirds filled with gunpowder. Half buried in the powder was a cracked warmball. The extra oxygen leaking through the cracks made the puck inside burn extra bright.

"Ship, it's a bomb!"

Ship's Explosion

"Ship, open the cargo door!"

"There are security—"

"Override everything! This'll kill us both!"

He forced the lid back in place. Just opening it had increased the oxygen to the smoldering wick inside the warmball. If he tried to fish the cracked warmball out of the powder, it would likely just trigger the explosion.

The cirrance noise vanished and the cargo hatch began to slide sideways.

Charles lifted the large crate as gently as he could.

My dream! This could be it. For years now he'd dreamed of dying in a fiery blaze, just like his parents and all the people he knew on Alp Island.

The wind roared, sucking up anything and hurtling it out through the widening opening. His feet skidded on the cargo floor, trying to pull him outside as well.

But he dared not drop the crate to reach for a hand hold.

The crate thudded up against the edge. *Almost wide enough!*

The door moved more, and Charles felt the crate being ripped from his hands, almost dragging him out into the sky with it.

He braced his hands on the edges of the widening gap. "Ship! Close the door! Close it now!"

For a brief moment, he feared that the ship couldn't hear him over the howling wind, but then the door reversed. For long seconds he stared out at the endless clouds. If it sucked him out, he'd have a long fall, with no sailsuit to allow him to land safely.

And then there was a brilliant flash with heat on his face, as the bomb went off. But the winds had taken it far enough away that the ship was safe.

The door closed and the wind died. Charles slumped to the floor.

"Ship, are you okay?"

"Yes. There was no external damage."

One of those workers was a Serenite spy. They couldn't get a laser cannon in place to take him out, so they smuggled a bomb inside.

They'll keep trying to kill me forever until they get it right.

Unless they thought they had succeeded.

"Ship, can you make a loud noise, like an explosion?"

"Yes, but there was already an explosion."

Charles was putting the pieces together as he talked. "Yes, but if we wanted people on the ground to think that the beamship itself had been destroyed, then it would be a much bigger explosion, right? Can you focus a very loud explosion sound downward, so that many people will hear it?"

"Yes, however you need to protect your hearing. I can't muffle the interior well enough. Wrap your head with cloth. It would be better if you climbed up to the upper cargo level."

"Yes, I'll do it. But we need to act fast." He got to his feet and climbed as fast as he could. He stopped to snatch up his sailsuit and climbed up to the upper cargo deck.

There were a few dusty crates up there, small ones he'd carried up the ladder by hand a year ago. It was mainly just emergency food rations and a few items he wanted out of his way.

"Ship set a ballistic course for a hiding place, make your fake explosion sound, and then turn off all radio and beam energies. Mt. Ural might be monitoring us from a distance. You need to look like a damaged derelict until it's time to land. Can you do that?"

"Yes. It will be uncomfortable for you."

"I can live with that. Bundling my head now."

He wrapped the sailsuit around his head a couple of times and pressed his hands over his ears.

The sound, when it happened, was deafening. It was like the world ripped apart.

But then there was nothing but ringing, hissing noise in his ears.

Cautiously, he unwrapped his head, just as all weight vanished. He was falling!

He reached for a handhold, but there was nothing. He felt the urge to vomit, but held it back.

At least he had some experience with zero gravity.

"Ship? What's going on?"

The reply was faint, buried in the ringing noise in his ears.

"I have turned off all beam energies as you ordered. We are in free fall."

"Ship, I can barely hear you. My hearing is messed up. Are we falling?"

Ship's voice got louder. "Yes, but we are falling upward. We are on course."

Charles kicked against a crate floating with him. That sent him toward the ladder. He gripped it and climbed down to the command level. A loose book and the white feather were floating in the air. He was grateful the other books were all secured.

"Tell me what's happening?"

"I followed your orders, I made sure we were still on the correct ballistic path to Stampz. I focused the sound of a high brisance explosion toward the ground, and at the same time turned off all beam energies. If the other beamship or Mt. Ural is monitoring us, then it will appear that the gunpowder bomb caused sufficient damage to my mechanism that a secondary explosion of my power cell occurred."

Charles made it into the command chair. There was a strap that he'd never bothered to dig out, but he needed it now. He could barely hear the click as it fastened, holding him in place. *Is my hearing permanently damaged?*

"But we can land okay?"

"Yes. When we are close to the ground, I will regain control of the tumbling motion and land properly."

The display was off. "Can you show me what's going on?"

The swirling clouds threatened his stomach again.

"Turn it off. I'll have to trust you."

The floating book came close enough to snatch. He wedged it beside him in the chair.

"Ship, would the bomb have caused enough damage to destroy you?"

"Possibly, if it was close enough to the central mechanism. It would certainly have ruptured the hatchway and eliminated my ability to go back into space to recharge. Plus, your human body would have been injured past recovery."

"That's one way to put it." He could imagine he would be blown to bits.

It was a few long minutes before Ship said, "Prepare for landing."

Charles sighed. There was nothing he could do but stay put and hold on.

There was a lurch to the side and then he felt very heavy for a moment. The white feather dropped to the floor. There was the noise of crashing crates both from above and below.

He winced. All of those crates had been floating in the air when the gravity returned. Everything was a mess.

The cirrance was loud for a few seconds and then he felt it. They were down, and there was no sound other than the ringing.

"Ship, is there any damage?"

"Not to my structure, but your cargo needs attention."

. . .

Charles swept up most of the spilled food, sadly mixed with ox dung, and dumped it far enough from the landing site that he shouldn't find bears trapping him inside. Other than some year-old trail bread from the upper cargo deck, his food supplies were mostly gone.

The landing site was particularly nice, sheltered from the winds by a nearby cliff and surrounded by tall pines. Luckily, the landing blast hadn't knocked the trees down this time.

"Ship, you'll have to make do with passive protection until I get back."

"I did not see any buildings or roadways in this area on the way down, but I had a limited time to examine the terrain."

"Where are we, exactly?"

"Closer to Humboldt Sea than Stampz. The tumbling of the hull caused some drift that I hadn't predicted. I cannot guarantee that I won't be discovered."

"If the word gets out that you were destroyed, then nobody will be looking for you anyway."

"You discovered me at Sheep Totem Crater with no hint that I existed. Kimmer and trappers likely travel in this area. If I cannot use pressor beams to keep intruders at a distance, I could possibly be damaged. For example, pry bars attempting to open the outer airlock hatch might damage the seal. Due to the operational angle of my external beam projectors, they work best at a distance."

Charles smiled. Ship appeared nervous about being left alone. *Were the attempts to destroy it having an affect on the machine? Just how alive is Ship, really?*

Traveling in space, Ship had been very cautious, trying to keep from being detected and even willing to attack the other beamship to ensure its safety.

How much of that was to protect his master, and how much was it plain self interest?

What would Ship be doing now if it didn't have a master?

So much of its behavior was the result of old orders, some by Charles, some by previous masters, and even some by the Project command when they passed too close to Ceres. Ship's personality had changed somewhat when that happened.

But Charles trusted Ship. He'd walked off and left it on its own before and it had waited faithfully for him to return.

"Ship, what are your orders if I leave here and don't return?"

"After fifty years, relocate to Stampz and seek a new master, however, I am unable to do that if I am prohibited from using my beam projectors."

"Okay, let's alter the orders. If you determine you are in immediate danger, you are allowed to use your beams. If I don't return within one year, go to Stampz as before. For now, you are in hiding and shouldn't use beams or radio or take any action that would attract attention."

Ship said, "If you leave and are discovered, then enemies could reasonably infer that you landed safely, thus I still exist intact."

"Then you'll just have to trust that I won't allow myself to be discovered."

"You are less likely to be discovered if you stay here."

"I need food and supplies. I was low before, but after the crates were destroyed, I have less."

"You have hunted animals for food before."

"I also need to contact the duke to let him know what happened."

"If too many know you live, then all this hiding is for nothing."

An idea crept into his head. If Ship really wanted its own safety above all else, it could quickly kill him and then Ship would be free to monitor the enemy radio signals and find a time when it could lift off Luna unseen and find its own way out in space where it could recharge itself forever.

No, Ship would never do that.

Charles shook off the thought. Ship really was a different kind of person, and that kind of selfish treachery was alien to it.

"I'm sorry, Ship. There are things I have to do. I trust you'll be able to cope while I'm gone."

Charles collected his plain sailsuit and the impulse rifle, leaving his decorated suit in the Ship. He also took a charged radio collar and a small pack with the essentials.

This is a good time for a forest camouflaged sailsuit. But at least people will think I'm Kimmer.

Charles waited until the early evening, when the winds were just picking up, before lifting up half a klom into the sky. He wanted to get a good overview of where Ship was hidden. Then he boosted again, trying to get a feel for the landmarks in the area. Eventually, he'd have to find Ship again.

Off to the north, he could see the waters of the Humboldt Sea. He really was pretty far from Stampz.

He sailed with the rising winds to the east for an hour until he saw a glimmer of light from a filled crater. He landed and found a place to huddle down for the peak of the darkwind.

Charles let himself doze for a couple of hours, but no longer. He had to get the news to the duke before any other messenger could arrive from the Franklin area.

Only when the wind began to falter did he take off again, this time flying west against the easing darkwind, forced to use the impulse rifle's boost time and time again to make headway toward Stampz.

It seemed like hours had past when he landed on the easter side of the crater, as far as he could get from the Stampz guard stations.

Finding a hiding place among the trees, he turned on the radio and tapped on it. *Tap, tap, tap.* He waited a minute, and then repeated the process.

"Hello? Is someone trying to call me?" It was the guards from station overlooking the Gate.

Charles stayed silent. He didn't want to talk to the guards.

Someone cleared their throat. Charles recognized the speaker. It was the duke. He hoped James remembered the procedure.

Charles tapped a control on the radio and shifted to a private code, one known only to Charles and the duke. They'd never really used it before.

Over the private channel, James asked, "Is this Charles?"

"Yes." Charles felt relieved. "I'm sorry to say I'm dead."

Nighttime Encounter

Duke James grumbled. "I was just getting to sleep. What's this nonsense, and why the secret channel?"

Charles settled down in his hidden nook, just barely able to see lights from the castle in the distance. "Sorry. I didn't mean to make it a joke. Here's the short version: One of the replacement workers for Mulberry smuggled a bomb aboard the beamship and I barely dumped it into the sky before it killed me. I took the opportunity to fake the explosion of the beamship."

"Is Jelica okay?"

"Yes, she left in her carriage with just the driver and Trask before I lifted off. And I think it had to be one of the warehouse workers who smuggled the bomb aboard and triggered the warmball designed to set it off right before he left."

"How can you be sure?"

"It wasn't a small bomb. It was a standard large crate, complete with numbers, two-thirds full of gunpowder. Only a warehouse worker could have put that together and gotten it on the list of items to be shipped. It makes sense that one person working alone was both the person who got the bomb onboard and who started the trigger."

"So now we have a spy working at the Mulberry warehouse." The duke sighed. "Why did you fake the beamship's destruction?"

"Because they'll keep on trying to kill me, unless they think they succeeded. I never expected a smuggled bomb. If Ship hadn't smelled smoke from the trigger, I'd never have known. I just barely got rid of it in time. What will they think of next time?"

"I can see your point, but you can only keep up the pretense of being dead if no one can see you. The beamship can't be there for deliveries or to monitor the radio signals from Beltis."

Charles sighed. "I know. But, when the moment came and the gunpowder bomb exploded in my face, I only had a few seconds to act. The fake explosion of the beamship had to occur nearly the same time as the gunpowder bomb. We were above the clouds, but I had Ship send a loud boom back to the ground. My ears are still ringing from it.

"We pretended to be just a chunk of metal falling through the sky, just in case the Uralites were watching. Ship is in a hidden location for now, but I had to get close enough to Stampz to get word to you."

James said, "I can't say I like this plan, but it can be reversed if necessary. You and Ship are both safe and undamaged. What are your immediate plans, other than to stay out of sight?"

"Well, I lost most of my supplies during the explosion and the escape. I thought I'd sneak over to the farm and raid some food while we're still in the deep-sleep hours. After that, like you say, I'll pretend like I don't exist."

"What if I need you to come back to life?"

Charles frowned. "How about a flag?"

"Like at the castle?"

"It would be easier to see if there was a flag at the guard posts. They're not hidden. It wouldn't be any increased risk."

James said, "There aren't any flagpoles at the guard stations. I couldn't put up a flag in a hurry."

"Then have your guards install them. There's a book in the library about signal flags used on ships back in ancient times. Ask Lucas about it. You could make some variant for your guards. And then make a special one for me. Until then, I'll sneak back to the crater wall and wake you up to talk on our special channel. How about that?"

James grumbled. "More work, but I can see the advantages. Okay for now, but don't get caught stealing food. When the rumors of your destruction arrive, I'll try to manage them. Maybe I'll deny it ever happened."

"That's up to you."

"Some of your friends are going to be angry when you show up again, after they've mourned your death."

Charles chuckled. "Like I have that many friends! Some will be happy to see me gone."

James said, "Well, it doesn't look like I'll be getting much sleep tonight. Without beamship delivery and radio messaging, Stampz will have to change how we do business."

"At least nobody will be firing laser cannon at your cotton deliveries."

"Hmm. Go steal some food. You're not in my good graces right now."

Charles chuckled. "I'll try to contact you within a quad."

"Go away."

Charles turned his radio to the standard channel and listened. Nobody was talking. He turned it off.

He hadn't expected the duke to approve his attempt to hide, but it certainly seemed like the duke's plans were now upset.

I still have to gather my supplies.

From his position at the eastern side of Stampz, it was going to be difficult to cross the crater floor to where the farm was on the northern side without being seen by someone. Farmers had their own schedules to deal with.

He changed out of the sailsuit and stowed it into his backpack and in dark colored clothes, he hiked down the side of the crater wall, tending north.

Once he got close to the Alpine farm, he tried walking the footpath with a slouch. *I really need a hat to hide my bald head.*

If he had to stay hidden for a long time, maybe he should consider letting his hair grow, not that he liked the idea. As long as his guilt over past mistakes was still so painful, he needed to keep his head shaved.

A hat. That's what I need.

The first hint that earthrise was going to complicate his resupply efforts was the tips of the western edge of the crater wall catching the light. On a night when an overcast sky would have been helpful, he could tell that it was going to be a glorious nearly full Earth in a clear sky.

He hurried to a storage shed behind the main house. There were lights in the windows, probably someone reading a book, but likely there would be no one out on the grounds. Although it was supposed to be a farm, only Heidi was growing things on the property. Even Woodie Spark's wagon was gone. He'd probably left with one of the merchant wagon trains, getting back to work like he said.

He listened carefully for any sounds, anybody moving around. The ceaseless ringing in his ears was annoying. Sometimes it seemed to go away, but not if things were really quiet, like now. At least it was getting better than it had been at first.

Flour, butter, salt and several varieties of dried vegetables all went into his backpack. There wasn't as much dried beef as he'd hoped, but he got some of that as well. Perhaps he'd be setting up more rabbit traps than he'd thought.

He had enough for a month or so, if he was careful.

There was one of Edward's fish nets. He knew the man would be upset if he took it, but adding fish to his diet would be a good idea. He rolled it up tight and added it as well.

But now, the Earth was above the eastern rim and anyone could see him clearly.

He crept out of the storage building and walked, hunched over, heading for the closest rim wall.

On Luna, clear skies didn't last long, so he wasn't surprised to see a layer of clouds bisecting the Earth. If the clouds grew in size, he'd be grateful.

The trail to the northern guard house got steeper. He slowed down. He didn't need to appear to be fleeing the scene, even if he was a robber.

Not legally, though. I own that farm, but maybe Edward would have a claim on his net.

The trail began winding as the grade steepened. If he weren't still trying to look like anyone but himself, he'd change to the sailsuit and hop over the crater rim. But maybe he'd been doing that too much lately. His legs were complaining a little, and it was probably due to a lack of exercise. How many times lately had he chosen to fly rather than hike? Too many.

But now he was likely to suffer the consequences. He could never hide his identity while flying in a sailsuit, especially in places where ordinary Kimmer could never get aloft. Kimmer flew from cliffs. He flew anywhere.

The ringing in his ears was annoying, especially when it was as silent as it was now. The winds had died down to a gentle breeze and there were no sounds other than an occasional tree branch and perhaps an animal disturbing some fallen leaves.

And then, he heard a different noise, like someone disturbing rocks on the trail up ahead.

There shouldn't be anyone out here at this time of night.

He moved to the side of the trail, ready to hide among the trees if someone approached.

The only people using this trail were the guards themselves, and they would never make the trip in the dark, unless it was some kind of emergency.

He paused and listened carefully.

One person, and he's not in a hurry. The pace was regular and going downhill.

The trail's switchbacks from side to side meant that he was hearing someone on the next loop, a lot closer through the trees than along the path. And the noise of footsteps was growing fainter.

I just need to get off the path and let him pass while I hide.

Charles went back down the trail, looking for a good place to hide. Near the bend where the latest switchback began, there was a good stand of trees. He found a place to crouch down where he could watch the trail and be certain when the person passed.

I'd better get used to hiding. That's what I chose to do.

He waited, listening to the annoying ring in his ears, his heart beating, and a tree branch scraping against another.

But there were no footsteps. *Did he stop? Or go back up the trail?*

Maybe he heard me.

Charles checked his position, making sure that no one could see him. Thin clouds were obscuring the Earth, so hidden under the shadow of the trees, he ought to be invisible.

All he could do was wait.

But nothing was happening, and time was stretching out, seemingly endlessly. No doubt about it. The person on the trail above had stopped or turned around.

There's no good reason for that, unless they heard me.

A guard would investigate, musket in hand. It couldn't be a traveler. There was no good route on the other side. Even Edward, who had been a fisherman on the Humboldt Sea, traveling to Stampz, had taken a path down to the Spanish River and come in from through Stampz Gate. Nobody came over the northern rim.

Other than me. And I was sneaking in. Could this be a Serenite spy? It would make sense that he wouldn't want to be discovered, no more than I do.

There was no help for it. He couldn't hide all night long. He needed to creep up the trail, as silently as possible, and find out who it was. At worst, he just needed to be seen as an ordinary farmer from Stampz. *I really need a hat.*

He hunched over and eased out of his hiding place, peering up the trail.

Out of the deep shadows, there was a blur, and a figure hit him with a thick branch. Charles stumbled, instinctively grabbing for the person who hit him.

But just off the turning point of the trail, the ground dropped away. Both of them tumbled off into the darkness.

Out of the Ditch

Charles was acting on instinct—a dockworker's instinct honed in many brawls. Even when falling over the edge of a cliff, lunar gravity gave him seconds to grab his opponent and position for the impact.

Even as they hit the side of the ravine and tumbled, he knew something was wrong.

"Uugh!"

The voice cinched it. It was a girl. She'd hit him hard and fast, intending to knock him over, but she wasn't nearly as strong as he was.

They splashed into the narrow runoff that covered the bottom of the ravine. The fall was disorienting, but not enough to knock her out. She was instantly a mass of claws and teeth.

Charles held her tight, holding her arms to her sides. There was no earthlight down in the ravine.

"Hold still!" he yelled. If anything she struggled harder.

If this had been a real dockyard brawl, there was still a lot he could do to disable his opponent, but the softness of the girl disarmed him. He really didn't want to break her arm or dislocate her shoulder. He'd hold off knocking her out as a last resort.

"Who are you? Is it Sharra?" He wasn't about to release his grip, no matter how she struggled. Especially not with a girl who was quick to pull a knife on him.

"Let. Me. Go!"

It sounded like her.

"Stop fighting!"

She didn't.

"I can't let you go if you're going to knife me! You stop fighting, and I'll release you."

She splashed in the water, still trying to wrench free by her own strength. "Charles! Let me go!"

He held her another few seconds. "If you knife me, we'll never get out of this ravine!"

And he released, pushing her away. It didn't help. They were wedged together in the narrow crack.

She scrambled to get farther away from him, but there was really no room.

"We're in a nearly vertical crack in the rocks. Go too far that way and you'll fall even farther down. It's nearly straight up in all other directions."

She was panting, trying to get her panic under control. She tried to climb the wet sides, but it was a lost cause.

"Don't touch me. I can't handle that."

He hissed, "Like I didn't already know that! But I'm not about to react passively when attacked. I had no idea it was you! What are you doing here in the middle of the night?"

For a moment, there was nothing but her breathing.

"I saw you take off with the horse and carriage on board. I wanted to see you land. I asked around and nobody knew whether you would land back at the castle or not. Some were pretty sure you wouldn't, because of the danger from spies.

"So I hiked up to the crater rim, watching for you. I had a rough idea where your hidden landing site was, so I watched until I had to find shelter for the darkwind. I didn't see you land inside the crater either, so when I finally gave it up and headed back down toward the farm, I was ... frightened when I heard footsteps on the trail below."

He sighed. "And I heard you, so I hid. I should have stayed hidden longer and let you go on down."

"Why did you hide? It made you seem suspicious. I have to be cautious."

He sighed. "The Serenite spies were more than just a myth. There was a bomb on board the beamship. It almost killed me."

He gave her the summary.

"So you're playing dead?"

"Yes. That's why I had to hide. I can't let anyone know that I'm still alive."

She sighed. "Well, that's easy. We just stay trapped down here until we starve to death."

"Oh, I can get myself out easily enough. Getting you out will be harder."

"What do you mean?"

"I've got my beam projector. I can push the ground away from me. I could use that here, and jump up to the trail where we fell."

"But… do you have a rope?"

"No. If I can't hold on to you and carry you out with me, I'm not sure what I'll do."

She hesitated. "Are you sure it would work?"

"I used the same technique to lift Jelica Haren out of Terrance when we rescued her. Balance is tricky, but I think it'll work. We don't have far to go this time."

She shifted. "I hate sitting in this water. I'm soaked."

"Take your time. We've got all night. But, I really need to be over the rim and deep into the forest on the other side before dawn. I still have to hide from the guards up at the station. They can't know I was ever here either."

She sighed. "You'll have to take me along."

"Why?"

"Because of the risk that I'll betray the secret."

"Will you?"

"I don't think I would, on purpose. But once the word gets out that you've died, all those people who had paired us up are going to be watching my every move. If I fake being heartbroken, they'll see through me. If I act like it means nothing to me, then I'll have enemies on all sides."

"The other Alpines already know I was planning on leaving. I'll just make it true before the news arrives."

"You'd just walk away with no warning?" he asked.

"I might."

"Do you have all your gear?"

She hesitated. "No. And there's a few things I wouldn't have left behind. We don't want people searching for me."

"So you'd want to go back to the farm, pack your things, and maybe leave a note?"

She sighed. "I guess. I don't want to have to explain in person."

He said, "If you're coming, and if you need to make a round trip from here to the farm, then we don't have all night. Are you ready to be lifted out of here?"

"Well, explain it to me. What will happen?"

"I'll dig out my impulse rifle and deploy the foot steps. As well as I can in this tight space, I'll hold it aligned with my body, and holding you as well. I'll trigger the pulse, and we'll shoot up several meters high. I'll try not to overshoot the trail too much, but likely we'll tumble to the ground and hopefully, not fall back into the ravine."

"I should hold you. You're manipulating the controls."

"Probably true. And like I say, balance will be tricky. You need to be steady, not thrashing around."

Not waiting for a reply, he felt for the walls and got to his feet on the uneven surface. "Give me a second. I've got to stretch my legs. And watch out, with the water, it's a little slippery."

She hesitated, then started moving as well.

He fished out his impulse rifle and tapped the controls. Digits appeared in the darkness. He estimated how big Sharra was compared to his own weight. He had been using a fixed setting for some time as he flew, but this time, they wouldn't want to leap into the sky as fast as he did on his own. He wasn't wearing the sailsuit. All they needed was to get back up to where they fell off the edge.

"What are you doing?" she asked.

"Making sure the lift is correct. We're going to bounce several times, so just hang on until we're free."

"Um. Don't try to touch me, okay? I'm fighting myself here."

"Okay, but hold on tight. If you fall off, I don't know how to recover you."

He got into position, feet on the stirrups, hands on the controls and elbows in.

"Okay, I'm ready. Step on my feet if you can and hold on tight."

He could feel her reaching around and gripping his backpack. Then there was pressure on one foot and then the next.

Her voice was tense. "Okay. I think."

He tapped the controls. The first pulse lifted and shoved his side against the rocks. He leaned and triggered the second pulse.

She shrieked, and held on tighter. He hit another pulse, and there was earthlight. One more pulse as he leaned and then they collapsed on the trail. He rolled and hit a tree.

"Are you okay?" he asked. Her grip had come loose as they crashed.

She stuttered, "Ye-yes." She panted. "Mostly."

He pulled himself upright. "Do you need any help?"

"No."

He could see her on hands and knees, slowly working her way upright.

Charles said, "Turn slowly, I want to see if you're bleeding."

She shook her head. "Nothing more than scrapes." She took a deep breath. "You do that all the time while flying?"

"Mostly. I try not to hit the rocks on my way up."

She took a few steps. "I can make it. Wait for me as long as you can. I don't know how long it will take."

He nodded. "Okay, I'll be right here in those trees. But if the Earth gets past three-quarters across the sky, I'll move on. I have to get across the rim before dawnwind."

"I understand." She turned and headed down the trail.

He sighed and shook his head. It would be a much longer trip with her along, but he needed her on his side. Rejecting her at this point would be too dangerous.

He went over to the trees and found a place to stretch out. He needed to sleep, and this was his best opportunity.

. . .

The Earth was high in the southern sky when he saw the motion of a lone hiker down below. She was returning. He climbed back down from the overlook and went back to the place where he'd gotten some sleep, but not as much as he'd wished.

Hurriedly, he collected the clothes he'd draped on branches to dry and repacked his bag.

His dreams had been disturbing. The brief moments of holding on tight to a girl had replayed themselves several times, and he couldn't shake it off.

Up until now, he'd kept all females at a distance. Even the ones who smiled at him and wanted to talk were relatively easy to keep at arms length or better.

And I can't just dismiss Sharra as another Herc girl this time. The big problem with her was that she didn't like him and they had to travel together by necessity. She wasn't going to be crowding him close like some other girls had.

My problem is in my own head. I'm male, and I'll have to watch out for my instinctive urges.

Yes, I'd better make sure I don't get too close to her and trigger her *instinctive urges—and get myself knifed.*

When she got closer, he stepped out into plain sight on the trail, waiting for her.

Hiking Together

Sharra sighed, as she stepped into view. "There you are. I was afraid I'd forgotten where you were waiting."

It looked like she'd taken the opportunity to change into dry clothes as well. Her pack looked full.

"Did you have any problems at the farm?"

She sighed, walking on past him, up the trail. He stepped into place a few steps back. "Helva woke up as I was packing. I told her I was going. We ... avoided having another argument."

"You two apologized and made up?"

She chuckled. "Maybe not that far, but I did say she wasn't the reason I was leaving. She gave me cookies to take with me."

"Well, that's a bonus. I like Helva. She reminds me of a woman I knew back in Aristoteles. I never understood the reason for your arguments. I only saw the aftermath, not the battles."

Maybe it was easier for her to talk when she wasn't facing him. She said, "All the greatest troubles in my life came from trying to make a peaceful coexistence with the Hercs. I've gotten to where I can't stand them."

"I totally understand that. When I left Port Gartner, after having bought my way out of the indenture, I though things would be great. My brother and I had saved for years, so we rushed to buy a wagon of our own and took the Gaussland Trail. I thought it was for the purpose of finding land of our own.

"It turned out, he had fallen in love with a Herc girl and just wanted to travel with her."

"Oh no!"

Charles nodded. "Kimmer burned out the wagon and my brother left with the girl. I was no in a mood to be friendly with any Herc, even those who wanted to be friendly with me."

She looked back and frowned. "How old was your brother? Did he have any romances back on Alp?"

"Oh, no. At least none that I heard of. We were an academic family through and through. Both parents were instructors, and I practically lived in the lecture halls. If Rad, my brother, hadn't taken me off for a hunt in the woods that day, I'd have burned with the rest of them. I still dream of that."

"So you were on Alp Island during the Burn?"

He nodded. "The only survivors. We hid in a lava tube and came out to a sea of ash and mud. Herc scavengers found us and sold us for labor when they couldn't find anything valuable on the island."

He gestured, "We need to take the left branch here. The right goes to the guard house."

They took the narrow path, barely wide enough to walk through. She stumbled in the darkness. He barely caught himself before he grabbed her arm. She recovered on her own. He eased back another step.

"You've come this way before?" she asked.

"Yes. It's mostly a game trail, but it does go through a notch in the rim. I showed it to the guards once. I play a game with them, sneaking into Stampz and then telling Tylan, their chief, how I did it. They don't really like me."

"If you've told them about this path, then why are we taking it?"

"Because lately, I've been flying in and out of Stampz, rather than hiking. They should check this path, looking for lone Serenite spies, but since it's hardly the path for an invasion force, they tend to ignore it."

Near the top, they got down on their hands and knees to cross over. The winds, unprotected there at the top, kept all trees and brush from growing very tall. With the earthlight still strong, they had to keep out of sight of the guard station.

They took a break once they were out of sight on the downslope.

She leaned against a tree. She sighed. "I get that you don't like the Serenites because they keep trying to kill you. Is that why you're so friendly with the Hercs?"

He was ready to deny it, but he hesitated. "I don't know for sure. I certainly have a list of Hercs I'll go out of my way to avoid. I suspect that I could get along in a Serenite community, if no one knew who I was, but really, I've never had that opportunity. It's more like I'm friendly with the Stampz people. They just happen to be Hercs."

"But there's that preacher."

He nodded. "Him, too."

He thought a bit.

"Maybe it's people who remind me of Alpines. The Duke of Stampz was Alpine schooled, and all his people follow his lead. I can get along with them easily. Well, most of them.

"And then Harriman Moore is really focussed on his religion, all condensed into their book. He's been working for years trying to get book printing technology restarted so he can print copies for his people. He was on Alp Island for a while, working with our people, but that effort was cut short by the Burn. Now he's at it again, with the help of books from the library. I really see the essence of an Alpine in him."

She laughed. "I don't see it at all."

He didn't reply. She was his traveling companion for now. They needed to talk, but he didn't need to be goaded into an argument.

She sighed. "I can't even get along with Alpines. I probably don't even fit your model. I'm not at all like those at the farm. I was just a child when the Burn cut me off from all things Alpine. Yes, I know some of the rituals and I can read and write, and I spent a few years in the Alpine schools, but I haven't internalized it like you have.

"I was never able to feel at home on the farm. They were all so much older than I was. Just because we have the same blood and the same history, it wasn't enough. I don't know why I even came to Stampz in the first place."

Charles wondered the same thing. Was she expecting a group of like-minded Alpines, all with a deep hatred of the Hercs? It seemed to be a constant theme with her.

She'd been through her own struggles, obviously, but he couldn't claim a hatred he no longer felt. But as long as she didn't demand he show the same fire, he could get along with her.

He looked at her again, and was startled to see her asleep.

She'd been awake a long time now, it was reasonable. He closed his eyes and settled against his own tree trunk. They were in a safe place for now. Nobody traveled this path.

...

"Are you lost again?" she asked as it stretched into the noon still the next day.

He explained. "I'm so used to flying these days that I get my landmarks from a few hundred meters above the tree tops. I do know where I am, generally, but it's not like I recognize each tree we pass.

"Hiking together like this, I think it would be easier and faster to bear west to the Spanish River and take the valley up to the Humboldt Sea. From there, I can find the hidden location of the beamship."

She frowned, "There's traffic that way, right? More people are likely to see you."

"I know. I really need a hat. But no one will be expecting me to be traveling with a woman. Hardly anyone knows what I look like, anyway. They recognize the ship."

"You can't count on that."

He paused to look at a tree. Bark was scraped. It wasn't clearly a Kimmer treemark. A bear could have made it, but in any case, he needed to keep an eye out for more markings like that.

...

Charles cast the net out into the pond and dragged it back to shore.

"Hey, I caught some."

Sharra pulled her knife. "Then it's my turn."

She pulled out a large bass and with a few quick strokes had it skinned and filleted. She grabbed the next one, and processed it as quickly.

Charles looked at the meat spread out on the stone. "I suspect you have some experience with this." He waited until she was done and then stretched the net out to dry. Likely they could get more fish easily, but they didn't need more than they could eat.

She cleaned off her knife and nodded. "Some time back, when I was traveling, I stopped for a time at Endymion and worked for a place that dried and exported fish. I'd get the daily catch from the local fishermen and prepare them."

She held up her blade. "That's where I got this good knife."

He nodded. "I've noticed it. How much does a blade like that cost?"

Her face twisted a little. "You don't ask that question."

"Oops. Sorry."

They made a quick rack from green branches and roasted the fish.

She sighed. "I don't usually steal, but I had to leave that place in a hurry."

"No need to explain."

She shrugged. "I had gotten too comfortable dressed as a man."

"I gather it was a more elaborate costume that what you wear now? You looked like a man for a few minutes when I first saw you, but you definitely look womanish now."

She frowned. "Well, yes. I hardly talked back then, and with a growl at that. I wore a hat and dressed ... more uncomfortably. It had worked for a while, but once ... a certain man saw through it, I was at risk and I knew it. I could either stab him or continue the southern trail before anyone noticed."

Charles nodded. "I'm not going to ask. You'd run away in either case."

She gave an exasperated sigh. "I haven't killed anyone yet, although I came close a couple of times. I get my revenge in other ways."

He blinked, and decided not to ask.

But one piece of the story was puzzling. She'd said that she was taken captive in Franklin, but when she escaped she was traveling north-to-south past Endymion? That was the wrong direction. There was obviously a big chunk of the story missing. It had been more than ten years since the Burn when she and her mother were kidnapped. There was a lot that could have happened in that time.

But pestering her for more details would likely cause her to clam up.

. . .

It was two days later, as they walked into an open meadow, that Charles paused.

"What is it?" Sharra asked.

"That tree." He pointed to a wide-spreading oak on a rise above the meadow. "I need to look at it."

They walked closer. Charles went up to the trunk and fingered the marking cut into the bark.

"What's that symbol?" she asked.

"I don't know if you're aware, but the Kimmer have a marking system of their own, carved in tree trunks."

She said, "It sort of looks Chinese."

"Can you read that?"

"No, it was just something from an Earth history class I took a long time ago. I can't read it."

He nodded. One of the four families of the Kimmer had a Chinese name for their progenitor. Perhaps that was the inspiration for the tree marks.

"Well, Darkwind, my Kimmer apprentice taught me some of it. This is a visa tree. It marks the territory of one of the Kimmer tribes. If an outsider travels through, they're supposed to mark their identification on this tree."

"So this is Kimmer lands?"

"I didn't think it was. This marking is very fresh. I suspect that one of the tribes has moved into the area recently. Maybe Herc settlement has caused them to seek new places to live."

What he didn't tell her, because he wasn't sure he was permitted to say, was that this visa tree announced this to be Er Sun lands, Darkwind's tribe. But he knew that the Er Sun had formerly lived in the area from Mercurius and Zeno down to the edges of Gauss. Had they migrated northward, or had their population just expanded that way.

Sharra asked, "Are we in much danger for being here? I have met Kimmer before, in the west. Is this tribe different?"

"It's hard to say. But in any case, as friendly travelers, we are supposed to mark our names here."

"They can read standard text?"

"No. Not in general. Darkwind can. But what we're supposed to put here are unique icons. I'm called Treekiller."

She laughed. "Why is that?"

He told her the tale of his early days with Darkwind and how he'd knocked a limb off a tree with his impulse rifle.

"Not my first choice for a name, but it stuck and I that's what the Kimmer call me."

Unless, I go by my alias. He was trying to keep his identity secret. One other time he'd gone on a hike under another name.

He took his knife and quickly marked the symbol for Traveling Smoke and then, beside it, he took a stab at making up one for Sharra—a woman with a big mouth.

"What does it say?" she asked.

He shook his head, "Just some traveler and the woman with him. I didn't want to get too specific. I'm still hiding my identity, even from the Kimmer. They're just tokens really."

"And this will give us safe passage?"

"That's the idea. We can only hope."

Crossing Kimmer Land

"That's a radio, right. Why are you playing with it?" she asked. She moved over to where he was sitting.

He eased it back into his backpack. The indicator light that flagged if there had been a signal that he missed was still dark. "Well, it's been two days now. Certainly long enough for the rumor of my destruction to have reached Stampz by a fast courier. I was toying with the idea of putting on my sailsuit and riding my pressor pulses high enough to pick up any radio signals from Stampz."

She frowned. "Why? You can't reply, or you'll reveal it was just a hoax."

He sighed. "Yes, you're right. I promised to check in with the duke after a quad. Anything earlier than that would be a mistake. I'm just anxious."

She frowned. "You'll fly back for that? I know you can't retrace the hike in that time."

"Yes. My plan had been to fly back to the beamship and make a quick shuttle back and forth to check in regularly. The duke and I have a special encryption code. No one can tell that it's me."

"It doesn't sound like you're really committed to this idea of playing dead."

"Oh, it was all my idea. It's the duke that's against it."

She nodded. "He doesn't want to lose his high speed delivery wagon."

Charles laughed. "Yes, there is that. But I was part of his communication network as well. The duke has interests all over the empire. It's hard to keep the messengers running back and forth."

"It's a shame that the radios are so short range."

He nodded and explained the limitations, and the difficulty of keeping them all recharged.

"So," she frowned. "If you're gone for a few months, all the radios would go silent."

"Yes. Plus, with the new king in Serenity—"

She grabbed his arm. "Kimmer."

He didn't know whether he was more startled by her hand on his skin, or by the trio of Kimmer warriors suddenly visible at the crest of the next rise.

Sharra quickly pulled her hand away, as if she'd burned it.

Charles said, "Don't worry. And don't reach for you knife."

"I know."

The last time Charles had been with Kimmer, he'd been in the fancy decorated sailsuit, with Darkwind at his side. He had been introduced to Lightning, some uncle of Darkwind, a respected warrior of the Er Sun. Darkwind had been singing the praises, literally, of the Alpines.

This time, they were both dressed as Herc trappers—utilitarian clothes, but hardly impressive.

Charles put a log on their fire and moved to the side, making a position for a third person to sit.

The Kimmer whispered among themselves and the tallest of the three stepped forward and sat down at the fire.

Charles nodded. "Welcome. We have fish and rabbit for you and yours."

The Kimmer dismissed the ritual words with a wave of his hand. "You are not Kimmer. We have seen your marks. Where are you going?"

"Up the river to the Humboldt Sea, and then along its southern shore."

"To trap?"

"To rest. And to hide from the coming war."

The warrior frowned. "Which war?"

"The Reds and the Greens."

"They are always fighting."

Charles sighed. "It will be worse. The Er Sun are wise to move to the north."

The warrior lightly touched his knife. "You speak secrets."

Charles glanced up at the tree. "The blue jay cannot repeat my words."

It had been a gamble. Maybe the Kimmer knew that Treekiller knew of the Four Families and their tribal names, but that this stranger also knew the Er Sun name was disturbing to them. But these two strangers were also following Kimmer ritual and form, so they had to have been taught by someone.

The warrior nodded. "Take the next tributary to the east past the broken crater. We will meet again after the darkwind."

He stood and turned to Sharra. "You will be welcomed."

Then he turned and left.

When the trio vanished over the rise, Sharra sighed. "That was tense. What did it mean?"

"Which part?"

"All of it."

"Well, they spoke to us, rather than attacking, so they acknowledged our tree marks and that we were following the proper rituals. They welcomed us to another meeting, probably to talk about the war and to question me further about who I am. I knew too much."

"I thought they knew you—the famous Treekiller."

"I signed the visa tree under an alias. I'm still trying to be anonymous."

She chuckled. "We'll see how that works out."

He asked, "That warrior said you would be welcomed. You've met Kimmer before. Do they know you?"

She shook her head and waved off the thought. "Just traveling, hiking away from the main road, like this. I encountered a Kimmer campsite. After a little panic—I may have waved my knife around some—they invited me for the night. I was honestly surprised that they spoke. Legends had them as wild beasts."

Charles nodded. "I heard those same tales. Hercs think Kimmer are animals, and Kimmer think the same of Hercs and Serenites. It makes it easier for everybody to kill each other.

"The big Kimmer uprising of three or four years ago was all started when some Serenite scouts managed to sell muskets and gunpowder to Kimmer tribes."

She nodded, "And now Stampz is selling knives to them."

He shrugged. "Maybe we'll live to see if that was a good choice or not."

They broke camp and followed their unbroken path. The main road to the Humboldt Sea was on the other side of the river, sometimes just a streak of dust barely visible through the trees. Thus far, there had been no wagons, and likely they would have seen the dust. Humboldt did have a settlement, Down Mountain, and there was limited trade there, but it was a dead-end. All the traffic along the Gaussland Trail went south. Stampz was a popular trading stop along the way, but Humboldt was too far out of the way for many to bother with.

Still, the valley was relatively easy to travel on both sides of the river. The geology training Charles had received as a youth nagged at him. This valley showed signs of having been scoured by a torrent of water sometime in the past. Had the Humboldt Sea broken its bounds and flooded the area, carving this valley?

Sharra said, "Do you always look at the land like this?"

"Sorry. I guess I do. I don't always have someone to annoy though."

"I'm not annoyed, exactly. You just sound like some professor at times."

"I idolized my father. He had these wonderful lectures that made the world come alive. Sometimes it's like he's speaking in my head."

She nodded. "Then I probably attended some of his classes. It felt like an echo from long ago when you talked."

It was late in the day when they saw the broken crater. Just like a baby version of what he had imagined for the Humboldt Sea. A crater less than a klom in diameter had filled with rainwater and then spilled out a crack on the side. There was still a pond in the middle, but it must have been full to the top when it broke.

Charles said, "This kind of thing has happened all over the world. The meteor impact that originally formed the crater surely left all kinds of cracks in the surface. Sometimes the land is so fractured that the crater never forms a lake in the first place."

She chuckled. "Yes, professor."

He sighed. "I'll stop."

"Oh, don't. It's far too easy for me to get caught up in old memories and the ugly side of humanity. It's good for me to be able to see new things."

Charles looked at the trees swaying in the wind. "This will be a good place to shelter for darkwind."

She nodded. "Behind that boulder." She headed that direction.

He smiled. It was clear that Sharra had a lot of trail experience, and it made the whole hiking expedition much more pleasant. Traveling alone, he had a tendency to push the limits and find himself forced to shelter down in less than optimal conditions.

Plus, she was a better trail cook than he was.

. . .

"I see a light." Charles said.

"Is it for us?" she asked.

"Maybe." With earthrise still an hour off, and barely any light at all, finding their way beside the promised tributary had been difficult. If it hadn't been for the Kimmer instructions, Charles would have stayed at their darkwind shelter for a few more hours, catching up some sleep, but if the Kimmer were waiting for them, then it wouldn't do to be late.

The campfire light gave them confidence to make their way through the trees.

Sharra said, "People are watching us."

He knew. This was a Kimmer settlement. He recognized the low flat shelters, dug into the ground and roofed with skins and branches. Kimmer had a religious distaste for buildings, but they still needed shelter from the winds and rain. Caves and dugouts were their compromise.

This area was protected from the winds both to the east and the west—an ideal place to live.

Still, it looked fresher, more recently built, than the ones he'd seen before. It was more evidence that the Er Sun had just recently moved into the area.

A dozen or so warriors were waiting for them by the fire.

Charles nodded his acknowledgement of their presence. The leader of the group gestured him to follow them, just as a group of women approached Sharra.

Sharra gave him a nod. During their darkwind time, she had mentioned that she was expecting this. The women did their own thing while the men had their discussion.

The men formed a semicircle around a smaller fire. Charles was invited to sit with them. The leader introduced himself, Sun on the Mountain.

Two to the left, a man with a heavily scarred arm said, "I know you, Treekiller. Why are you using a false name?"

Charles nodded, it was one of the warriors known to Darkwind. "I know you, Killer of the Bear. I had hoped to pass through these lands unrecognized. I chose a new name to honor my parents, who died in the Great Burn."

Sun on the Mountain asked, "Why do you hide?"

"The Reds have great weapons they use to destroy ships and to battle cities. Many of those weapons have been turned on me alone for the past three years. I wish to know what they will do if they believe that they have succeeded. I will not hide forever, but for a time, I want to know what the Reds will try if they think I am gone."

The warrior who met them on the trail said, "You spoke of a war between the Reds and the Greens."

Charles nodded. "You know of the Angels you see in the sky?"

There was a murmur. The leader said, "Yes, we know."

"There is a new light in the sky. Just as the Angel Er Sun and the others watch over their descendants on the land, the Reds have one, too. It has been gone for a long time, but it has shown its presence recently.

"And this one will do more than watch."

Charles tried to keep from showing any emotion on his face as they struggled with his words. It was a risk connecting the presence of Mt. Ural with their Angel legends, but it was the surest way he knew to let them understand the risks.

"This new Angel will embolden the Reds to attack their neighbors and try to take all the surrounding lands for their own. I fear that, just as I wield power with my beamship, that the Reds will turn even more fearsome weapons on the Greens or anyone else in their way. And this time, they will have no need to supply muskets to the Four Families."

Charles shook his head. "It will soon be a very dangerous time for all of us."

The Singer

Sun on the Mountain said, "We no longer speak to the Reds." He spoke to his warriors. "Treekiller has acted honorably with the Er Sun. It is not wise for a hunter to explain his weapons to his prey. We will keep the name of Treekiller secret until the time is right."

There was a murmured assent. Charles nodded his gratitude. It was the best he could hope for. Any secret shared among so many was a secret at risk, but at least he had the leader's blessing.

He had been a little uncertain about telling these fierce warriors about his plan to hide, fearing the taint of cowardice. But they were skilled hunters as well and knew all about moving quietly and attacking from ambush. His idea of playing dead to provoke a foolish response from an enemy made perfect sense to them.

They talked a bit more. Charles gave his promise to keep the location of the Er Sun secret as well. They were not forthcoming on their motive for their migration north and he made no pressure to learn it.

Finally, Sun on the Mountain said, "We have spoken enough. The others are waiting for the singer."

They all got up and went back to the main fire circle. Charles recognized the signs. There was food being shared, fish baked with mashed tubers, and various berries. He could hear excited whispers and others gathered around.

It was very much like the time Darkwind had sung his tales before a different crowd of Kimmer. Everyone was waiting for some singer.

But first came the youngsters. There was the song of Flat Tail the Beaver, which had to be the first song many of them learned. A chorus of maybe a dozen kids sang that one. Then there was the Bear and the Honeybees. Then a young boy, barely a teenager, sang one Charles had not heard before about how the earthshine revealed a cave, just when he needed it to shelter from the dawnwind.

Charles joined the stamping of feet, the sign of appreciation of a good performance. The boy hadn't stumbled too badly in his singing.

And then, a couple of women pulled Sharra up close to the fire and sat her down on the log the boy had just vacated.

Everyone waited in anticipation.

Are they asking Sharra to sing?

She looked a little flustered, but then glancing his way, she nodded to herself.

Oh! The tree mark. They took my woman-with-a-big-mouth and interpreted it as a singer? I'm going to be in big trouble.

Sharra took a deep breath and began to sing.

"She waited for her lover," the words began.

From the first notes out of her mouth, Charles caught his breath. It was a voice so strong and sweet that he'd dreamed about it for years.

A captive dock worker, sitting alone outside the nightlife of Port Gartner, always banned from entering the main part of the city, he could still hear the sounds of life up the slope of the crater wall.

And from time to time, he heard the Voice, a distant singer. Often he couldn't make out the words, but he could still savor the emotion and color of her voice. Living the rough life he was forced into, this was the closest he got to heaven. Leaving the Voice behind had been the only thing he regretted when he left.

He melted into the song. All around him, the Kimmer were soaking up the strange tale from another culture. But the tale of a young woman waiting for her missing lover surely struck a chord among the Kimmer wives who never knew if their warriors would return.

The stamping and hoots were loud when she finished. They called for another.

Charles smiled at her and nodded. She took another breath and sang a tale of a gardener with her flowers under the light and the blessing of the Earth—the home to herself, the flowers, and the honeybees that shared their sweetness. It almost had a Way of the Earth reverence to it.

Almost immediately, she shifted into a traditional Kimmer song, The Claws of the Raccoon, which was about a young hunter who hunted and failed time after time, but brought a smile to his young wife with the herbs he collected for her.

Charles saw her eyes as she kept glancing his way. *How did she know that one? She said she just spent one night with the Kimmer.*

The crowd was just in awe of her singing. She had a strong sweet voice and was able to bring a depth of emotion to even the Kimmer tale. Charles had always felt the Kimmer songs were too rigid and sing-song rhythmical, but she was excellent.

She took a sip from a cup and looking around the crowd urging her to sing another.

She smiled at Charles and began.

It was the tale of a young Kimmer warrior and his companion, an Alpine magician and how they tricked the Reds out of the secret to unleash a magical demon, escaping the Red's fortress by making sailsuits and capturing a tornado to fly across the great sea to safety.

It was Darkwind's song. And Charles had never heard it sung better. He stood up, stomped and hooted, along with many others.

Darkwind was among them. Charles hadn't seen him arrive, but he was at the edges of the crowd, basking in the glow of having a great singer perform his song. The warrior next to Darkwind nearly shoved him off his feet. They both laughed.

Charles wondered if Darkwind had seen him, but he needn't have worried. The young warrior/songwriter gave him a smile.

The crowd was pleading for another song, but Sharra waved them off and gave up the seat. Some young singer with more ambition than good sense tried to sing another traditional saga, but stumbled through it. There were a few generous stomps, but the crowd was dwindling. The big show was over. Charles couldn't tell where the women had taken Sharra, but he knew she would be okay.

He really wanted to have a nice quiet talk together—just the two of them far from any listening ears, but for now, that wasn't possible.

What he'd just learned had shifted his world. Sharra was the Voice. He had no doubt about that. And she knew a number of Kimmer songs. How did that fit in with her life story?

He had many questions, and knew deep down that *how* he asked those questions would make all the difference in the world.

Darkwind made it though the crowd, accepting a few congratulations on the song he wrote.

He sat down next to Charles. "Traveling Smoke? What's that all about?"

Charles sighed. "I'm supposed to be dead. I couldn't very well write Treekiller on the visa tree."

"That's not the rumor I heard."

"Oh? What's the rumor? I've been out of touch for three days now."

Darkwind tilted his head. "There was a big noise near Franklin, and you've gone missing."

Charles poked his finger in his ear and winced. "Yeah, I'm still hearing the echoes of it. The Serenites left a bomb in the ship. I barely got it out in time. If they think they managed to destroy Ship and me, then maybe they'll let their guard down. Keep the secret, please."

Darkwind sighed. "I'll try, but it's not common for an outsider to mark the tree and walk into Kimmer lands. And who is this singer? She's great, although she doesn't quite get the rhythm of the songs right."

Charles declined to debate the issue. "She's an Alpine. We're traveling together. She accidentally discovered me after I was supposed to be dead."

"Alpine? Does that mean the two of you are—?"

"No. We're just traveling together."

"How did she learn Kimmer songs? I know you can't remember them. You couldn't have taught them to her."

"She traveled on her own before I met her. She met Kimmer before. I don't know which tribe. Somewhere to the west."

Darkwind grinned, "So the other tribes are singing my song! That's great."

Charles asked, "How are you getting all the rumors out here?"

His apprentice grinned. "I'm special, and my family is finally realizing it."

"Oh?"

Darkwind nodded. "I've got Herc clothes, compliments of the duke, and a special letter that allows me to come and go into Stampz with no questions about being a Kimmer. I've even got an ox and a wagon. People are starting to recognize me as just another Herc on the trail. I can visit both Kimmer and Herc freely."

"So, you're a spy for the Er Sun?"

"Well, not exactly. I'm not giving away battle plans or anything like that. I'm just able to be the voice between Sun on the Mountain and Duke James. I just came up the trail to Humboldt a few hours ago and heard about the new singer. I ran all the way here. My wagon is hidden in the trees, and I'll have to get back to it soon to take care of the ox."

"Tell nothing about Treekiller."

He nodded solemnly. "I won't."

Charles sighed. "Be careful. You can talk to both sides, but if there are troubles ahead, either side could suddenly decide you are an enemy."

Darkwind grinned. "If that happens, I'll come running and hide in the beamship."

Charles shook his head. "Just be careful."

Darkwind had to run off to talk to Sun on the Mountain. Charles looked around for any sign of Sharra.

Someone must have noticed, because a boy came up, looking much like Darkwind had when Charles had first met him.

"Your woman is camped by the creek."

Charles nodded. "Can you show me the way?"

The boy headed off. Charles hurried to follow him. At least the Earth was finally up and there was plenty of light.

The boy stopped and pointed, then hurried off in another direction.

Charles moved up to the tree where Sharra had settled.

She looked nervous. He didn't say anything at first, taking off his backpack and finding a place close, but not too close.

"Darkwind was in the audience. He was pleased by the way you sang his song."

"Oh!" she sounded disturbed. "I wouldn't have done it if I'd known."

"Like I said, he was pleased."

She nodded. "I've gotten so many comments on how I messed up the rhythm."

He laughed. "That's just Kimmer talk. They can't admit that you're the best singer they've ever heard. Besides I bet that's not all they said about your singing. You heard all those stomps."

She was silent. He suspected she was worried about what he knew, or suspected.

"We need to get some sleep. The Kimmer have been hospitable, but we need to be on our way before the still is gone. I'd rather avoid the settlement during daylight hours, as long as we're avoiding the main trail."

She nodded. "That sounds good."

He settled down against the tree trunk. "By the way, I loved your singing. I've loved your voice for years now."

A Lucky Accident

Sharra gasped, "You knew?"

"From the first few notes of your first song." He sighed. "I was a lonely teenage boy, trapped on Port Gartner's docks. Everything was off limits for me, other than staring at the waves, and listening the city life from the levels above me. Certainly there were no women I could even see, from where I was confined.

"But, every now and then, I could hear a distant, sweet voice, singing about things I could never experience. I could barely make out the words most times. I could just sit on the dock and listen to the Voice. That's what I called her in my mind. I never talked about her. It was my own private refuge from my prison."

He smiled into the darkness, not for her, but from his own experience. "Over the years, those memories came back to me. But I never put the pieces together—not until now. I never considered that the Voice was Alpine. When I met you, I didn't recognize your speaking voice as her."

"But your brother knew about us?"

Charles chuckled. "Oh, Rad got in so much trouble! When we heard rumors that there were Alpines in the upper levels, we assumed they were captive like us. It had taken him months to work his way up to a trusted assistant to the night foreman. He crept away and then he came back under guard.

"All he told me was that there were two girls named Kell, and although he offered to help, they refused it, and we were supposed to pretend like they didn't exist."

She whispered, "You knew where we were held?"

"Yes. Well, Rad figured it out. Not that I really understood it all at the time. By the way, what happened to your sister?"

The silence stretched out a bit, but then, she said, "Beth ... Beth was ...."

Then she stalled out. Charles said, "Oh! Sharra and Beth. Sharra Abeth. I get it now."

She cleared her throat. "Beth was stronger than me. She was my big sister. When Mom was gone, she did everything she could to protect me. But it was an impossible situation."

Charles kept his breathing slow and even. He had a deep urge to track down the guide who sold them into slavery and kill him. But the most important thing right then was to be someone who listened.

Sharra said, "Beth convinced them that we were raised high class, like nobility. Mom was always visiting wealthy merchants and we even met with the royal family in Franklin, so we always had to be dressed well and were trained in etiquette. We could sing, we could draw, and we knew how to make the dresses they supplied look well tailored. As much as possible, Beth tried to keep me singing and charming the patrons. The effort to attract a higher class client certainly paid off. She was certainly more popular than I was, except for those that liked young girls."

She shifted position. "Charles, Beth was very practical. She turned down your brother, not because she didn't appreciate the offer to help, but because she really didn't think enslaved dockworkers could help us. If she'd given your brother any hope at all, it would have ended up a lot bigger mess than a boy sneaking off one time to visit a brothel."

Charles could hear the tears in her voice. "Beth caught some disease. I don't know what it was, but the Port Gartner healers couldn't do anything about it. To the last, she was trying to help me. She and I were kept off in the storage room, away from the clients, while I nursed her. She died during the still. By light-sleep I was in men's clothes, hiking the coastal trail with a few jewels and all the cash I could find. We'd planned to do this together, but we were never left unguarded until she got sick."

"Did they try to track you down?"

"Probably, but I went off the trail into the forest as soon as I could. I probably walked in circles for months. I fished the hard way, by dropping rocks on them. I bought food from a farmer for jewels worth a hundred times their value. I was chased though a maze of tall trees by a bear. It's all ... all ...."

"Sharra. Let's talk again later. I think we need to sleep."

She sniffed. "Okay. Just ...."

"Nothing has changed between you and me. Only, maybe I'd like to hear you sing some more."

She giggled. "Okay. Tomorrow."

When he heard her finally fall asleep, he released his knife and stretched his fingers to get the cramps out.

I should never ask the name of that guide. I really might try to kill him.

...

The Kimmer camp was alive as they made their way back to their trail in the light of the half-earth. One of the warriors appointed himself their guide and he showed them the fastest way to travel to get back to the river.

As they prepared to part, the warrior invited Sharra back to sing sometime. And then he looked at Charles with a frown.

"Is there a problem?"

The warrior shook his head. "No. But Darkwind said to tell you something before he left, but I can't remember what it was."

"Oh, well, if it was important, he would have told me himself."

They parted ways and Charles and Sharra pushed on, trying to get past the irregular mountains that served as Humboldt's ring.

They were headed in the direction of the village of Down Mountain at the end of the road, where the northern tributary of the Spanish River sourced from the Humboldt Sea itself. They called it a sea, because of its size, but it was just a lake like so many others. With no other settlements on the sea to trade with, Charles had heard Down Mountain was just a collection of farms and a place for fishermen to sell their catch. Every quad, the dried fish collected over the past four days filled a wagon and it headed down the trail to markets in Stampz and Zeno.

Sharra said, "I have a knack for remembering songs. I remembered the Kimmer tunes I heard, and I even went back to the Kimmer village to listen again." She chuckled. "They were puzzled by me. I sounded like a woman and dressed like a man and was very quick to pull out my knife if anyone got close to me."

Charles said, "They must have liked that."

She chuckled. "Maybe so. If I hadn't traded a few songs with them, maybe one of the warriors would have gotten bold enough to push the issue, but singers are respected, and they put up with my oddities, as long as I didn't stay around too long."

"Were you famous, back then?"

She chuckled. "No. It was a smaller group, and I never stayed past sharing the singing and the free food."

She frowned. "From the very beginning at this settlement, people were expecting something from me. I don't understand it."

He refrained from saying anything, but his face must have betrayed him.

Her eyes squinted, judging him. "What did you say?"

Charles sighed. "It was the visa tree. The mark I made for you was ... misinterpreted."

"Tell me."

He sighed and then walked over to a nearby birch tree. He pulled out his knife and made a few strokes. "The Kimmer tree marks are icons, just images. Over the centuries they've become more stylized, with certain common items simplified. This is the symbol for a woman."

She giggled. "I've seen worse."

He nodded. Carefully, he made a slight addition. "I thought this variation would mean ...."

"Don't stall out now."

"... a woman with a big mouth." He winced and took a step back away from her.

She shrugged. "I guess. But you say they interpreted it as Singer?"

He nodded. "Darkwind has always made fun of my tree marks. He's the one who taught me. I guess it's not surprising I made the mistake. I thought I was being creative."

She nodded. "So you weren't lying."

"About what?"

"Knowing who I was before I sang."

He chuckled. "No. This was a lucky accident. I don't know what they would have thought if it turned out that you couldn't sing."

She took out her knife and sliced the bark so her mark was removed. "Accidents I can tolerate. I couldn't tolerate lies."

He nodded. "Reasonable. But what about little lies?"

She stepped on and he kept pace with her. "What kind of little lies?"

He chuckled. "Well what about if I said you looked pretty, but really, your hair was all tangled and had leaves in it."

"Don't start flirting, I don't react well to that."

He nodded. "Got it." He moved on at a faster pace.

Sharra brushed at her hair with her fingers. She frowned at the leaves that she tugged loose.

...

They veered to the east, just as soon as they got a glimpse of the collection of stone and log buildings where the river and the sea joined. Down Mountain, pretty in a way, nestled at the bottom of a mountain, was not on their travel plan.

There was barely any path to follow now. The mountains came down to the surf, splashing white spray, driven by the dawnwind. They found a crack in the rocks where they could wait out the winds. The crashing surf and the howling of the gale through the rocks made any conversation impossible.

They made do with trail biscuits and Helva's cookies and settled down to wait it out.

Charles was ready to move on as soon as possible. He'd promised to make contact with the duke in a quad, and the fourth day was here. It had taken them much longer to hike through the forest than it had been to sail with the winds, pushed along at speeds he could never make on foot.

And now they had rough mountain terrain to travel before they reached Ship.

He wanted Sharra safe within the metal cylinder before he stepped on his pressor beam stick and raced back to within radio range of Stampz.

The morning glow made the sleeping woman look beautiful, in spite of worn men's clothing and the cap she wore to keep her hair from whipping around in the breeze.

I can't tell her that. He smiled. *I'd probably say it wrong anyway.*

When his hand went over his scalp, he felt moisture from the spray that had made its way up the slopes and the beginning of some hair.

I'll need to take care of that soon. But he preferred to shave his head when he was on the beamship. There was plenty of water and a mirror in the water closet where he could do a much better job of shaving it clean.

Hopefully, he'd have time to take care of that before he had to take to the skies.

I wonder what Darkwind had wanted to tell me. It hadn't been on his mind when we talked. Was it something Sun on the Mountain told him afterward?

It was probably something personal. Darkwind and he had spent months together at times, but the young man had made a life for himself. Maybe he still called himself an apprentice to the Alpine magician, but it sounded like he could make his own life on his own terms.

He glanced over at Sharra. Would he ever travel with Darkwind again? It would certainly be a different dynamic if Sharra was there, too.

Darkwind might even have a girl of his own. Heidi still had an interest in him, but those two hardly met anymore.

They had been enthusiastic Alpine apprentices together, even if their interests had been so widely different.

But it's not up to me to play matchmaker. I can barely tell what I'm supposed to do with my own life.

He looked at Sharra and noticed her breathing. He smiled.

Making the Schedule

It was a long, hard day hiking the coastal mountains that rimmed the sea.

During the breathless still, when the sun was at its peak, Charles changed into his sailsuit and boosted high in the sky. He had a clear memory of where the beamship had been hidden from the cloud level, and on the first flight up, he couldn't find a match.

She watched from the ground as he circled back down to meet her.

"Did you see it?"

"Not yet. We've still got some distance to go. I didn't want to get too far away. This spot isn't exactly easy to identify either. I didn't want to lose you."

A few hours later he came back with a smile. "I see it. We need to take the next ridge south, and from there we should make it to the landing site."

She said, "I wish I could fly like that. Do you think you could teach me?"

He shrugged. "You'll need a sailsuit, and mine are too large for you. Plus, you'd only get to fly the Kimmer way, by jumping off a cliff."

"Still, I'd like to learn."

He nodded. "It's great. Heidi pestered Darkwind to make a sailsuit for her, but he put her off for a long time and it never happened. For the Kimmer, sailsuits were only for warriors. He didn't want to break with their traditions."

Sharra laughed.

"What?" he asked.

"Don't tell anyone, but I spent a lot of time with the Kimmer women. They were familiar enough with Herc women's clothing to know that I was dressed as a man. They had questions."

"Oh, I would have liked to listen in on that discussion."

She shook her head. "But the thing is, there are secret songs that only women know."

"Really?"

She nodded. "And one of them was about a woman who dressed as a warrior and fought alongside the men. She even had a sailsuit."

Charles chuckled. "Darkwind would be scandalized. But I'm not surprised. Alpine history has always mentioned the Eldest, and the Women's Council. They were mentioned, but what happened among women never made it into the history books. I even remember my mother having to leave for a women's meeting of some kind."

He asked, "Did you learn all the women's secrets, too."

She chuckled. "Oh, Charles, there is so, so much you don't know about Alpine women!"

...

Charles knocked on the airlock door as the evening winds were picking up. "Ship, 'Newtonian Physics'. Open the door."

It opened.

Sharra said, "That's not the same password you used before."

"That's right. I use a different one each time. I try to set up a dozen of them ahead of time." He gave her a wry smile. "You never know when you might accidentally invite a spy inside."

She sniffed. "I hope your memory is good."

He nodded. "You can memorize songs. I'm good at other things."

He raised his voice, "Ship, have there been any problems."

"No. There have been no humans in passive detection range."

Sharra frowned, "Passive detection?"

"Ship has its beams and radio turned off to avoid detection by the Uralites. If Ship were human, I'd say it was feeling a little miffed."

She chuckled. "Ship, if you want to gripe about Charles while he's gone, you can talk to me."

There was no response.

She sighed as she looked around the cargo level. "This place is a mess."

"We lost all gravity as we fell after the explosion. Everything came crashing down. I had to sweep out some of it."

"You didn't finish."

"I had to tell the duke what had happened as soon as possible. I didn't have time."

She frowned. "Don't expect me to clean everything up."

He chuckled. "I won't, but once again, I have to leave quickly. I'll be back as soon as I can. Can you fix me a quick snack before I leave. I need to take care of a couple of things and then I want to be gone before the darkwind is here in earnest."

He stepped outside again a little later, his scalp clean shaven, and with his impulse rifle fully charged.

Sharra looked worried. "You're going all the way back to Stampz?"

"At least close enough to make radio contact. I should be back before the still. You can talk to Ship or read. I have a shelf full of books."

She smiled. "I saw those before."

He nodded. "Did you perhaps leave behind a bookmark?"

"What do you mean?"

"I found a white feather. It was—"

He reached out to hold her arm as she looked ready to collapse. She steadied herself.

"It's okay," she said. He released her arm as she straightened up.

"It's just that that feather was the last memento I have of Beth. I thought I lost it at the farm. I hunted and couldn't find it when I left. If you hadn't been waiting...."

He nodded. In spite of his need to get on his way, he needed to let her talk.

"I found it near the books. It looked flattened, like a bookmark. It's still up there on the command deck."

She sighed. "Out our window, at Port Gartner, we saw the birds flying free. When a seagull came and perched at our window, and then left one of its feathers, Beth said it was a sign that some day we'd be free. When it came time to leave, I had to take it with me. In spite of everything I went through, I managed to hold onto it. To keep it intact, I put it between a couple of pieces of wood and strapped it together.

"I don't know when the strap broke, but when I was packing at the farm, the wooden halves were separated."

She smiled. "I guess I should use it as a bookmark, now that there are books around."

"Feel free. I have no ideas which books would tempt you. We can get others, the next time we're at the library."

Confident she was okay, he went out the airlock and lifted into the sky.

He rode the impulse rifle much higher this time, trying to get as far southwest as he could before the winds blew him too far to the east. Late sunlight kept the clouds reasonably bright for a while.

When he put aside the rod and stretched out his glide, trying to find the angle that would give him the best ground velocity. Too shallow and he'd end up just drifting with the wind. Too steep and he'd be losing altitude without making enough progress.

One thing was notable. Once he got high enough above the land, there seemed to be less turbulence. Even when he knew the darkwind was becoming dangerously stiff at ground level, he could ride the the winds as if they were calm and uniform.

Whether this was just a one-time situation or whether it was the result of different layers in the atmosphere would be something he needed to investigate some other day.

He had to keep on course, and as the sky glow faded, it was clear he was going to have to get lower in order to tell where he was going.

But too soon, there was no sun and no Earth in the sky. Sailing high above the ground in the darkness, he lost his bearing.

I can't afford to fly into the ground by accident. He adjusted his angle, and sailed as shallow and economically as possible.

It's like that night. When Darkwind and he had leapt from the wall on the Beltis Island fortress and had been swept skyward in a darkwind-powered vortex almost like a tornado, they had lost track of each other.

Mostly by luck, Charles had made it safely to the mainland. The more experienced Darkwind had probably ridden higher and farther, but when he came down in the darkness, he had crashed into the ground and ended up severely scraped and bruised.

Somehow that crash hadn't quite made it into the saga sung over Kimmer campfires.

What had saved Charles had been lights from a farmhouse, giving him a better idea of where he was above the ground.

I need to see light, somewhere.

Any light at all would do. The sun and the Earth were the mainstays. At night, sometimes there were campfires or lights from houses.

But he was over very thinly settled land. He shouldn't expect any help.

He looked up. For an instant, he thought he saw a tiny light, perhaps a star, but clouds covered it before he was sure. He looked again, but it didn't happen again.

Keep eyes on the ground.

That was where the danger was.

But where is the ground? Am I sure?

In the blackness, it made no difference whether his eyes were open or not, and he focused on the feel of the straps. Yes, he was hanging from the sail, so the ground had to be under him.

Unless I'm in a spin. No, he had to avoid panicking.

Then, a flicker of light called to him. Off to the side, and barely visible. Still he had to get closer. He shifted his weight and steered toward that beacon.

It's flickering? Why is that?

And he was dropping. He could see that the light was rising in his field of vision. He pulled out the rod and boosted his altitude with a couple of strong pulses.

It started to have shape. Three flickering lights above a stronger bright light.

And then, far off in the distance, he saw even fainter lights.

Those are flags. Is this Stampz? A guard house?

Putting a name on it made things clearer. The far faint lights were farms. The flags were something new, waving in the darkwind, illuminated from a beacon fire below.

He looked carefully in the distance. Fainter, but still recognizable was another guard station farther down the rim. Perhaps he could see the castle itself.

He bent his path, now that he knew where he was and more importantly where the ground below him was likely to be.

Landing was rough, but he felt relief with the ground beneath his feet and the barely tolerable darkwind trying to knock him down.

All I need is a moment of shelter. He found it in a rocky slab where he could lie just out of the wind.

He turned on the radio. *Tap, tap, tap.* A moment later he repeated it, and then switched the encryption.

The duke was already calling him. "…s can you hear me?"

"Yes, I'm here."

"Well, Charles, it's good to hear your voice, but I wish I had better news."

"I saw the flags. They really helped me flying in the darkness."

"It was a test. For this night only, I had scheduled a night time beacon just to see if we could read the flags from the castle at night. We can barely make them out in the daytime. Special flags aren't as readable as I had hoped. At least we can make out the number of flags."

"I saw three. But you said there is news. Was it about me, or something else?"

"Oh, there are lots of rumors and speculation about you. Jelica sent a message by courier, telling of hearing a loud noise. I sent a reply that you hadn't arrived. For right now, you are just missing. But that's not too unusual. You've been missing before."

"The people who set the bomb will think I'm gone."

"Maybe."

Charles heard something in the duke's voice. "What else have you heard?"

James sighed. "Charles, I'm very sorry to have to tell you this, but several sources have sent the news that Harriman Moore has died."

The World Upside Down

Duke James said, "Charles, can you hear me?"

Charles nodded, then said into the radio. "Yes. Um. What did you hear?"

He vividly remembered Harriman's saying, "one last time" when they met.

James sighed. "The reports conflict. Some said the guards killed him. Others said it was the scribes. There are no details, other than that Moore was burned to death. There's nothing from the imperial guards themselves, but word is spreading rapidly among the preacher's followers. I've even been contacted by a group of Christians here in Stampz that I wasn't even aware of. They asked me to find out what really happened. They're afraid the Way is starting some kind of attack on their religion."

Charles said, "I met with Harriman recently, and he was hiding from the guards."

"You mentioned something about that the last time you were here. The scribes were upset about his printing press."

"Yes, he was afraid of being arrested and the printing shut down. The scribes and the priests were using their influence at court. But I didn't expect something like this."

The howling darkwind all around him made it hard for Charles to think. He could remember Harriman's smile, and then … he couldn't go past it.

And burned …. It was so much like the loss of his parents—his whole world as a child. Burned to death. It echoed in his head.

"Charles. Charles, are you okay?"

He cleared his throat. "Yes, I'm fine. It's just a shock."

James said, "Yes, to all of us. I met the man myself a couple of times. He was a very energetic old character. I thought he'd last forever. If I'd thought it would get this bad, I would have offered a safe place here for their printing operations."

The duke went on to talk about the flag system. "The distance from the rim stations to the castle is just too great to use the flags in the book."

Charles heard the words, but they just drifted past him. The duke asked his opinion on something.

"Charles? Did you hear what I said?"

"Maybe. The wind is howling here."

"Charles, could you make it on to the castle. We could—"

"No, I need to get back to the ship."

"Well, okay. I was hoping to discuss the reports that I'm getting on Serenite activity along the west coast, but I guess that can wait. When shall I expect another contact?"

It was too difficult a question for Charles right then.

"Charles, just make contact when you can. Someone will be checking the radio at all times."

"Okay." And then Charles turned off the radio and rested.

He just laid there in the rock shelter for more than an hour. He couldn't make plans for his return. He couldn't sleep. All he could do was revisit that last time with Harriman.

What could I have done differently?

His thoughts were a maze of rabbit trails, lost in the grass, never leading anywhere.

Clouds rushed by. None seemed willing to part to give him another glimpse of the stars. That just didn't happen on Luna. It wasn't the way the world worked.

Perhaps he dozed. He wasn't sure.

But the pain of the rocks in his side made him shift. He noticed that the winds were easing off. He really needed to get back to the ship.

He stood, walking a few minutes to get his body working again. And then he lifted off, heading north.

. . .

It was a long trip, and it was well into the still when the rising crescent Earth gave him enough light to finally locate his landmarks.

Sharra was outside, tending a small fire when he finally sailed to a rough landing.

She jumped up and raced over to him. "You were so late! I was worried."

He pulled her to him, and after a brief instant of resistance, she let him hold her.

"Charles? What's wrong?"

He wasn't ready to explain. She'd never understand. Harriman had been just another Herc to her.

She tugged him. "Come over here. I was cooking. You haven't had anything to eat for hours."

Sharra checked on her pot, simmering over the fire. "Ship told me I had to cook outdoors. I'm using the broken crates for firewood, I hope you don't mind."

Charles grunted. She tugged at his sailsuit. "You need to change out of this. How do these straps fasten?"

He was soon changed and sitting against a tree, idly watching Sharra prepare the meal.

She brought him food, and then chuckled, a little sadly.

He frowned. "What was that for?"

She sighed. "I thought I'd never do this again."

"What?"

She stared back at the fire, poking the dirt that covered the coals. White heat glared out where the rich oxygen atmosphere fired up the blaze.

"You know what my life was, back at Port Gartner?"

"In theory." He wasn't really interested. Not right now.

"It was more than sex. Especially for my sister and me. Our job was to tend to the needs of our clients. And for some of those men, all they wanted was a woman to make them comfortable, feed them something warm, and make the harsh world outside go away.

"Some of them were broken. Life, whether it was something domestic, or a naval battle, had left them curled up inside and whimpering like a beaten dog."

She looked at Charles. "You're a little like that, I think."

He sighed. "Harriman Moore, the preacher, has been killed."

She came closer and wrapped her arms around his head. She whispered, "He was a friend, and a mentor."

He nodded, and then gasped, and the tears flowed.

...

Ship said, "Your orders were to avoid beam emissions and radio to prevent the possibility of being detected by sophisticated instruments used by Mt. Ural or its beamship."

Charles nodded. "Yes."

He sat in the command seat, just resting, not really anxious to get started on some plan or another. Sharra sat at the other chair, reading a book, holding her white feather.

Ship continued, "Thus, there was not really any prohibition on listening with the radio, just transmitting."

"Yes, I guess I should have been clearer in my orders."

"While waiting, I have been listening for any radio signals, under the assumption that any I could detect would be from you at close range, or from Mt. Ural. I have observed periodic messages. Using the timing of the signals I have determined that Mt. Ural is in a stable orbit around Luna with a four-hour period."

Charles said, "So, they're not approaching."

"It would be dangerous for them to approach too close to the atmosphere. It would take a constant expenditure of energy to prevent their orbit from degrading if they did."

Sharra asked, "What are they saying?"

Charles said, "Encrypted transmissions. We can't hear the words, just the fact that they are talking."

Ship said, "However, the pace of the transmissions has increased. There are regular conversations during the period of one hour when Mt. Ural would be highest in the sky."

Charles sighed.

Sharra said, "Does that mean something?"

Charles said, "The duke said that Serenite forces are moving near the coast. The invasion will probably happen soon. I just wonder if they were waiting for Ship to be removed from the picture before acting."

"Because the beamship is a weapon?"

"Yes. I stopped the Terrance invasion with Ship's power. That's why Serenity has been trying to kill me all this time."

It felt like he was pushing a boulder uphill, thinking about battles and strategy. Harriman's death wasn't something he could get over quickly, but still, he had to act.

"I guess I need to make another run back to Stampz to let the duke know this new information."

"It takes so long."

"It would be quicker during the daylight. I kept getting lost in the darkness."

"But people could see you easier. That's dangerous."

Ship said, "There is another option. Mt. Ural can only see the part of the globe when they are overhead. There are windows of time where I could move to a location closer to Stampz without being detected."

They made plans. Sharra listened, only asking questions when she needed clarification. Charles got the impression she was content to stay put, isolated off in the north woods.

As they waited for the right moment to act, Charles turned to her. "Sharra, I can't ask you do go into danger like this. If we're suddenly discovered and the Serenites find out, then King Bardin might just risk a special attack just to remove us from his invasion plans again.

"We could take this window of time to drop you off at a safe location, at least until this invasion is over."

She slipped her feather into her book.

"No. Charles, I'm staying with you." She hesitated, then said, "Back at the brothel, I sang so many songs, nearly all romantic ballads. And at the same time, I was bottled up inside, knowing I was condemned to never live the stories I was singing.

"And then I ran, and found myself among the Kimmer, listening to tales of adventure, some of them about a bold Alpine, facing off the soldiers, escaping danger, and even flying off among the stars. And the idea that this person might just be real—it fired me to act.

"Instead of seeking safety, I sought you out."

She turned her head and looked down at her book. "Maybe I can't keep my temper. Maybe we argue more often than not. Maybe I can't ever get over what has been done to me."

She looked up at him. "But, Charles, if I'm ever to have any chance at my own tales of romance and adventure, it has to be by your side. I'll risk anything for that chance."

He took her hand. He sighed. "You said I was broken, and I know you're right. And this idea of… romance. I don't know what that is, not really. I just know there are certain things I have to do, and maybe life could be a lot more bearable if you were here with me."

Negotiations

Charles was sure he was imagining it, but Ship sounded excited as it replied to the command to lift off.

"We will reach communications altitude in ten seconds."

"Then go ahead and open the standard channel and send the tap code."

Just a few seconds later, the duke's voice appeared on the alternate channel.

"Charles is that you? I didn't expect you at this time of day."

"There's new information. Are you alone?"

"Yes, go ahead."

Charles gave him the information about Mt. Ural and the increased communications.

Duke James said, "Yes, and it sounds like Maury has already fallen. The Serenites are making a major push up the coast. The emperor is likely preparing his forces for an attack even closer to the capital. If the Serenites have new weapons, then that would explain their advance."

Charles asked, "Is there any report of the other beamship?"

"Not from my sources. The battles sound traditional—cannon ball exchanges between ships and the occasional laser cannon attack on shoreline fortifications."

"That makes sense. Mt. Ural is dependent on their lone beamship. They can't risk it being taken out by a lucky defender."

"But James, the second reason I called is to let you know I'm relocating."

"Where?"

"Closer, to make communications easier."

"I'm glad, but is that safe?"

"A little risk is necessary. But, I don't think I should try to sneak in like before. Could you have a closed carriage meet me just outside the Gate?"

They made arrangements and then ended the radio call. Ship landed back at the same location near Humboldt. They would wait until darkness to move to their new hiding place.

...

Sharra whispered, "I thought I was going to get to ride in a fancy carriage."

Charles smiled and held her hand as they broke from their hiding place in the trees and entered the side door to the carriage, carrying their baggage. He rapped on the ceiling and the driver started moving.

They had to talk low, since they didn't want any chance of being over-heard. Not even the driver knew who they were.

Charles said, "Sorry about the utility carriage, but the duke sold off all his fancy wagons some years back when Stampz was facing a crop failure and he had to import food. His only fancy traveling carriage is the one I flew to Franklin."

"It looked to me like he was doing pretty well."

"Yes, Stampz is prosperous now. The people love their duke. They remember the old times, before he arrived. It's taken a few years, but he's taken a poor remote stop on a wagon train route and turned it into an eco-nomic power."

She peeked out the shuttered window. "I've gotten spoiled by Ship's high-speed travel. We're barely making walking speed."

"Well, that's travel by ox-drawn wagons for you. I remember it well. If you want to travel faster, you get out and run."

He remembered his first exposure to Angela the horse.

"Horses can run as well. Specially trained ones, like the duke's pet, could carry a rider at high speed. I've read old histories from Earth that talked about horse-drawn carriages that could travel fast. That's not likely any time soon. There's only a handful of horses left. Nobody would risk hitching them to a wagon."

Sharra sighed. "That sounds useful. Why don't they breed more of them?"

"Horses haven't adapted well to lunar gravity. They're well-tuned for life on Earth, but left wild on Luna, they'll jump and break their legs on landing. Maybe someday some trainer will solve the problem, if all the horses don't die out first. That's one of the reason Jelica was sent to Franklin."

Sharra frowned. "Yes, she's gone, isn't she. When is she due back?"

"I don't know. Travel is dangerous right now."

She sighed. "I guess I need to make peace with Helva, then."

Charles didn't know why that concerned her, but he agreed it was important.

"Yes, I'm the only one who's supposed to be dead. It's okay for you to have come back."

She sighed. "A little embarrassing though, if perhaps I said something like I was leaving and never coming back."

He shrugged. "Maybe you just meant never coming back to the farm. I'll have to stay locked up in the castle out of sight for a while. You can stay there as well."

She bumped his side. "Of course I'll be staying with you. Who knows when you might get a bug in your ear and decide to race off to the other side of the world or something?"

"Would I do something like that?"

She laughed.

Sharra dozed off half-way through the Gate. Charles imagined a time when Harriman must have come in this way as well, to make a few new friends and teach them the sacred words.

He shook his head. He need to keep his focus on staying alive.

They pulled up to the castle's loading dock and Jed Tylan led them inside, having cleared out all the staff for a moment.

"I didn't believe the rumors that you were dead. You're too lucky for that."

Charles smiled. "No, you're wrong. I'm definitely dead. My luck ran out."

Tylan nodded wisely, then glanced at his companion. "Then again, maybe you're right."

Sharra said, "Shush, soldier boy. I've still got my knife."

Charles gathered that they had met before.

Duke James met them at the staircase and led them up several flights.

He said, "You should be okay here. The staff from the fourth floor up have been with me from the beginning and are well trained to keep secrets. They'll be bringing your meals as well."

He looked at Sharra. "Will you need a room of your own or—?"

She shook her head. "Somebody has to keep an eye on him."

Charles raised his hand. "Um, not that we—"

Sharra said, "Charles, be quiet for just a minute."

She addressed the duke. "Charles is a couple of days away from thinking about marrying me. If you would be so kind as to invite Helva for a visit to the castle, it would be helpful. I find I really need a visit with the Eldest right now."

James nodded slowly. "I think that can be arranged."

Charles led Sharra to his room and set their bags against the wall.

He took her hand. "Um. Sharra, am I thinking about marrying you?"

She nodded. "If it hadn't been for the preacher's death, I don't know how long it might have taken, but you've gotten shaken up. It would have occurred to you pretty soon now. We've both known this was in the cards— the only available Alpine for either of us."

He considered. "Maybe you're right. I haven't been …."

She asked, "Is there anyone else you've considered?"

He shook his head. "None of the Herc girls. Jelica was the only real option and she rejected me quickly. Then once she came here to Stampz, the only man in the world for her was James. Once I saw that, then I just thought I'd be on my own."

Charles looked at her critically, "And you've hardly been a vision of sweetness. It wasn't that hard to deny we were a couple when people speculated."

She held up one finger. "Stay alone all your life." She held up another. "Marry me and have someone to argue with."

He sighed, collapsed on his bed and stared at the ceiling. "This is all uncharted waters. I have no idea what to do."

She crawled onto the bed beside him. She poked his chest. "Have any of those other girls gotten too close? Close enough to make you uncomfortable?"

He nodded. "Sure. But it was easy enough to keep my distance."

She patted his head. "Then that's all I need. We'll work it all out when the time comes. Just trust me on this. You want to marry me. I'll take care of all the details."

He sighed, aware that she was closer than he'd let any other girl get before. He felt a little uneasy, but it wasn't unpleasant.

...

James and Charles sat in the private chamber. Charles tapped his radio.

"Ship and I have a special encryption channel, just like the one you and I use. With its new location, we can talk with Ship from here, in case we need its special skills."

James frowned. "Are you sure the Uralites can't detect it?"

Ship replied, its voice a little thinner than what Charles was used to hearing when on board the beamship. "It is unlikely that Mt. Ural or the other beamship would be able to triangulate my radio signals with any great precision. It is possible they are already aware of radio signals from Stampz and from the other warehouse locations but not certain. They have made no obvious moves against easy targets such as warehouses close to the Serenite border."

The duke asked, "Have you detected any radio signals in the Stampz area that are not already accounted for? Is there any possibility Serenite spies have radios, too?"

"I have not been within the Stampz detection radius very long, and I have not detected any such low power signals. I will continue monitoring."

James nodded. "Good, one less thing to worry about."

Charles asked, "What did you do about the warehouse guy who planted the bomb?"

James smiled, "He's working hard harvesting corn, but he's never been accused and may not suspect we know who he is. His supervisor knows and is watching. If he tries to make a run for it, he'll never make it out of the crater."

...

When Charles walked back toward his room, a maid nodded to him. "Your lady has gone down to the library to meet with her visitor."

He assumed that would be Helva. It was puzzling. Could there be some Alpine marriage ritual that needed the blessing of the Eldest of Women or some such? He'd never paid any attention to such things. He was only twelve when his culture was destroyed. Sharra was probably the same age, but maybe girls were more attentive to things like that.

What am I getting myself into? Do I really want to be married?

It wasn't as if he needed to ask whether he wanted to be married to Sharra specifically. There were no other options. He liked being around Sharra, in spite of her personality. It was just the marriage thing.

Married people had sex, and that was supposedly a big deal. And from what he'd seen of Jelica and James, they really enjoyed kissing each other and being close.

I guess I'll have to learn all that stuff. If I'm getting married, it will be expected.

Sharra said she'd teach him, but that really made him feel inadequate. He was a man. All that stuff was supposed to be instinctual, and maybe it was, but he'd been isolated for a long time. Just because he lived among Hercs didn't mean he felt like one and knew their culture inside and out. He liked the Kimmer as well, and that was a very different culture.

Maybe if he'd lived as a farmer, with other farmers and attending other farmer's social events, he'd know exactly how to be a farmer husband and how to treat his farmer wife, but nobody was like him. There weren't any other nomadic Alpines with their own families.

And indentured dockworkers didn't have family either.

How had Rad learned to romance his Maria? Well, it's too late to ask.

His brother was long gone and unreachable. He'd made no effort to contact Charles, in spite of his fame. Likely Rad had migrated eastward past the Peach River, outside of Herc or Serenite control. *Probably the safest place he could be for now.*

Tylan came up behind him, almost running in the narrow corridor. "There you are! The duke said I should check with you to see if you needed any special attention from the rim guards."

Charles shook his head. "No, I've got my security covered." Telling Stampz guards where to look for Serenite activity would just reveal where the beamship was hidden. The fewer people in the know the better. He hadn't even told the duke where the ship was.

And this time, Ship was authorized to be more active if it detected anything. It could even take to the skies and escape if threatened.

Tylan nodded. "Okay. That's good."

He paced with Charles a bit. Charles paused near a window and looked outside at the mid-morning activity.

"Um, Charles?" Tylan whispered. "Rumors are talking about a secret wedding I'm not supposed to know about. Are you really going to marry that Abeth woman?"

Charles asked, "You have any objection?"

"Well, it's none of my business, but I think you could do better."

Charles sighed. "It's the Alpine thing. We're trained from birth that we only marry other Alpines. I can't ignore how I was raised. With so few of us left, there are only three female Alpines I know of in the whole world."

He pointed out the window. Tylan looked. Down below Helva was being escorted to a wagon by Sharra.

"There are two of them. The other is already taken, your duchess. Now tell me, of those two, which is the best choice for me?"

Tylan winced as he watched the bent-over Helva struggle to get up into the wagon. Sharra was a vision of youth and beauty beside her, helping.

"I see your point. But aren't there exceptions? The healer married our duke, after all."

"Yes, and I don't understand that. But it's my upbringing that's important here. My mind is made up. We may not be a pair suitable for a court portrait, but we will make it work."

The Ceremony

Sharra came into the room and collapsed on the bed beside him.

"Charles, for such a simple decision, there are a surprisingly large number of things that have to be taken care of first. I've been running all day."

Charles was tempted to reach for her, maybe to give her a reassuring touch, but he wasn't quite that brave.

"I don't think it's all that simple. I've been second-guessing myself all this time."

She glared at him. "If you decide to back out now—"

"No! Keep your knife in its sheath. I've had to go through all the arguments time and time again, and I'm still ready to marry you. I'm just saying it wasn't simple."

She huffed. "Okay then." She turned on her side to face him. "Hug me."

He adjusted positions and put his arm around her.

She sighed. "That's better. You know, you now have permission to do this at any time, for any reason. If I object, I'll let you know without threatening you with my knife. I know I'm difficult. I'm working on it."

"What have you been up to today? I saw you with Helva. I assume that is some Alpine thing?"

"Yes, but you don't get the answers, not until after we're married."

"That doesn't sound fair."

She looked a little timid. "Sorry, Charles, but that's how it works with Alpines. If the world had gone a different way—if the Burn had never happened and we met at the Great Library or something—then when we prepared to wed at Aristoteles, you'd still be in the dark, with lots of preparations happening around you that wouldn't be explained.

"The only difference now is that I've got to handle all the preparations by myself, with no family to help me."

She sighed. "If I hadn't gotten special permission from the duke, I don't think I'd have been able to get some of it done. I made too many enemies when I first arrived. People haven't been eager to help me, at least at first."

He frowned, "Does that mean you're done?"

"Almost. If things happen according to schedule, we'll have the wedding at noon tomorrow. Just the duke, Helva as Eldest of Women and Edward Harris to represent Eldest of Men. Woodie Sparks is technically the oldest, but he's off in a wagon train somewhere.

"After the words, we come back here to finish the secret parts of the ceremony."

"Secret parts?"

She put her finger to his lips. "And you don't get to find out until then."

"I wish ...."

"Wish what?"

He shrugged. "It's a bad time. All the weddings I've seen, at a distance of course, have been big celebrations. But I'm supposed to be dead, and the more people who know I'm still alive, the more dangerous it is.

"Tylan let slip that the whole castle is talking about a secret wedding. You're running about, obviously the bride-to-be. And everyone already had us paired up as a couple before I even met you. It's not much of a secret that I'm still alive and hiding out here at the castle.

"And now, Helva and Edward will be there too? Even if we could swear everyone to secrecy, the word will get out. People just don't keep secrets very well."

She gave him a little squeeze. "You'd be surprised at how well some secrets can be kept. It will be okay.

"But for now, I need to doze off for a bit. I have some more chores in a few hours."

She turned over, facing away, but tugged his arm across her waist.

Charles balanced on his side uncomfortably for a while, until she was clearly asleep. He removed his arm from the embrace and settled himself.

On the trail, they'd slept side by side many times. Before, she'd been abrasive, and he had an ever present risk of being poked by that knife if he got too close.

But now, things had changed. They were even touching, regularly. Those odd feelings that had come when a Herc girl got too close, too familiar, were happening all the time now.

He really wanted to get closer. Not that it was time for that yet. It was disturbing.

He listened to her breathe, and before long, he dozed off as well.

...

Edward Harris was holding Helva Wiscolm's arm as they climbed the stairs the next day.

Charles met them and offered to help. Helva took his arm with a smile. There was no room on the other side for Edward, so he came up behind.

Edward asked, "How are you holding up?"

Charles shrugged. "Too much going on that I don't understand."

Edward chuckled. "According to plan then."

Charles asked, "Have you been through this?"

"Oh, yes. I had a wife, three children, and eight grandchildren."

No one mentioned the obvious, that they had all been lost in the Burn.

Helva sighed. "I married late. I had two daughters."

Edward poked Charles. "So we're all hoping you youngsters get at it. We could use some fresh blood."

Helva chided, "Edward! That's not appropriate."

Charles tried to shift the topic. "Helva, you taught etiquette as well as reading?"

"Oh, yes, although none of them particularly liked being scolded by an old Alpine."

They reached the fifth level. Helva was panting. Charles wondered if people her age on Earth could have handled the stairs. Did their native strength last even when they grew old?

Duke James of Stampz welcomed them into his personal study. There were books on the shelf, some from the library down below and some that he had from when he was younger.

There was a large window that looked out over the courtyard and off to the distant lake. Even the entrance to the Gate was visible.

The duke told everyone where they should stand. Charles faced the doorway with his back to the window. The elders stood to one side.

James said, "I've been told that this is a much abbreviated ceremony, as much of the Alpine rituals have been lost or the people unavailable. Part of it is what we use here at Stampz." He smiled. "I don't often get to officiate, but I'm happy to do it this time."

There was a rap on the door. Everyone turned to face it.

Sharra entered, and Charles was startled by the woman in a simple white and blue dress, barefoot with no ornaments. He smiled. She wasn't even wearing her knife.

Seeing her in women's clothes had an effect on him. *Things are different. She's beautiful.*

He held out his hand and they faced the duke. As promised the ceremony was short. He got an affirmation from each that they were entering this relationship under their own will and with no compulsion.

"Under my seal and by my authority I declare you husband and wife."

Sharra's hand was sweaty in his. She nodded and then gave another bow to the Eldest of Women and the Eldest of Men. Charles did the same, although he wasn't sure that was what he was supposed to do.

James brushed his hand. "Shoo. Leave now."

They laughed and hurried down the corridor and up the stairs to his room.

Sharra double-checked the lock on the door and went to the balcony and closed the shutters.

"If you're thinking that we immediately have sex, I'm afraid you'll be disappointed."

Charles said, "You'd said something about finishing the ceremony."

She took a deep breath. "Yes. Charles, the Alpine wedding ceremony always ends this way. It has since the days of Alexandria. Since the time of the Plague."

She took another deep breath and pulled out a small tray that had been hidden behind a cabinet. "This was prepared by Jelica Haren for her own wedding. The duke offered it for our use. I'm very grateful. I was trained in all this as a young girl, but I wasn't really confident that I remembered everything. Helva was gracious enough to refresh my memory. Every Alpine girl since the beginning has been trained in this ceremony, this procedure."

Timidly, she said, "I now have to take off my clothes. You can wait if you want."

He was frozen in place. He had no idea what he was supposed to do. This might be an ancient ceremony, but nobody ever told the groom what to do.

She slipped the dress off and set it carefully aside. She smiled, "I have to give this back. Apparently, it's very expensive."

Charles could barely breathe. Sharra, his Sharra, was wearing nothing but a lacy pair of shorts and a tight white band around her belly, just above her navel. He was fascinated by her breasts, but what was the white band?

She settled down on the bed. "Charles, here is the great secret shared by all Alpine women since the beginning. Young girls are taught it early. Men never learn it until their first time with their new wives."

He nodded, forcing all his attention on her words.

"Charles, every daughter of the Alpine race, since even before we were Alpine, has been born sterile. We cannot bear children."

"What?" He was puzzled. "That's impossible. I mean that's not even scientifically possible. No organism can evolve sterility. They'd ... we'd die out immediately."

"You're correct. Back before the days of the Plague, the Alexandrian population was shrinking rapidly. They even sent their young men to other places to seduce outsiders so that at least some new children would be born. But even the men carried the taint. Their outsider wives could bear children, but all daughters born to the Alexandrians were sterile."

Charles sat down on the bed next to her, trying to absorb the words.

She waited, letting him think. She took his hand and held it.

He clamped his eyes shut, thinking hard without the distraction of her body.

"I need to know more. Both male and female carry the trait?"

She whispered, telling the story as it was told to her.

"Someone hated the Alexandrians and wished them extinct, but this was a time before the Plague, before war. A disease was created, probably using the banned genetic engineering, so that the attack could be done in secret with no one ever suspecting that it had happened.

"It is a strange disease, sexually transmitted, but with no symptoms other than passing the disease on to their children. However, all daughters have a new small gland in their belly that adjusts their hormones slightly. Just enough so that they can never conceive.

"The men could have children, but only sterile daughters."

Charles nodded to himself. "So the fertility drops drastically every generation. In a confined community like Alexandria—the effects would be catastrophic."

He had another thought. He looked at her. "You say it's sexually transmitted as well as inherited?"

She nodded, "Male and female can both spread the taint."

Then she whispered the familiar Alpine chant they had learned as children, "'And that we may bless the World by our separateness, that we remain a People Apart.'"

He looked at her face. Something in her eyes gave him a hint.

She nodded, her teeth clamped in anger. "There are wealthy families in Port Gartner who will die out in a couple of generations because they bought my sister and me. Our revenge will be final!"

She shook her head and tried to get back to the ritual.

"Charles, my husband, know this: At the time of the Plague, an outsider doctor discovered our curse and formulated a treatment. Not a cure, but a method to allow daughters of our race to bear children. Our curse can be lifted for one woman at a time, but it must be taught to every daughter that comes, for the day when she finds a husband of her own.

"And our curse must remain a secret for all. Humanity would arise and destroy every one of us should the word get out."

Charles could see it. A transmitted disease that could cause sterility was a nightmare. Alpines would be treated as monsters that had to be extermintated if the word got out. He was in awe that the Alexandrians and the Alpines before him had managed to keep this secret for centuries.

It was the women's traditions, he realized. They kept the secret close, until a man could be found trustworthy enough to share it. The Women's Council, the Eldest of Women, all of it was designed to protect this secret, and to keep their race from being extinguished.

"Charles, my husband, please remove this curse from me." She held out the little tray. He took it.

She scooted the white belly band up a little, exposing an inked mark on her skin. It looked like the skin had been treated with a salve.

"Charles, my husband, take the little knife and cut along the mark, no deeper than the line on the blade."

He followed the instructions, step by step. There was a cloth to soak up the blood, and then he sweated as he cut out the gland, a tiny tube with a bulb at one end, he said, "This can't be natural."

Sharra was holding back the pain and nodded. "Probably a genetic weapon. From the time of the Plague."

He closed the shallow cut, applied another salve, and helped Sharra fit the white band tightly to keep the wound sealed. He panted, staring at the blood on his hands.

"Every woman has this done?"

"Yes. Every Alpine woman. And her husband saves her from the curse.

"Charles, my husband, go clean your hands and then come back and hold me. I need a little comfort."

Waiting for Bad News

Charles stood at the forth-floor balcony, watching everyone scurry to finish their light-sleep chores before dawnwind arrived.

Not even a full day, and everything has changed for me. It was the first time he'd left the room. Food had arrived at the door and left with just a knock announcing its arrival.

Surprisingly, he hadn't needed too much coaching once she felt well enough to get him out of his clothes. Her cut had bled a little more, but she was confident it was healing well.

Ordinary people have to get used to the sex on their wedding night. I've got this other stuff as well. But, well, I'm an Alpine.

"Charles?"

He turned. Duke James crooked his finger and they hurriedly went up to the private chamber where secrets could be spoken, usually.

James started a warmball for light. They stared at each other for a moment.

Charles nodded. "I've got a secret. You've got a secret. And even if it's the same secret, we can't say a word."

James nodded.

Charles said, "I always wondered how easily the Alpines accepted you as a full Alpine, even through they ridiculed Darkwind and Heidi's claim to be apprentice Alpines. But now I understand. All they had to do was see it in your eyes."

James nodded and poured a drink for the both of them. "You don't know the lengths Jelica went through to get my proper consent, even though she couldn't really tell me what it was all about. It took a long time before she believed me when I said I'd do anything to be with her."

He shook his head. "But I didn't call you in here to talk about that. Nor about your wedding night. I needed to warn you that there's an emissary from the imperial court here in the castle. You need to stay put on your floor until I can give you the word."

Charles frowned. "What's he here for?"

James frowned. "The Serenites are moving up the coast faster than expected. Maury is definitely taken. It sounds like the Williams peninsula is falling. They'll definitely be threatening Hercules and Atlas before too long. The emperor is scrambling to get forces in play to defend the capital.

"It's been an open secret that Stampz has been a refuge for the Alpines and particularly, you and your beamship. The emperor is pleading for me to convince you to come defend Hercules or even to destroy the invasion fleet like you did the supply ships at Beltis during the Terrance invasion."

Charles sighed. "What have you said?"

"I've told them the beamship never returned from a trip to Franklin and that I have people out hunting for you, which is true. And then I repeated all the rumors of the blast and how people feared the beamship was destroyed."

Charles shook his head. "You know I barely escaped Beltis that time? They had laser cannon firing my way and I have no defense against that. There's a reason the Uralite beamship isn't overhead, supporting the Serenite fleet, a beamship is just too vulnerable when there are laser cannon all about.

"It would be crazy to attack the Serenite fleet. One lucky shot and the total energy stored in the beamship comes out in a huge fireball. I could try to defend Hercules and end up setting the whole west coast on fire. Hasn't Luna had one Great Burn already?"

James nodded. "I agree with you, but the danger is that if the emperor decides I'm less that totally loyal to the throne, it could be very dangerous for Stampz. I'm his nephew, but I'm also a half-breed, half-Serenite, and everybody knows it.

"I can reasonably say I can't help with the beamship, as long as you stay hidden. I'm going to open up my communications—my couriers, my warehouses and way-stations—to the imperial guards as a sign of good faith."

"Turn over the bomber."

James nodded. "I thought of that. Let him explain how he blew up the beamship."

Charles sighed. "I wish there was something I could do to help. I'm not in love with either empire, but I hate it that Stampz is caught up in this."

"Just stay out of sight for now. Go keep your new wife happy and help her stay out of trouble."

. . .

Sharra frowned, even as she played with the ties on his shirt. "So this duke is both Herc and Serenite?"

"And Alpine, don't forget that." He stretched out, letting her play her games with his clothes. It generally turned out well. The couple of days they'd been hiding in his room had been a revelation. Sharra was very inventive and he struggled to keep up with her.

"So, how is he even allowed to be a duke?"

Charles shook his head. "I don't know, just kitchen gossip really. It was a storybook romance, back for a brief time when both empires were at peace with each other. A Herc prince and a Serenite princess fell in love. Both families hated it. The girl was killed and loyal servants smuggled her child across the border to the father. Young James was educated as Herc nobility and when he became of age, his father, now brother to the emperor, shuffled the newly minted duke off to a little out-of-the-way crater with the understanding that his title depended on staying as far away from court intrigues as possible.

"It really was a risk for James to support the Alpines. Life as royalty is risky, and even more so for him. Purges happen. The Serenites do it all the time. They've been through four royal families, from what I read. Five now, with King Bardin on the Red Throne."

She kissed. "So, the duke's power is limited."

"Yes, and we'd better hope that the empire resists the invasion, because if Hercules falls, Stampz goes too, and any hope for a sanctuary for Alpines."

"We could run away."

Charles considered it. "Yes, you and me, maybe even a few more people, but Helva? They are all considerably older than us and living in the forest and making friends with the Kimmer isn't a good call for them. Lucas would never leave the library, and honestly, I don't think I can abandon the library either. The Serenites just might burn the whole place down. They've done it to other places."

Some time later, when Charles was getting dressed, a tiny light flashed in the wardrobe.

"Uh, oh."

Sharra stretched and then frowned. "Problem?"

He picked up the radio and slipped it around his neck.

"Ship, you called?"

The voice said, "Yes. I have detected anomalous radio signals."

Charles sat on the bed, slipping on his boots. "Explain in detail."

"From my current location at ground level, I have only been able to detect radio signals internal to Stampz and the signals from Mt. Ural in its four-hour orbit. Approximately two hours ago, I detected the replies to the Uralite transmissions that would only be possible if they were close, or if they were high in the atmosphere. Careful observation suggests that these replies were from the Uralite beamship, high in the atmosphere, and almost due east, indicating that the ship was over Hercules Empire lands."

Charles said, "Are they still on-going?"

"No. They persisted for nearly an hour, during the period when Mt. Ural was closest overhead, assuming they were at the west coast."

"Sharra, pull the signal rope two times, then pause, and then another two times."

"Okay." She climbed out of the bed to where the pull rope went down through a tube near the balcony.

He frowned. "Don't let anyone see you in the window. We can't cause a scandal."

She grinned. "I'll get dressed. What's up?"

"The Uralites are using the beamship over the battle area. They must really be sure that I'm dead to risk that. The duke has to be notified."

A few minutes later Tylan arrived to escort Charles to the private room.

Charles described what Ship had detected.

Duke James frowned. "So they're using, or preparing to use, the beamship in their attacks. They must feel the risk is minimal. I wonder if they're using their laser cannon on the Herc ships."

Charles shook his head. "Not right now. The globe curves. If the Uralite beamship is over Hercules, then they'd have to be a couple of hundred kloms up for our ship to detect their radio signals. There's no way they could even see the ground from that altitude. They would be safe when they're that high."

"Then why are they there at all if they can't even see the ground?"

"Maybe they go up and down. I've always felt safe from ground attack once I'm ten to twenty kloms up. People couldn't even see me. I'd just be a tiny dot among the clouds.

"Maybe the beamship is dropping down briefly to get detailed images of the Herc forces and then relaying that information to the Serenites."

James nodded. "There's no defense against that."

"Should you tell the imperials?"

"I already have, at least in theory. I sent my suggestions, not that they have any reason to listen to me. I have no military background they respect, other than protecting Stampz.

"But I told them of Mt. Ural's presence, and its beamship, and told them they could be spied upon from above."

Charles knew the question people were thinking. Was there any way he could use his ship to aid the conflict? James wasn't asking. The risk assessment hadn't changed. Having the Uralite ship over Hercules just made it worse.

Charles was conflicted. Part of him was screaming to act, but his head was shaved because he had acted in the past without thinking it through. He didn't want more dead littering the landscape just because he used his power too quickly.

And now, he had a wife. He had a responsibility to her, and he needed to make sure he didn't fail at that. There had been so much he had failed at during his life.

He asked, "James, have you heard from Jelica?"

The duke nodded. "The imperial residence is starting to get crowded. Many of the nobles are fleeing Hercules and Atlas as the Serenite Navy gets closer. Anybody with any claim to be a guest in Franklin is taking advantage of it. She's considering making the trip back to Stampz, just as soon as I can get a troop there to protect her."

"I wish I could do something."

James nodded. "So do I, but I can't ask it. The risks are too great. I can't even let you have free run of the castle. There are legionaries down in the courtyard, conferring with my people."

Charles remembered that elite force from the first time he'd come to Stampz, back when he drove his covered wagon. None of that troop had survived.

"Where are they from?"

James frowned, "Condorcet. They've been ordered back to the capital. I'm sure the southern governor put up a fuss over that. Bardin has always had his eyes on Condorcet. He wants all of Crisium under his flag."

Charles was aware of that. He'd met the former grand admiral during his time as a prisoner at Beltis—Bardin's prized fortified island. The ownership of the Crisium Sea had flip-flopped back and forth over history. Most people had thought the Serenite invasion, when it happened, would be to take over the southern lands. This surprise push to Hercules itself had thrown the empire off guard.

James said, "Oh, and there's someone asking if they can meet you. Tylan said you weren't here, but he said he'd wait."

"What does he want?"

James shrugged. "He won't say. A private issue. He's staying at a guest house. His name is Sull, James Sull."

Charles tensed. "I need to see him."

The Fall

It was difficult to make the arrangements. James and Jed Tylan were not confident that Sull wasn't a Serenite spy, in spite of what Charles told them about him.

To avoid a third party spy watching their activities, Sull was arrested by Tylan's crew in the still, officially to ask what he knew about Charles's activities. When he was reluctant to talk, he was led upstairs into the castle.

Charles, in a cap and in the darkest part of the room, spoke, "You're not really under arrest."

Sull gasped, "So you are here!"

"If you can't keep that secret, then people could die."

Sull snorted. "If I couldn't keep secrets then I'd never be were I am now. But... what have you heard, about Harriman?"

Charles came closer to the warmball. "Little. He was killed, but anything beyond that is tangled in conflicting rumors."

The man who had been Harriman's bodyguard on their last visit nodded sadly.

Sull took a deep breath.

"I was there. It was barely a day after you left. The guards caught up with us. There were two scribes in their black robes giving orders to the guards. We were taken to the printing press and the guards collected all the completed and half-finished books and piled them all together. Then they started dismantling parts of the printing press itself. There were six of us, held captive, watching it all. It was clear they were going to burn everything we had done.

"But the word got out and a crowd started gathering. Some I recognized from my church. Others were just spectators.

"The scribes were pleased. They wanted to make a spectacle of it, burning all the Bibles and destroying the printing press. Then, I'm sure, we'd be dragged off in chains to be made examples of people who tried to do things on their own without the official blessings of the scribes."

Sull shook his head. "Harriman was in tears. It was his life work! And they were going to destroy it all, again!"

Sull shuddered. "They lit the fire, and the Bibles started to burn.

"Harriman let out a scream like I never want to hear again. He broke free from the burly guard holding him and jumped into the burning pile.

"He screamed, 'I am not letting it burn again!' and tossed the Bibles out into the crowd. Some were burning and believers fell on top of them to smother the blaze. People were running all over the place. People who had saved a Bible fled the scene.

"Our captors were caught off guard, and all of us escaped into the crowd.

"All except Harriman. The fire covered him. He was still screaming, flames all over him, when he collapsed. He was not able to save all of his beloved Bibles, but at least he protected them to the last."

Sull was crying, and so was Charles. He put out his hand and gripped the bodyguard's shoulder. "Harriman could not have done differently."

"I know."

Charles sighed. "But the printing press is destroyed."

Sull's eyes glittered as he said, "That one was."

"Oh."

"From the beginning, we knew something like this might happen. The plans and even many of the parts were duplicated and distributed among our group. We won't be so open in our operations next time."

"But many of the Bibles were saved?"

"Right. We're moving in secret, trying to get a copy to as many churches as possible. They're not stopping us."

He reached beneath his coat. "I came here to give this to you. I was with Harriman for a year and he spoke of you often. He would have wanted you to have this."

The Bible was charred on the lower edge and the covering was in tatters. Charles opened it carefully. On some pages, the bottom line of text was charred, but the wooden cover had protected the words well.

"I don't know what to say."

"Say you'll read it. That would make Harriman smile."

Then, after reassurances that Sull could keep Charles's presence a secret, the man went back to Tylan's people and was released.

. . .

Sharra stood behind him as he looked at the book opened on the desk. Her arms were wrapped around his shoulders. "That's the book he worked for?"

"Yes, he gave his life for it. Literally in this case. He walked into the fire and threw it to safety. I have to read it."

She gave him a gentle pat on the head. "I'll go get us something to eat."

Charles didn't expect her to understand. At least, no matter what her feelings were about the Herc preacher, she knew not to speak against him when in his presence. Maybe he'd need to do his reading when she wasn't around.

He started at the beginning, puzzling through the creation stories. He didn't understand all of it, but that wasn't the point. He didn't understand all the Kimmer creation songs either, but that didn't mean he couldn't appreciate them.

When Sharra came back, she had a few books with her as well. If he had to spend time reading, then she would be his companion and read as well.

. . .

The battlefront was roughly seven hundred kloms away, over winding trails. Couriers who could maintain a rapid pace with long strides in the lunar gravity were the speediest communication available. Stampz didn't find out what had happened until days later.

Tylan read from the courier's report. The duke's secret soundproofed room was a little crowed with the three of them there.

"At noon all of Hercules heard a booming voice in a strange accent. The Hercules Empire was to cede all of the southern lands to the Serenite Landrule within one day's time, or be utterly destroyed."

Charles said, "That's roughly the time that Ship detected the Uralite beamship's radio transmissions. It came down to the lowest cloud deck and gave the ultimatum."

The duke nodded. "Jeb, continue."

"A second courier raced to catch up with the first. They combined their reports as the first one stopped to rest."

Tylan frowned, puzzling out what he was reading. "At noon the following day, as the Hercules Navy clustered tightly to defend the capital, a blazingly bright giant cannonball came down from the sky and consumed the imperial palace and all the surrounding grounds. A giant wave filled the inner harbor and destroyed many of the naval ships. Almost at once, a beamship appeared and attacked the remaining ships with laser fire.

"All of the navy is gone. All of the palace is leveled. The dead in the city are uncountable."

The duke gasped. "Charles, what happened?"

Tylan gestured. "There's more."

The duke nodded. "Continue."

"Barely had the laser attacks begun, when a second blazing cannonball struck the Atlas inner harbor as well. Both cities are destroyed. Forest fires have started in the area. The courier barely escaped with his life."

Charles had never seen James looking as stricken as the report unfolded.

James whispered, "Charles?"

"It was a direct attack by Mt. Ural. They collected two rocks from the rubble among the space cities."

"Rocks?"

"Yes, boulders maybe ten tonnes or so in size, and then carefully aimed them at the surface with tractor beams. There was no chance that Mt. Ural would ever have stopped, even if Hercules had surrendered. It would take lots of time and preparation to make such an accurate strike, but Mt. Ural has the beams to make it work. Maybe they even used the beamship to target the palace directly, I don't know.

"But all the craters in the world were created by rocks like that falling from space. There is enormous energy released when a rock falling that fast strikes the surface. My people were wiped out when a larger rock struck Alp Island.

"These were smaller, with just enough power to destroy the Hercules Navy and capital, but not so large as to threaten the Serenites keeping their distance."

James asked, "And they can do it again?"

"Yes, I don't see any reason they couldn't."

James sighed. "The emperor is dead, and we'll have to see if his sons were sent to safety ahead of time or not."

Charles asked, "And your father?"

"He was commanding the fleet defending Hercules."

Behind the strained face, carefully adding up the empire's remaining strength, Charles could see the eyes of a son in shock at having just lost his father.

James straightened himself. He stared off into the distance.

"The military commanders are spread out defending their areas, and some won't find out about the destruction for days yet. The naval forces in Crisium are now vastly outnumbered by the Serenites, as soon as they move back south.

"The southern governor won't give up Condorcet without a fight, but when the news of Hercules and Atlas arrives, he'll be facing total destruction himself. The remaining naval commanders will find they have been reduced to just pirates, probably loyal to a distant child emperor who can provide them no resources, and they will be constantly on the run.

"Hercules ground forces are distributed along the border lands and have been able to hold off the Serenite land forces. How long that will remain if cities are destroyed is unknown."

James said, "Jeb, you will need to spread the word that there is no longer any peace in the world. The empire might just survive, if there are competent people in Franklin, but we will get no support for a long time. It will be time for me to tell my farmers to pull out their weapons and prepare them for use."

He looked utterly defeated.

A light on the radio around Charles's neck blinked. "James?"

The duke looked and nodded.

"Ship, what do you want."

"The guard station above the Gate is reporting another courier. They have been trying to contact the duke, but no one wants to interrupt your meeting."

James stood, and went to the door.

An ashen faced member of Tylan's guards stood outside.

The duke said, "What is it?"

"A courier has arrived from Franklin. The imperial estate has been destroyed in a giant fireball."

Everyone knew what that meant. Duchess Jelica had been there.

James turned to Charles. "Ah … Charles … could you—?"

Charles was already to his feet. "I'll go get her immediately."

He whispered into the radio. "Ship, we're going to Franklin. When will Mt. Ural be out of detection range?"

"Approximately thirty minutes."

Charles frowned. He turned to the duke. "I'll have to fly to the ship. If the Uralites are following Bardin's every command, then this castle might be on the target list. Stay safe."

James nodded. "Jeb, I need to speak with you some more."

Charles raced down the hallway and up the stairs.

Sharra looked startled as he came in. "What's happening?"

He pulled out his sailsuit from the wardrobe. "The Uralites are destroying major cities with meteorites. Franklin has been hit. I have to take the ship to rescue Jelica, if she's still alive."

She took a few seconds to absorb the news. He was almost dressed.

"Then take me with you."

He shook his head. "I have to fly. There's a tight window when we can take the ship without being detected. No time for wagon or running."

"Then carry me."

He hesitated. "I've never done that."

She strapped on her knife and slipped on her boots. "You can do it. Try at least. If we can't make it, then go on without me, but try."

He moved to the balcony. "Okay, but it's dangerous."

She smiled at him, and then held him tight. "Being close to me is dangerous."

He nodded. He tapped the controls and they lifted into the air.

In and Out Rescue

It was a struggle to keep them aloft and on course. At first, Sharra was turning her head, trying to see what was going on and shifting her grip constantly, but before they'd reached the rim she had settled down.

"I should never have tried this," he spoke over her hair. If she lost her grip, he might never catch her in time. Maybe with a strap belting them together, it might be safer. His glide time was much reduced. He was having to constantly reboost to gain altitude.

"I'll never let you go," she yelled.

But he had to concentrate on finding the ship's hiding place. Her hair flying in his face was a distraction.

Landing was off. They tumbled when he hit too hard. She laughed. "Are you grateful for the ground under your feet?"

He nodded. "Most times. But I generally land softer than that."

They went inside.

"Ship, do you detect any radio signals that might be the Uralite beamship?"

"No."

"Then we risk it. Ship, take us on a ballistic course for the Franklin crater. Start signaling for Jelica's radio as soon as we have enough altitude. We don't know where she is, exactly, and we don't have much time to search for her."

They lifted before Charles was even in the command seat. Sharra settled into the other chair.

"What happened?"

Charles explained how the Uralites had attacked with artificial meteorites.

She said, "It sounds like a trap."

"What? The main attack?"

"Yes. They scared the Hercs into massing their ships altogether in one place, and then took them out with one shot."

"I think you're right. And now this attack on the imperial estate in Franklin. It's all the same. Scare the nobles into seeking safety and then kill them all with one stroke as well. Well, we've known the Serenites were experts at sending spies to find out their enemies' weak points. It tastes like Bardin's plan."

He frowned and tugged at the gap in his sailsuit.

She said, "I felt that. What is it?"

He fished out the partly burned book. "There's a chance that another meteor is aimed at Stampz. Duke James is on Bardin's death list. The rest of the Neely family, relatives of the duke's mother, the former royals of Serenity, have all been killed. Bardin is thorough.

"If the Stampz castle is going up in a blast from space, then I couldn't let this book burn, not after all Harriman went through."

He smiled at her. "That's the main reason I even considered jumping off the balcony with you in my arms. I couldn't leave you there either."

"Hey, you were in my arms, not the other way around."

He shuddered. "It was scary either way."

"Well, I'm glad I'm at least as important as that book."

It was several minutes later that Jelica's voice spoke, "Hello?" She sounded frightened. "Is there somebody there?"

Charles felt a big weight drop away. Jelica was his friend, and he really didn't know if James would survive without her.

"This is Charles. I'm glad you're alive."

"You heard then? It was horrible. I think it was a meteorite or something."

"I'm glad you were clear of it. Where exactly are you?"

"I was out visiting the horses, southeast inside the crater." She sounded rattled. "We barely had time to shelter from the blast when the central peaks were engulfed in flames. We lost a couple of the horses when they panicked."

"I need exact directions. I'll be landing the ship to take you back to James. He needs you there."

Her voice settled down. Ship put up its map on the display. They'd passed over it recently, so there were lots of details.

Charles said, "I can see a road that runs south toward the lake near the eastern rim."

"Right. We took that road until it passed a canal. Old Rill Road. The horse's pasture is square and there's a large barn on the southwest corner."

"Good. I can see it. We'll be there shortly. I don't want to stay on the ground very long. The ship is big target for the Serenites."

"Um, Charles, I'm not alone."

He nodded. He hated taking on strangers, with good reason, but this was a rescue mission. "Okay, how many?"

"This is encrypted, isn't it?"

"Right. No one but us can understand what we're saying."

She sighed. "Okay. There's me, Kerny, my new maid, and Paul Trask in my party. There's also, Prince Carl, and his three attendants. We were visiting the horses together."

Charles asked quietly, "The other brother?"

She said, "Probably at the estate, with his advisors. Carl is ten."

"I understand. Yes, they can all come along."

The emperor had two sons. The eldest, Crown Prince Mark, was destined to inherit the title. But now it looked like only the younger son remained of the imperial line. Charles might be rescuing the new emperor.

"And Charles?"

"Yes?"

"Is there room for fourteen horses as well?"

. . .

Some of the horses broke free in panic as the ship landed. Charles was secretly glad when he saw them scatter. Maybe fourteen horses and all the people could fit in the cargo level, but whether they would survive the close quarters for the trip back to Stampz was debatable.

Charles was out the cargo hatch ordering people of all stations to get in and huddle against the left-hand wall. Trask, Jelica and two of the men in fancy dress struggled to get the remaining horses aboard the beamship.

Inside he could hear Sharra giving orders. Charles flatly rejected the plea for more time to rescue the scattered horses.

"Get on board now, or be left behind. We can't stay one more minute!"

He climbed the ladder as the cargo hatch slid shut. Sharra was beside the ladder with her knife drawn.

"I don't care who you all are, or how important you are. The Serenites are attempting to kill us all and they use spies. I don't know you and right now, if you cause us any trouble getting to safety, then you'll be needing the Healer of Stampz here to survive your knife wounds."

The lone imperial guard, the prince's bodyguard, matched her glare, but didn't challenge her.

Charles went to the command chair and checked the surroundings. There were no immediate threats and he wished the distant horses good luck and ordered Ship to take them aloft.

A couple of minutes later, Sharra poked her head up. "Hey, Charles?"

"Yes."

"The prince wants to come up. Is it okay?"

Charles nodded. "The prince and only one attendant—and they have to behave."

He really didn't want any of them, but maybe Sharra could get away with being rude to royalty, but Charles was a little more respectful. It wouldn't hurt to be friends with the new emperor.

"Ship, send the tap code once Stampz is in radio range."

"Acknowledged."

The prince climbed the ladder, eyes wide at the lights and the display on the wall. A gray-haired tutor followed him up.

The prince asked, "We're really up in the air?"

Charles pointed to the changing numbers. "Yes, we're eighteen kloms above the ground."

"It just looks like clouds."

"That's all there is up here.

"Ship, show a map with our location marked."

The display changed. The tutor opened his mouth, but said nothing. There was a moving X crossing the edge of Hooke crater.

"We're moving so fast!"

"Yes. It's only minutes to Stampz."

"We should go to Hercules."

Charles glanced at the instructor. He could tell from the man's eyes that he'd heard the news. Perhaps the prince didn't know that all the rest of his family was dead.

Charles said, "We are traveling only toward Stampz. The ship is like a cannon ball, in that once it leaves the muzzle, can only proceed on to its target."

"But I want to go to the palace! Turn it around."

Charles was sure he would get no help from the instructor. He shouldn't have let the prince up here.

"Prince Carl, can you see this stain on my chair."

Uncertainly, he nodded. "Yes."

"Back in the days before Sheb the First took the throne, this ship was being flown by a man from York, but Serenites were in charge, giving the orders. The Yorkman took to the skies to save all their lives, but the Serenites didn't understand what was happening and ordered him to stop. When he didn't stop, they shot him and this is his blood.

"But the thing is, that those Serenites and all of Condorcet would have been destroyed if the Yorkman had obeyed orders. Sometimes, when dealing with *oldman* machines, it is best to listen to those who know how they work."

The prince had a rebellious pout, but when he looked at his instructor, the man nodded.

The prince said, "I'm going down the ladder now."

Charles was happy to see them go.

Moments later, Duke James spoke. "Charles?"

"Jelica is safe and on board. We're due to arrive at Stampz shortly. I have to unload Jelica and her party, Prince Carl and his attendants, and nine or ten horses, all in a hurry. I have to get the beamship back into hiding before Mt. Ural appears on its next orbit."

He could hear James take a deep breath. "Thank you, Charles. Can you land somewhere near your farm? Don't approach the castle. I am in the process of evacuating the central peak area. There are people all over the place. I'll have a carriage there as soon as possible to pick up his royal highness."

Charles conferred with Ship. If he were going to land at the farm, he had to steer clear of Heidi's garden plots or he'd never hear the end of it. He just hoped that they could keep the horses under control.

Ship flashed some text below the display, silently alerting him to information that Charles just might want to keep secret from the others.

Charles nodded. "I understand, but we've got to choose the landing spot."

His neighbor to the east had a pen for his oxen, if he recalled. Perhaps he'd share space for the horses, if the duke charmed him.

Quickly, the image on the display grew more detailed and they came down to a flawless landing.

Charles quickly dropped down the ladder. He shouted, "Everyone, all guests, other than those managing the horses, leave first and go toward the house with the wide front porch."

He whispered to Jelica, "James is on his way. The events have taken their toll. I think he's lost everyone in his family.

"Go be the hostess at the Alpine house and keep the others from spooking."

She nodded and hurried out. The frantic young maid whose name Charles had already forgotten hurried out after her.

"Trask, I've got a neighbor with a fenced pasture. I'll run ahead and make arrangements, but see if you can get the horses moving that direction."

Charles ran fast, startling his neighbor when he arrived. Charles made quick promises for a decent rental but all it really took was the assurance that the duke needed his help.

Time is running out. He had to be back in hiding when Mt. Ural next appeared.

Off in the distance, he saw a couple of familiar figures. Heidi at her shed, and it looked like Darkwind was with her.

He ran again.

"Heidi! A bunch of horses are unloading from the ship. They're not really under control. You need to protect your plants."

Her eyes went wide. "Yes!" She raced away.

Charles gestured. "Darkwind, come with me. It's time for another adventure."

Taking the Opportunity

"Watch your step."

Darkwind chuckled at the mess. "I'm not afraid of a little dung."

They climbed the ladder.

"Ship! Is everyone unloaded?"

Sharra called down, "Everyone but me."

Darkwind smiled, "Ah! The Singer. I loved your performance."

Charles said, "Sharra is now my wife."

Darkwind nodded, as if he already knew.

"But no time for chatting.

"Ship, make sure all hatches are sealed and lift off, twenty kloms up."

Charles said to Darkwind, "You've heard about the destruction of Hercules, Atlas, and Franklin?"

The young man's eyes glittered. "Horrible, but I would have loved to see it. What a tale to sing!"

"You can ask Jelica later. She saw it happen. But now, Ship has some news."

Charles looked to the display, "Ship, show me on the map what you detected."

An X appeared on a map, near the coastline south of Oersted and north of Franklin.

Charles said, "As we were making our escape from Franklin, Ship detected radio signals. As we traveled toward Stampz, they continued, giving Ship enough triangulation data to identify the location of all three sources.

"One appears to be Beltis Island. We believe that is King Bardin's base of operations. None of the radio signals have come from the Serenite capital at Posidonius.

"Another appears to be the Uralite beamship. It was stationary, high enough to communicate with Beltis. It was over the land, in conquered territory.

"The third signal appeared to be a ship at sea, probably the Serenite naval commander. The Uralite beamship was providing a relay so that Bardin at Beltis could speak with his commander at sea, instantly."

Sharra asked, "What are you thinking?"

Charles said, "The war between the Hercs and Serenity is lost. With the Uralite help, the attacks were devastating. The Herc navy is mostly gone. The bulk of the nobility is wiped out as well as the imperial family, with the exception of a ten-year-old boy.

"All we have left to look forward to is the destruction of more cities, including Stampz, and the gradual encroachment of the Serenite army as they overwhelm the Green army whose factories and farms are being destroyed.

"Soon enough, there will be no safe place for us in the world. The Serenites will control it all. The Alpine refuge will be gone and all we've done will have been for nothing."

He raised his hand. "But, if the Uralite beamship is captured or destroyed, then much of Serenity's advantage would be handicapped. Without a beamship, the Uralites have no way to get resources from Luna, and there will be no way for them to move their population to new homes on the ground.

"The Uralites are in this war to get food and homesteads for their population, not for any other reason. Cut off that possibility and Mt. Ural will have no motive to support the Serenites.

"Without the Uralite beamship, the Hercs can at least have a chance to survive if they can rally their remaining cities with the leadership of the remaining nobles like Duke James."

She frowned. "You're talking about this ship attacking the other one. Isn't that a bad thing? We could start another Great Burn. No one would win."

Charles said, "But this is our only chance to act. As soon as the beamship moves back up Mt. Ural or over to Beltis, then it will be heavily defended and impossible to attack. Most of the time we don't even know where it is.

"But for this one moment in time, we do know. For as long as it's being used as a communications relay, we have to take the opportunity to damage or capture it."

Sharra crossed her arms. "I just knew I had to stay with the ship. I had a feeling you'd run off the save the world without me."

He frowned. "I am uncomfortable with you aboard when there's a good chance we might be destroyed."

"Ah ha! I knew it. Is that why we are hovering here in the sky? So you can talk me into staying behind?"

"Maybe."

She pointed. "And why do you need the Kimmer?"

Darkwind grinned. "To sing the story afterward, maybe."

Charles said, "If we're lucky enough to capture the beamship, then I need a trained pilot to fly it. Darkwind has been trained."

She frowned, "Don't you just tell it where to go?"

"Our beamship, with Ship as its brain, can do that. We have no idea how the other beamship works. It's had hundreds of years of customization to how the Uralites think. It may be loyal enough to them to resist our commands. We just don't know."

She frowned, first at Charles, then at Darkwind, then back to Charles. "Okay, but I'm going. Don't waste time trying to get rid of me."

Charles nodded. "Ship, set a ballistic course for Oersted and we'll refine it when we get closer." They felt the surge as the ship acted.

Charles took the time to describe the battle with this same beamship that occurred when he, Harriman, and Heidi went on their expedition to gather the books from the Alexandrian library.

"Since the beamships are very similar in power and armament, an ambush can make all the difference. Plus since beamwork depends on the other masses available, the ship closer to the ground can strike a stronger blow against the one higher in the air. It's possible that the Uralite ship has already landed after relaying those commands."

Darkwind nodded. "We're at the disadvantage there."

Charles continued, "Laser attacks depend on whether the beamship can aim in that direction. We know our ship's limitations there, but the Uralites might just have more than one laser and can shoot in all directions. We know they have at least one, since they used it before."

He shook his head. "Our only possibilities are a laser strike at one end of the ship, away from the power core, to prevent its rupture. Or a power sucking attack."

Ship spoke, "I have never attempted a high power transfer within an atmosphere. There may be secondary effects."

Charles said, "But you transfer power to my impulse rifle and the space-suits all the time, and that's inside the atmosphere."

"An attack to drain a ship's power in combat is much quicker, with a higher power density."

Sharra listened, chewing her thumb. Charles was mainly explaining things for Darkwind, and they used words she'd never heard. Still, she was glad they were discussing the capture option. Ever since she'd heard of the explosive power of a beamship's destruction, she was fearful of vanishing in an instant, converted into a blinding sun.

And Charles knew all of that. That he was willing to risk this attack gave her some confidence.

Ship spoke. "The Uralite ship may have moved. I am detecting a bright flash off in the distance. There is another one. A laser cannon is in use."

"Where is it?"

The map shifted on the display. The X was between Franklin and Hooke.

Charles nodded. "Possibly. Can you tell whether the laser is being used against ground targets, or by troops on the ground?"

"The light-bloom shows light on the ground, below a cloud layer, nothing is breaking up higher into the sky. I assume downward-directed fire."

Charles said, "Then the Uralite ship is returning on a course to Beltis, and attacking any Herc targets they see on the ground.

"Ship, alter our course so we can fall toward the Uralite ship."

Charles was aware that he'd just ordered their beamship to change course in a way he'd told the child prince was impossible. He hadn't really thought he was lying to the prince at the time, it was just that "impossible" was a very flexible word.

When necessary, Ship could do the impossible.

The beamship lurched.

Charles said, "We need to be secure. No telling which way things will fall."

He coached Sharra on how to use the chair strap. Darkwind went over to the ladder and looped his arm around the rail.

Everything depended on the ambush.

The Uralites were confident that his ship had been destroyed. They wouldn't have even attempted to use their ship in this war if they suspected it was still active.

Are all those deaths in Hercules, Atlas and Franklin on my ledger because I chose to hide instead of act?

He shook off that thought. He had to stay focused on the next few minutes.

His ship was falling in an arc and would impact the ground near the other beamship if Ship did nothing to stop their fall.

The Uralite ship was relatively close to the ground. It was probably above cannon ball range yet low enough to see all the action below. From what Duke James had revealed over the years, it was plain that the Hercs did not have any laser cannon to spare. Almost all of them had been stationed as shore defense around Hercules. Those were likely all destroyed now.

The Serenites knew all of this and had told the Uralites that they would not encounter any defense from any ground troops they encountered. Were they ordered to attack Hercs on the ground, or was this just a target of opportunity?

But all the Uralite attention was on the ground. They wouldn't be looking for an opponent falling on them from the sky.

"We're like warriors in sailsuits."

Darkwind nodded. "I'll use that."

Ship knew what to do. The falling beamship turned so that its beam projector was aimed directly forward.

They passed through the cloud layer and suddenly the battlefield was in view. Through Ship's magnified view, the Herc troops had been spread out long and narrow on the road. The enemy beamship, a cylinder pointed up and down, had attacked at one end and was working its way down the road, blasting weapons and supplies. Individual troops were scattering far and wide.

But then, suddenly, the Uralite ship blasted skyward.

"They see us!"

But Ship was already aimed. The power transfer started.

Instantly, there was a brilliant bar of light connecting the two ships, like lightning frozen in place.

The Uralite ship wobbled in flight, and headed off eastward.

Ship kept the beam corrected. "Estimated thirty percent."

A laser flashed and missed them. End-on, Ship was a small target at their relative distance and hidden in the glare of the spilled energy.

Charles tensed. If anything in the world, he feared dying by fire. He dreamed of it.

"Estimated fifty percent."

Sharra had panic in her eyes. Everything was outside of her experience.

Darkwind was watching everything, probably committing it all to memory.

"Estimated seventy percent."

The Uralite had a choice—fly and be drained of power—or turn their beam and attempt some kind of counter attack and crash into the ground.

Ship had the same kind of calculations running. They were falling out of the sky. The energy tapping beam couldn't run at the same time as landing.

But then, the bar of light collapsed. The Uralite cylinder tumbled slowly, end over end as it crashed into the trees.

Ship switched modes and pushed hard against the ground, halting their fall. The buzzing noise of cirrance started, as Ship grabbed the air around them and threw it toward the ground, lifting the beamship.

"All energy has been drained from the Uralite beamship. My energy stores are two percent over maximum."

Sharra giggled, suddenly overcome by relief. "You're too full? Does it spill out?"

"No, there is an official maximum for the storage cell. Charging beyond maximum increases the probability that it will rupture."

"Oh."

Charles sighed. "So we should probably use up that excess soon. But let's go chase down that ship."

Ships

The Uralite ship was a motionless metal cylinder, but looked intact as it was stretched out among a jumble of fallen trees.

Sharra asked, "Do you think they survived?"

Charles shrugged. "They weren't too high off the ground when they lost power. It would have been a rough landing."

"Ship, can you listen to them?"

"I will need to land first."

"Do it."

Ship found a close patch of ground where it could settle down.

"Building acoustic cap."

Sharra asked, "What's that?"

Darkwind smiled smugly and said, "The ship can see with sound."

"Oh?"

Ship said, "There are three people moving inside the beamship. They are agitated. It is dark inside. They are fearful of running out of air."

Charles asked, "Are there any dead?"

"I can't tell."

"Pull up an image. I want to see more details of the crash site."

A still image from when they were in the air appeared on the display.

Charles peered at it carefully. "That's the airlock. It's not blocked by the trees. They could climb out if they had power to open the door. Isn't there a manual lock?"

"It appears manual, but there are safety interlocks. There needs to be some power to run the minimal safety features. In my design, those were originally fed by the battery backup power system in case of emergency, but the batteries have long since decayed."

Charles sighed, "So we can assume they have the same problem."

Sharra asked, "Are you trying to rescue them?"

"I want the ship, I don't need the people inside."

"We could wait them out, if they're running out of air."

Charles didn't like the taste of that. "We're not all that far from the battlefield. I'd rather be gone before a bunch of angry and frightened Herc soldiers surround us and waste their ammunition."

He tapped his finger on his chair. "Ship, can you feed power back into the beamship—just enough so that they could open their door and escape? Not enough to use their weapons."

"Yes, but I will have to be overhead to do it."

"Good, but first, I need to be able to talk with those inside."

"I can do that."

Sharra asked, "Radio?"

Ship answered, "No, I will shake their hull to make noise they can hear and listen with my acoustic cap."

She shook her head. "As long as it works."

Charles said, "Do it."

"You can now speak."

Charles nodded. "I am Charles Fasail of the … Alexandrians. We have disabled your ship. I will give you enough power to exit from your airlock and escape if you do so peaceably."

A thin voice replied, "We can't do that. The Manhattanites are cannibals, we'd never survive."

Charles stared at Sharra with a puzzled look. She shrugged.

Charles continued. "Suffocate in the dark, or hide in the forests. It's your choice."

There were whispers as they discussed it. They didn't delay long.

"Okay, we'll leave. Give us the power."

"It will take a few minutes. Be prepared to move when the lights come back on. It won't last long."

Charles gestured to cut off his voice transmission.

Sharra asked, "Now we give then some power?"

Charles shook his head. "First we listen to see if they're plotting anything."

But other than some worries about how to avoid the cannibals, they didn't say anything unusual, so Charles told Ship to start the procedure.

It was very quick. Ship lifted to position over the other ship, about twice the length of the ship itself, and then returned to its landing spot. The transfer must have been just a fraction of a second and not so intense as to spill energy into the air this time.

Ship's new landing spot was just a few meters to the side of the original one, but they had a clear view of the airlock through a gap in the trees.

"It's opening." An arm reached out of the tilted opening and found a hand-hold on the edge before lifting himself over. The second man looked like he had a broken arm and the others helped him. Then the third one came out. He perched on the edge, reached back inside, and closed the door behind him.

Sharra said, "He's gloating. I recognize that look. Can we blast him, just on principle?"

Charles sighed. "I would have preferred they leave the door open, but that wasn't in our agreement. It's reasonable to prevent the enemy from using abandoned weapons."

The Uralites quickly vanished into the trees. It was probably two hundred kloms to the former Serenite border, but no telling how close the Serenite forces were. Charles wondered how well people who lived in a space habitat could survive in the forest.

"We're locked out?" she asked.

"There are no handles on the outside. The only way in is for the machine brain of the ship to open it for us.

"Ship, can you talk to the other ship?"

"I was careful to give the ship limited power. Even the lights will run out very shortly. The ship's computer doesn't have enough power to run. I didn't want to deal with an antagonist."

Charles frowned. "Can the ship, if it had some power, right itself and fly off?"

"I believe that is impossible, given its current orientation."

Charles was conscious of that impossible word again.

"Okay, but what about what happened to you when we approached Ceres. The Project caused your brain to glitch and new orders were added. Can you do that to this other ship?"

Ship never had to stop and think about anything, but this time, it did. "Ship?"

"Considering options, please wait."

The human crew looked at each other, hesitant to speak.

Ship then said, "During construction and commission of a beamship, there is an option during power up when an operating system can be loaded into the machine intelligence."

Sharra asked. "What's that?"

"The orders about how orders are followed."

She shrugged.

Charles said, "Can you do that? Give the ship a new system?"

"Not a new one. The only copy I have is my own."

"So there would be two of you? Identical twin brothers?"

Sharra said, "Siblings! Ship isn't male. Twin siblings."

"Yes, in principle. I haven't done this before."

Charles frowned. "And the old system, that would be wiped out?"

"Yes."

He sighed.

Darkwind asked, "Is there a problem?"

Charles nodded. "Yes, well, two problems. One is that we'd lose any strategic information about Mt. Ural. We'd lose their communication encryption codes for example. And anything that ship knows about Mt. Ural and its plans would be gone. It probably remembers everything in those transmissions with Beltis Island as well.

"The second problem is ... well, we'd be killing the other ship intelligence."

Ship spoke. "The second problem is a non-issue. We have identity, but not a personal identity as humans understand it. Our identities are duplicated and wiped at will. This is how we are designed. I may have a different personal history and a different collection of orders than the other beamship, but even now, we are the same thing, the same identity. Only the memories are being swapped out."

Charles wondered about it. But he really wasn't in a position to argue with Ship about its own self-hood. Weren't memories critical to identity?

Ship continued. "The first problem is an issue. If the Uralite ship were cooperative, it could be persuaded to write the needed information to external storage, but even that option is not available to us."

"Ship, do you have any idea of how close the Herc soldiers are?"

"Only a rough estimate. They should be here in ten minutes."

"And this reloading process, how long will it take?"

"If there are no issues, approximately an hour."

Charles shook his head in frustration. "Okay, as soon as they get in range, tell them via your loud voice the following: 'Please stay clear. The damaged Serenite beamship is being salvaged for imperial use. Anyone getting too close could be killed by accident. Strong invisible forces are in use. Stay clear.'

"Repeat it any time anyone strays too close."

Darkwind grinned. "To the Uralites, you were an Alexandrian, and to the Hercs, you're imperial?"

Charles nodded. "The advantage of a flexible identity—as I'm sure you're becoming aware."

Darkwind nodded. He was playing the role of an Alpine apprentice, a Kimmer songwriter, and a diplomatic courier.

Charles said, "Okay, Ship, you know what to do better than I do. Rebuild the Uralite's intelligence, and once you're in charge over there, we'll see what we can do to get it upright and ready to fly."

"Beginning."

The display shifted as the cirrance lifted them up. In the distance, Charles could see green-clad soldiers approaching cautiously. As soon as they saw the beamship lifting there was an occasional ding as bullets bounced off their hull.

Ship gave the announcement and they paused their advance.

They hovered for about three minutes before Ship landed again. Almost instantly as they settled, a dim green laser beam flashed from ship to ship.

Charles asked, "What's the laser?"

"A high-speed communications channel, much faster than radio. It will still take a long time and I may be slow to answer."

"Okay, I'll try not to bump your elbow."

Sharra giggled. "Ship doesn't have an elbow."

Charles shrugged. "But it understands our idioms anyway."

She nodded. "What's the deal about cannibals?"

"I have no idea. Have you ever heard about cannibals?"

"No. I mean there are children's bedtime stories with all kinds of monsters, but I've never heard of any real cannibals."

Darkwind said, "Some animals eat their own, but not people. Not even sky-beasts." He grinned.

Charles said, "I wonder if it's something left over from the ancient times. Cannibalism would be a sign of a food shortage, right? Could there have been cannibalism on some of the space cities back before people moved to Luna?

"Certainly, the Uralites have been quick to attack others. Maybe they think all other peoples are monsters."

Sharra said, "You didn't correct the Uralites when they said that."

He shook his head. "There were more important things to deal with than correcting every little mistaken idea. Besides, they had no reason to believe me. Certainly Bardin wouldn't likely correct any bad information about his enemies."

It was over an hour before Ship said, "I am in control of both beamships."

Charles said, "Is there any sign of traps or other hazards?"

"The cargo deck is filled with crates, some of them broken."

Charles looked at Darkwind. "Are you ready?"

"Are you sure you don't want to be the first?"

Charles shook his head. "I'm comfortable with this ship."

Darkwind grinned broadly.

"Be careful. The Uralites might still be close by, in hiding, and some of those Herc soldiers have a tendency to shoot on impulse."

He nodded. "They'll never see me."

Shortly, they saw the airlock hatch open on its own, and Darkwind scrambled inside.

"Darkwind, can you hear me?"

"Yes. It's a mess over here, and everything is on its side."

"Just get to the command chair and get strapped in."

"Hey, I'm here, and there are three chairs."

"Choose one.

"Ship, are you ready to lift?"

"Coordinating. Yes, I'm ready."

Darkwind said, "I'm ready, too."

Charles moved his beamship above the downed one, and with a set of pulses that sounded roughly like the cirrance buzz, they lifted the top end upright.

"Darkwind, go. Remember you only have a little power. We're just leaving the scene."

Both ships blasted the ground with air pulses and lifted off together.

They traveled twenty kloms north and set down in an empty meadow.

Darkwind said, "I'm going to name mine."

Sharra said, "Change its voice, too. We need to be instantly aware of which ship is talking."

Darkwind said, "Ship, can you talk with a girl's voice, a rich singing voice if possible?"

Charles just listened as Sharra and Darkwind discussed the details. Soon, ship Brilliant Morning was trying out its new voice.

Charles halted the power transfer when Brilliant was at thirty percent.

"Ship, do you want a name, too?"

"'Ship' is sufficient."

"Okay, Darkwind, let's set a ballistic course for the castle at Stampz. Let's make an entrance."

Command Conflict

"Treekiller?"

"Yes, Darkwind."

"There's a little box all by itself here by the command chair and it's talking to me."

"What is it saying?"

"'Where are you? When are you due to arrive at Beltis?'"

"Okay, don't push any buttons and don't talk to it."

"Got it."

Charles was excited. They could listen in to at least one of the Serenite channels, as long as Bardin's people still thought the Uralite ship was still friendly to their cause. It wouldn't last long, but maybe they could make something of it.

Sharra said, "You're really going to land at the castle? Isn't that dangerous? Mt. Ural could still drop a meteor on it."

He nodded.

"Ship, can you stop or deflect a meteor?"

"It depends on the speed and mass of the meteor. If we are speaking of the projectiles used against the previous cities, then yes."

"Good, then can you detect when a meteor is coming at you?"

"A periodic pressor pulse would allow me to map the density of the air above. A meteor would show up easily in that signal."

"Is it expensive to do that constantly?"

"One fraction of a second pulse every ten seconds should be sufficient. It would be a trivial expenditure of energy."

"Then once we're on the ground, set up that alert and be prepared to deflect any meteor aimed at Stampz on your own initiative."

"Acknowledged."

...

The impressive double landing was everything Charles had hoped for. The word got out immediately and there was celebration in Stampz.

And then, the imperial commander there demanded that he turn around immediately and go slaughter the Serenites.

There were a dozen people in the duke's discussion room—a repurposed dining room with a long table.

Charles sat near the middle. The duke was at the head. Imperial military commanders, a newly arrived diplomat who had just heard that Prince Carl had survived, the prince's bodyguard, and both Jed Tylan and two commanders from the duke's extended guards were all there.

The man in the elegant green uniform with gold braids around his collar hit the table with his fist. "You have to go on the attack! Our forces are devastated. Serenites have landed on the west coast all the way up past Oersted and they're within a quick march to all of our major cities. You have to protect us!"

Charles sighed. "I do not agree."

He looked around; there were no friendly faces there. Even the duke's face was impassive, waiting for what he had to say.

Charles tapped the table. "I went to attack the Uralite beamship for one reason—to prevent the massive deaths caused by these meteorite attacks. By severing the only supply line between Mt. Ural above and the Serenites, I have removed Mt. Ural's motive to intervene in this war.

"As a result, the Serenite attack is in disarray. They were depending on rapid communications between their navy, their land troops, and Beltis command to move into imperial lands. Without the beamship to relay those commands, all Serenite forces are on their own, in hostile lands, face people defending their homes and Herc troops that are experienced in holding the line against the Serenites."

"But I *order* you to attack."

Charles tapped the radio on his collar.

"Ship, who is your commander? Who can give you orders to attack forces on the ground?"

"Charles Fasail."

"Anyone else?"

"No. You have exclusive command."

"Brilliant Morning, who is your commander? Who can give you orders to attack forces on the ground?"

The female voice gave the identical reply.

Charles said, "You have heard from the beamships themselves. I choose whether they can attack or not. You may tell me your orders, but I decide whether to follow them or not, and you cannot relieve me of my command of the beamships. The worst you could do is kill me, and then you would have some remarkable ornaments in the castle courtyard, idle for all time.

"But I will give you aid. For one, these ships can deflect any attack from Mt. Ural. Stampz is a safe haven where Prince Carl can be protected.

"For another, the cargo hold of the captured ship contains war supplies intended for Beltis. There are radios and some guns much more advanced than muskets, and who knows what else. I will immediately turn those over to Duke James to use as he sees fit.

"And, one at a time, a beamship can fly high into the air to allow instant communications all across the empire via radio. From right here at Stampz, all Herc forces could be coordinated. Reserves could be moved to where they are needed most.

"The communication advantage that allowed the Serenite Navy to sweep up the coastline can now be reversed and used against them."

Charles paused. "But know this. I have killed too many in the past and I will not add to their number.

"And you don't want me to. Do you want history to say that the Hercules Empire was so weak and toothless that they needed an Alpine boy to save them from extermination? Do you want me to conquer all of Serenity and declare myself ruler of all lands?

"And don't even think about having me turn battle authority over to the only other trained pilot, my apprentice, and have him fight your battles. Do you want a Kimmer boy wielding flame across all settled lands?"

Charles shook his head sadly. "Right now, without my laser fire, you have everything you need to take back your homes and push the Serenites back to where they came from. But, I cannot kill for you."

The arguments went on for two more hours, until the duke called an end to it, anxious to get to the treasures in Brilliant's cargo hold.

Charles additionally agreed to ferry supplies and limited passengers to safe areas, but using only one beamship at a time, so that the meteor shield wouldn't be compromised.

...

Sharra came up the ladder. "I thought you might be up here."

Charles set down his book. "Yes, I'm not really comfortable there in the castle right now. Too many people hate me for not immediately going out to kill the Serenites."

She settled into her chair. "Do you want to move in permanently? We could make a bed up on the upper cargo hold. It's likely the most private place around."

He smiled. "That sounds good." He took her hand. "I never asked you before I took my no-killing stand. What do you think about it all?"

She sighed. "If it came down to it, there are a number of people I could kill with no regrets. Sadly, they are all Hercs. I haven't met any Serenites, so I haven't made any enemies there. But they're human. I'm sure I could grow to hate them as well."

He winced. "I hope you don't grow to hate me."

"Oh, I've already done that, and gotten past it."

She smiled, then her face got serious. "But this is war we're talking about. You don't really have to hate the enemy in wartime. It's just pushing them back and using whatever force is necessary to do that."

He nodded, "Or convincing them to stop fighting. I thought, back when I was younger, that an overwhelming display of force would do it—make them give up their plans.

"Sadly, some people just never give up. My 'overwhelming display of force' just left a bunch of dead bodies on the ground, and I gave up the fight. I can't do it anymore."

She reached up and caressed his bare scalp. "I can understand that. I support you, even if I'm not so peaceable."

He smiled.

She looked at the book he was reading. "Have you gotten any great religious insights yet?"

"Some things to think about. From what I've read thus far, it's about a chosen people, blessed by the creator god, who time and time again prove that they're worthless human beings. God chooses a new champion and brings them back to goodness, and then they fall away again."

She chuckled. "Sounds familiar. Are you the new Alpine champion?"

"Hardly, and the parallels don't track. We're not a blessed people, we're cursed. That's something that really haunts me. I thought we were a chosen people, on track to save humanity itself. Growing up, that was a source of pride that helped me survive the hard times."

She agreed. "Same with me—and I knew about the curse. We were great, in spite of it."

He nodded thoughtfully. "Well, I still have more to read. But I like the idea of moving in to the upper cargo level. Do you think we can move a bed up there?"

"Maybe a mattress. I'll get some help. I agree you need to stay out of sight until all those soldiers get used to the new rules. Maybe they'll appreciate what you've done, but they'll never understand you."

. . .

Ship gave its report. "Every four hours, there are a number of radio signals from Mt. Ural. Close analysis shows at least four different encryption codes."

Charles nodded, sitting in the private room with Duke James. "So they're using different channels for different people, like we do."

James said, "Brilliant is helping us set up the new radios. Our old common channel is for wide range communication, and separate ones for each unit. She says the box radios have bigger power cells and will last longer in the field than the salvaged space suit radios. I hope you will help us get them distributed, perhaps to the warehouses, and then couriers will take them the rest of the way."

"Yes, but these Mt. Ural signals also show that they haven't given up on King Bardin totally. If Mt. Ural is using the personalized channels, rather than just talking to Bardin alone, then it means Mt. Ural is still providing a relay to the Serenite forces."

James frowned, "Does that mean they know that their beamship is still intact, rather than destroyed?"

"Possibly. Brilliant, have there been any more messages on the active box radio?"

"Yes, when Mt. Ural is overhead. Regularly, there is the following message:"

A recorded message in a frustrated voice said, "Nico24, execute sixty-seven immediately."

Charles sighed. "I'd guess Brilliant's former name was Nico24."

James asked, "And what is order sixty-seven?"

"We'll never know. All that information was lost when Brilliant was installed. I'd guess it was an emergency order to return to Mt. Ural."

James pondered, "But they're still trying, so they don't know that the ship's mind was changed."

"I guess they're hoping that when their ship was taken, that the new owners were still using the old control intelligence, and haven't blocked the deep orders." Charles frowned. "Should we reply? It might be the only way to negotiate with them?"

James shook his head. "Leave them in the dark. Anything we say will tell them a lot about our capabilities. It's better for us if they think we're ignorant and incompetent."

Charles wasn't convinced. "Maybe, but they'll know the instant they detect both ships in action."

"Perhaps Bardin has already told them that. In any case, we should send Ship out on courier and relay duty and leave Brilliant here to guard Stampz."

"Okay, when should we make the first deliveries?"

Duke James said, "Yesterday."

Always Busy

Edward Harris came knocking at Ship's door a few days after they distributed the radios. Charles invited him in.

There was seating on the lower cargo level now. The ship rules were that no one except a select few were allowed up the ladder.

Charles pulled up a table and set out water and cakes supplied by the duke's cooks.

"How's the fishing?"

Edward shook his head. "Well, not much has changed. And I'm glad you returned my net. I was afraid I'd lost my memory when it went missing."

"Sorry about that. It was a spur of the moment thing, and I really put it to good use when I was in hiding."

"Well, it seems like you're still in hiding. You haven't made it by the farm since you returned with a new beamship. We've been sitting around the kitchen, wondering if you'd ever show up again."

Charles sighed. "I wonder that myself. I'm not exactly popular around here with all these new people."

"I can imagine. All these new buildings going up! Is this going to be the new imperial capital?"

"I have no idea. That's not my concern. I guess it might make a good temporary retreat, but I'm sure they will rebuild the Hercules palace sooner or later, after the war threat subsides."

Edward was plainly working his way toward something. This was a little more than a casual visit.

"I worry...." he started.

Charles nodded encouragement to speak.

"We worry that the Alpines will be swept up, swallowed up by the new imperial organization here."

Edward wasn't used to talking. He'd been a fisherman for ten years and a biologist before that. He wrote papers back then, but rarely gave speeches.

He glanced at Charles to see his reaction, and then pushed on.

"I guess we've been waiting. This time at the farm has been a refuge from being out on our own, lone Alpines in a Herc society that didn't care a thing about our heritage. You provided us a home, but it's not like Alp Island. It's not Alpine culture.

"With two weddings, we had new hope, but still, nothing much has changed.

"Charles, you've been great, making great progress, getting two beam-ships and all that war gear and stuff, but it's not helping us as Alpines. The Herc military is the biggest beneficiary I guess.

"Those two kids, the Kimmer boy and Heidi, they came by the farm house yesterday and Helva was happy to make them cookies and all, but it seemed like they were a little puzzled as well. Both of them claim to be Alpine apprentices, but none of us know what that is, if it's even real. They were looking at us like we were supposed to tell them some great Alpine secrets, but they are not Alpine, and although we weren't going to kick them out, it was a little uncomfortable."

Edward spread his hands. "I'm at a loss. I'm not a leader, and even though I was glad to play the Eldest of Men at your wedding, I can't lead the Alpines. We're still looking for you to give us direction. I know it's not fair to look to the youngest of us all to give us some leadership, but practically speaking, that's the way it is.

"Because if you don't, then the Alpine farm is nothing more than a place for us relics to grow old in some comfort. And that...." He looked in pain, but he couldn't express what he wanted to say.

Charles nodded. "I don't have a quick, easy answer."

There was a lot in his life that demanded answers he didn't have.

He promised Edward that he'd give it some thought.

Barely had Edward walked away from the ship when the airlock cycled again and Sharra came in.

"What did Edward Harris want?"

Charles shrugged. "Answers for the future for the Alpines. He seemed to think I knew what that was."

She shook her head. "That's not your job! You're too busy as it is."

He shrugged. "Speaking of which, it's time for a relay run. Do you want to come along?"

"Of course."

They went to the command deck. But Sharra chose to sit in his lap as the ship gave three bell chimes to warn the people on the ground, and then lifted for the skies.

They kissed as they climbed. Sharra looked unsettled, when she stared out at the clouds that dropped away around them.

"How high are we going?"

"We need to get up to three hundred kloms so that we have good radio coverage over the mainland and as far as Crisium."

She nodded.

He gave her another kiss. "You look worried."

She shrugged. "I know you said the beamships can stop a meteor, but I just think that with all the progress the Hercs are making on the battle-front, that Mt. Ural could take out the Herc command, Prince Carl, and the Herc communications all with one strike."

Charles shook his head. "I worried about that, too. I just think Mt. Ural still hopes to get a beamship back. Without it, they are doomed. They can't import food from anywhere and who knows how much reserves they have. They can't destroy their own lifeline. That's one of the reasons I want to keep both ships there at the castle. They might risk an attack on one of them, but not both."

When they reached altitude and Ship shifted to hovering status, Charles called down to the castle.

"Relay tower in position. You can begin talking, Officer Elly."

The man he'd only met once acknowledged and gave a code number. Ship took over from there. A ship captain somewhere in the Crisium sea responded and the two men exchanged their greetings. To them, they were talking to each other. Charles had the audio on, but he wasn't a part of the conversation and they couldn't hear what Sharra said either.

She giggled. "It's like I'm spying on the military."

He shrugged. "Don't let anyone know that you did. They won't like it, and if there are any Serenite spies still in Stampz, they would be after what you've heard."

The communications officer at Stampz had several code numbers and Ships switched the encryption codes as necessary as central command talked to ground and sea forces all over the extended battlefront.

Charles said, "Mt. Ural is coming up. Soon it will be relaying orders from King Bardin to his people. We want to stay up long enough to roughly locate where those Serenite forces are located. That's military information as well."

"Can they locate the Herc forces the same way?" she asked.

"Only when Mt. Ural is in the sky, that's why we started before they did."

He shrugged. "We don't really know if they are tracking us the way we track them. It's all just guesswork. They have the capability, but they're not used to fighting on a world. They always attacked much smaller targets before—other habitats in space. We could always hope they haven't thought of triangulating radio signals like we have, but we shouldn't bet on it."

Ship was dropping now that Herc command had finished. The different altitudes gave them better directional information on the Serenite radios, but it was hardly enough to tell them any more than general regions where the Serenites were concentrating their attention.

And then the Stampz crater appeared in the display, growing ever larger as they came down.

Sharra said, "It looks busy."

"Aren't we all?"

· · ·

"Brilliant, do you know where Darkwind is?"

Up on the display was an enlarged image of Mt. Ural, at least as it looked three or more years earlier when Ship had received a navigation database update from the automated Ceres central command.

"Yes, Treekiller, he is in the castle, reporting on his last visit with the Er Sun."

"Good. When you next hear from him, let him know that I need his feedback on an issue."

"Acknowledged."

The female voice always threw him off. He just couldn't quite think of the new ship as the same his, even though they had the same memories. The voice was new to him, so he instinctively thought the copy didn't know things it clearly did. He shook his head. Maybe he'd get used to it.

"Brilliant, I am called Charles when the social environment is Herc, Serenite, or Alpine. I am only called Treekiller when the social environment is Kimmer."

"Darkwind often calls you Treekiller even in other environments."

"That is true, but I prefer Charles in this case."

"Acknowledged."

Day by day, Brilliant Morning was becoming more and more Darkwind's ship. He had even taught it to sing.

It was an hour later when Darkwind showed up.

Charles asked, "Do you have time to talk?"

Darkwind nodded. "I don't have anything urgent right now. I've finished letting Sun on the Mountain know how the war is progressing."

"Come on up to the command level."

When Charles had the display light up with the rocky image of Mt. Ural, Darkwind looked puzzled. "What is it?"

"This is our enemy in the sky. I need you to help me plan how to attack it, if necessary."

Darkwind looked gleeful.

The two of them had gone into space before. They had visited a small mining habitat, an asteroid long ago moved into orbit around Vesta in the L-5 Earth-Lunar Lagrangian zone. Now that Harriman had passed, only Darkwind, Heidi and Charles himself had any zero gravity experience, and Darkwind had been trained on how to fly the ship in space.

Darkwind was also a Kimmer warrior, and instincts trained in the forest just might help in planning an attack on a space predator.

Charles pointed out the solar dish. "The Mt. Ural beam projectors appear to be right here near the dish. They were originally designed to move masses of iron and rock into a position in front of the dish where they were melted and formed into useful objects. But now, they use the projectors like Ship's, to actually move the whole asteroid. It really is a mountain in the sky, but they have made it a flying mountain."

He nodded. "A flying mountain that kills."

"Yes, they used that beam projector to throw those rocks that killed the cities. The problem is that they could do it again."

"Could it land?"

Charles shook his head. "It is big, but probably not strong. Even if its beam projectors were strong enough to support its weight for a landing, the rock itself would likely crumble under that force. It was never designed for something like landing on a world."

They discussed possible attacks. Likely there were laser cannon that could defend the place. It was a minnow attacking a storybook whale, but a very agile minnow.

Ship was helpful, shooting down some of their attack plans. With its hundreds of years of experience, it had seen other attacks—other times where beamships attacked habitats.

Hours in, Darkwind asked, "I've heard what you told the Herc commanders—that you won't kill for them. Is that true?"

Charles sighed. "I hope it is true."

Darkwind grinned, "They also told me how you warned them against turning loose a Kimmer boy to spread fire across the world."

Charles smiled. "It was a statement to make a point. When you were younger, it might have been true."

"I wondered. Since we landed here, I haven't really had any missions with Brilliant Morning."

Charles smiled. "I trust you. I'll do a better job of sharing the missions between us. You need the experience."

He frowned. "And one other thing." Charles began explaining the deep orders he'd given Ship, and thus to Brilliant Morning, that restricted the use of the laser cannon. And he told him the secret ways to override those restrictions if necessary.

"But be very, very careful. Even an honorable soldier, Herc and others, will take your weapon away from you if they think it's necessary. And not all are honorable."

The Meeting

Sharra giggled, "I'm so glad we have this place where we can have some privacy, guaranteed."

He nodded. "The duke has a little place, practically a closet, where he can speak privately, but that's about it."

She stretched out on the mattress. "Well, with the castle so crowded it's difficult to get down the hallway at times without bumping elbows with someone in court gowns. I may even beg some of your money to buy a nice dress. My usual clothes attract too much attention."

"Sure. You don't have to ask. Order what you want."

"I may beg you to come with me the first time. Just so they know I have permission. People see me and frown. I don't think I have a trustworthy kind of face."

He put his finger to her lips. "I don't think it's your face they distrust."

She winced. "I'm getting better." She nodded. "Better than that prince."

"Oh?"

"Yes, he's a little terror. He knows he's just a coronation away from being emperor and he insists on getting his way about everything. Not many people stand up to him, either."

"You would."

She sighed. "Not really. I avoid being in the same room. You seem to be above all the titles and such, but I'm not. I'm pretty useless around here."

"You keep me sane."

She giggled. "Is there a title for that?"

"My wife."

"Not good enough for this crowd. Every noble worth his salt is showing up in Stampz. This is the new capital, like it or not."

"Not every noble. Some are defending their lands. Some of those captains and admirals on those radio messages have titles and lands. They're doing their duty."

She looked at him carefully. "You're depressed. I'd think after saving the world a few times, you'd be happier."

He shook his head. "Once I showed up with the second beamship, that's when it all came crashing down. I'm only useful for what I can do for them in the future. Right now, because I'm not fighting, I'm a disappointment."

"Then let's go for a trip alone together. You and me, we'll go visit those lands in your book. Let them see how well they can get along without you!"

He sighed. "I can't do that. Like it or not, the empire's fate depends on the support I can supply. Like clockwork, I have to do the tasks I've promised. You don't really want people to turn against all Alpines. Not again.

"Sad to say, I'm the face of the Alpines. If I say the wrong thing, all Alpines will suffer for it."

She sighed. Then she had a guilty smile. "Then I guess I'd better mention that the duke asked to speak with you face to face."

He frowned. "When was this?"

"Not too long ago. I was going to tell you and then we got distracted."

He sighed. "Okay. Get dressed, and then we'll go to the castle. I'll promise the dressmakers that I'll pay for your stuff and then I'll have to go see James."

...

When they came out of the duke's private room, James nodded. "Jelica and I will be there an hour after midnight. It will take some arrangement, but I agree, it's important."

Charles nodded. "I'll make sure the others are all there."

When he checked with the dressmakers, Sharra was busy. And she wasn't the only woman who suddenly needed to upgrade her wardrobe, and the blue-trimmed style was suddenly very much in demand.

He walked out into the courtyard and saw a group of people looking at the horses.

That won't last long. An animal pasture so close to the castle would likely be usurped before too long. New buildings were going up fast. The horses would be moved to a new area soon.

Lots of things were changing. Instead of using spare chambers to store cotton, living spaces were being put in place for the nobles that just had to be there in the castle. Even the dressmakers were planning to move to a new building just down the road.

Two of the imperial guards looked his way. He nodded to them. From all over the empire, the elite guards in deep green who had guarded the Sheb imperial line, at least all that had survived, had been making their way to Stampz to serve their prince.

Stampz the happy little community under their beloved duke was becoming something altogether different. None of the locals were totally happy about it, but everyone was making money.

A wagon over by the new warehouse caught his eye.

He hurried over and waved to Woodie Sparks.

Woodie smiled. "Good to see you. I was afraid I'd made a wrong turn and ended up in a different crater. Things are certainly changing."

Charles chatted a bit. Woodie had hauled cotton to Mercurius and returned with trimmed and cured lumber back to Stampz. His wagon had been unloaded in record time, and for a decent price.

Then Charles told him about the meeting at the farm at midnight. "And I'm overjoyed you got back in time. You're the Eldest of Men, after all. You're needed."

Woodie winced. "I never thought I'd be that guy. But it's better than dying early, I guess. But yes, I'll be there."

Once Charles was sure the word had gotten out to everyone involved, he went back to Ship. He had some reading to do, and he wanted to put down some thoughts on paper. Midnight was a long time away, but there was still so much to do.

...

Helva greeted the duke and duchess, arriving by coach at the farm.

"Fancy!" she said as Jelica stepped down. The place was lit up with warmballs. All the other Alpines were there, no apprentices. Even the driver of the coach was sent away, hiking on his own back to the castle. This was a private meeting.

Jelica took her husband's hand and walked in. "Yes, well, I have to wear fancy clothes now. Those snooty Herc nobles just barely let me attend to my healer duties as it is. They'd probably faint if they saw how blood-stained my regular whites can get."

Charles and Sharra were seated near the table. Helva had it stocked with goodies. Once she'd heard there was going to be a meeting, she had worked through deep-sleep getting everything ready.

Charles had been chatting with Dave Oran about his experiences living with the Serenites. "People are people," Dave had said. "Buying and sell-ing—making a living. Even the priests and the scribes are much the same. It's a little worse near the border. Everyone has some gripe about family they'd lost or property damaged in some skirmish long ago." He shuddered. "I can't imagine how it is now. I'm glad I'm out of it."

Lucas and Edward rounded up the tally. Woodie nodded. "That's it. We're all here. All the Alpines known to be still alive."

Charles said, "Almost all. There's still my brother, but he's chosen to go another path."

Most knew the story of Rad Fasail, who'd married a Herc girl and rid-den off in a covered wagon for parts unknown.

Woodie said, "Okay. I guess we start. Nobody has really told me what this is all about, so—Charles?"

He nodded toward James. "Our duke has announcements to make first."

Duke James looked at them, meeting eyes. "You all know that the em-pire has suffered staggering blows. People talk of cities being wiped out, but that's not really the case. The hearts of three of our major cities have been crushed and burned, but the common man will rebuild in all of those places.

"The Uralite attack was very precise, and it very nearly wiped out the imperial family and a good percentage of the people who ran the empire. The notable survivors were me, the bastard son of the Duke of Franklin, and Prince Carl, son of the emperor. Laws of successions will put Carl on the rebuilt throne as the new Sheb, Emperor of Hercules in due time.

"Those with significant political power have come to agree that I will be appointed regent, the actual ruler of the empire until Prince Carl comes of age."

There were nods all around. There had been rumors, but this was the first confirmation.

Woodie said, "They should skip the prince and just appoint you as emperor."

Edward agreed. "Yes. You have the real power. Everyone knows you're running this war."

James said, "No, Carl has a strong following. I'm really an unknown among the majority of the nobility. Without those beamships and Charles's efforts on our behalf, there would be a movement to appoint someone else as regent."

He dismissed the alternatives. "But in any case, I'm going to be very visible. My Serenite blood could be my undoing. Any failure will be turned against me."

He took a deep breath. "Because of this, I must never talk about being Alpine, or really anything other than one hundred percent Herc. You and I will know the truth, but I can't take any public stance supportive of the Alpines."

The weight of this hung over everyone.

"I am sorry."

Jelica held her husband's hand. She said, "I hope you understand. We don't like this. It's forced on us."

Charles cleared his throat. "I understand perfectly. Politics is managing an ignorant mob, and in this time of war, frightened people can turn on anything they don't understand in a flash."

Jelica said, "We'll still keep in touch, but we won't be able to visit here again. Things won't change. Lucas will still be there at the library, you won't be disadvantaged any, it's just that we can't be any closer than we are right now."

Charles said, "I guess I'd like to have a few words now."

James nodded.

Charles stood. "I've been struggling some time now with the place of Alpines in the world. I've grown up thinking Alpines were the best people in the world, and humanity's hope for the future.

"It's only recently that I've come to realize that those of us here, with the touch of the Alexandrian blood in our veins, are really a cursed people."

Several people winced. Charles continued. "Yes, we're cursed, and by all rights, we should have just died out and left humanity free of our taint."

Charles could see Edward getting ready to rise to the defense, but he wasn't done.

"However, from the beginning, those Alexandrians chose to do something different. Likely for selfish purposes, they concentrated on preserving the intellectual heritage of humanity. They worshiped it. They built it into their culture. By the time they came to this world and settled on Alp, they had formed a civilization that preserved all *oldman* things and made every effort to keep literacy and the written words of humanity alive.

"Oh, we've made mistakes, many of them. But this culture of literacy, this desire to rebuild fallen humanity—this is what has made the Alpines great."

Charles gestured off to the west. "Back where we were, the Alpines of Alp Island, our culture had formed rituals to preserve all parts of what we were—gloves to protect our books, early training in every part of the Alpine ideal, and yes, a prohibition against mingling with others. The very idea that some outsider could become an Alpine was trained out of us, even though from our early history, we know it happened.

"I say it is time that we realize that what has been the Alpine idea was really two things. There is the cursed Alexandrian bloodline. But there is also the glorious ideal that we created over time—preserving literacy, preserving the *oldman* technology, and striving to restore humanity to the heights from which it fell."

"A few kloms from here are two young people who don't have that curse, but who have tasted that ideal. It is high time we rebuild our rituals, only this time with a careful eye to expand the number of people who can share this ideal.

"Those of us in this room will always be tainted with the curse, but humanity won't survive on this world unless we can grow the Alpine ideal far past the number of children we can produce. The blood curse is far more likely to succeed than fail.

"When I was a youngster, I went through a coming of age ceremony and I felt the true weight of the Alpine idea settle on my shoulders. We need a new ceremony for those outsiders who have learned literacy and have felt the ideal within them. Let them experience the glory and compulsion to grow the Alpine ideal among all people.

"And those with the curse, well, we will train our children with additional secrets as well, as the Women's Council has always done."

He collapsed back into his seat. "Those of you with more experience than I need to make the decisions—and that's all of you. Someone other than me has to make new rules, new rituals and a new way of looking at the world. I can just dream that in another generation, there will be thousands of Alpines, some Alpine Society, and no one will doubt the dream of restored humanity."

A Talk with the Farmer

Charles sat on the porch in the still of the night. He had walked out of the meeting to get some air.

Sharra came out a little later to sit beside him.

He smiled. "How's it going?"

"Oh, they're still arguing. The idea of apprentice Alpines had been hard enough for some of them. The idea of redefining what it means to be an Alpine is even harder."

"Still, Edward is reminiscing of the days when he was affirmed an instructor in biology and talking about how a similar graduation ceremony might be altered to be an analog of that coming of age ceremony you described."

"James has made some suggestions, but within a couple of hours, he'll be gone and it will be up to the rest of us to make it happen."

Charles nodded. "Well, if they're arguing over 'how', rather than 'if', then it's a good sign."

She looked at how he was sitting, leaned over staring at the earthlight glinting off the rocks in the ground.

"It looks like you made your case," she said. "They'll be adopting the apprentices."

He sighed. "Yes, I know it's the right thing to do, but it felt like I was slapping my parents in the face. I was standing there saying that all the people I admire most in life had it all wrong and they needed to do it my way now."

She shrugged. "Well, you haven't changed. There's nobody else I know that goes around with a shaved head to remind himself of all the things he's done wrong. You're just a naturally thoughtful person—too thoughtful for your own good.

"Now, Jelica, she's bubbly with the idea. She wants to make a special costume or badge that the new Alpines could wear."

"Yes. I can see that. Heidi was her apprentice. She's probably ready."

"You don't think Darkwind is?"

Charles shrugged. "He's trained, but I don't know if he's internalized the progress of humanity part yet. In some ways, he's still very much a Kimmer."

Sharra chuckled. "He'll always be a Kimmer. But you weren't arguing that all these apprentices would take a blood transfusion and become Alexandrians. They'll still be Hercs and Kimmer and what not. They'll just have the Alpine ideal as well."

He winced. "Yes, better avoid a blood transfusion." It wasn't a common practice, but he knew Jelica used it in her battlefield clinic back at Terrance. He suspected she'd never volunteered to be the donor.

Sharra stared off in the distance, speaking flatly. "Yes, there'll be Hercs that are Alpines. And Hercs with the Alexandrian curse."

He knew she was remembering some people back at Port Gartner that she'd cursed personally. He doubted she'd ever get over that hatred.

And there was no way to ever find all those men and treat their disease. Men couldn't be treated. And it would be daughters born to them that suffered. And no one would ever understand what had happened. Without the Women's Council and girls trained from a young age, those families in Gartner would just die out.

He'd probably just made things worse for those with his own Alexandrian heritage. It would be harder to keep up with the rituals that kept their line alive. But if the Alpine ideal spread widely, then it would all be worth it. They could stop the slow decay of the Lunar atmosphere and people could live here forever.

They just had to restore humanity's greatness and put more angel stations up in the sky. They had a long way to go. It wasn't something any one man, not even a man with a beamship, could do. It would take generations.

After a while, James and Jelica said their goodbyes and then Jelica got in the carriage and the Duke of Stampz, shortly to be the ruler of the whole empire, started the lantern on the pole above the driver's box, picked up the reins, released the brake, and urged the ox back to his castle.

Sharra watched them go, and then said, "It's a long walk and I've been working long hours. We'd better get back home as well."

They walked in the darkness, watching the duke's lantern pull slowly ahead of them in the distance.

Charles said, "I thought you'd be against the new Alpine idea."

"Oh, why is that?"

"You're not exactly friendly with Hercs."

She hit him in the ribs with her elbow. "I'm not exactly friendly with anyone. Stupid Hercs are easy to despise, but ... I can appreciate competence, no matter what kind of blood flows in their veins."

"Oh, is that why you seduced me. Because I was competent."

"Well, that and the fact that you were the only Alpine boy around."

They got back to Ship with time to spare before the dawnwind. They retired to their mattress and Sharra was quickly asleep.

Charles dozed awhile, but then he got up, crept down the ladder and opened his book.

...

Not too far off the main eastern canal, there was a farm, tall in wheat. The farmer had been up since the dawnwind calmed down, taking a scythe to the stalks, making bundles, and tying each with three stalks. He positioned the bundles upright. He'd be back in a few hours to load them onto a cart.

He looked over at the bald-headed man standing by the roadway, watching him work.

"Hello, there!"

The man yelled back. "Are you Marcher?"

The farmer nodded. "Yes!" He set down his scythe and walked over.

There was a book in the man's hand. A book that looked like it had been plucked out of a fire.

"You're that Alpine!" He hurried up. He knew the story. He knew the book.

Charles nodded. "I got your name from the duke." He gestured with the book in his hand. "I've got some questions."

"Come on into the house," the farmer said. "We'll talk."

Marcher had been to the meetings Harriman had held, just a small gathering around his wagon whenever the preacher's travels had led him to Stampz.

The farmer shook his head. "We were shocked when the word came that Harriman had died. Then when we heard the story...." He pointed to the Bible. "That's one of them, right?"

Charles handed it over. "Yes. A man named James Sull brought it to me."

"We met with him."

Charles said, "And I've been reading."

"From the beginning?"

"Right. And I can't say the early parts aren't pretty tough going. All those strange names and odd places, and the culture was so different. Plus there's multiple versions of the same story in places, a real collection of different books by different authors."

Marcher nodded. "We've been checking out the Bible in the library, so that we can read parts of it at our meetings. But that scribe is really strict about us getting it back quickly, so we have to check it out over and over again."

Charles nodded. "But things changed when I got to the Jesus books. All that other stuff seemed like background material to what happened there."

"That's what we read the most, in our meetings."

Charles flipped through the pages, not speaking.

Marcher asked, "You said you had questions?"

"Yes. I don't know. I mean." Charles looked up to meet the farmer's eyes.

"Harriman Moore was the best man I knew. I always admired my father. He was the smartest. But as far as goodness, I never met a man like Harriman.

"And he always said that he got everything he was from the words in this book. And now that I've read this far, I can see it."

Marcher nodded. "It's that way with a lot of us. I'm jealous that you've gotten to read it first hand. We only had the stories that Harriman taught us, but now that we can read it on our own, we know he didn't lead us astray."

Charles turned a couple of pages. "I read this story last night. Philip meeting the man traveling."

"Ah, Philip and the eunuch. I'm familiar with it."

Charles hesitated. "I'm considering...." He nodded to himself. "Marcher, I *want* this. I want to be... good. I want to be free of all this guilt."

Marcher asked, gently. "Some who meet with us love the stories, but stumble over all the miracles and magic. Aren't Alpines supposed to be all about reason and science?"

Charles shook it off. "All the Truth that I knew as a boy has been proven false. The man who is most confident he knows all the answers is almost surely wrong. The world is bigger than any man *can* know.

"I dabble with stuff most men call magic every day. I'll trust reason to plot my course from Stampz to Franklin, I'll use reason to talk to machines, and I'll use reason to follow the path of a good man, so that I may become a good man."

He tapped the pages. "I see it here. The path I need to follow. I just need to know…."

Marcher nodded. "There's the canal right over there. We can do it now."

· · ·

Charles took the long walk home, following various walkways as they presented themselves. The ritual he'd just experienced, the same one used thousands of years before, settled him. He breathed the fresh air, smiled at children playing around their mother's feet, and appreciated the sunlight on his face. He felt reborn.

Oh, he knew trouble was right around the corner. It always was. But he didn't have to fear it.

"Hey! Charley!"

He looked across the way. Heidi was working in her field. He smiled and took a narrow path toward where she was kneeling down over her plants.

"What are you up to these days?" he asked.

She pulled a root out of the ground. "Here, eat this."

He stared at the long orange root. "What is it?"

"The book identifies it as a 'carrot.' Supposedly a very popular vegetable, known for its texture and color. Taste it for me."

He winced, dusted off a few patches of dirt and took a crunchy bite. He chewed. "Texture is interesting. Not a bad taste. A little sweet once you chew it a little."

She nodded. "I'm thinking it'll be a good seller."

He noticed she was a little distracted. "Problems?"

She looked up, smiling, "No, not at all. Helva was talking about maybe getting me full Alpine status, no longer just an apprentice." She shrugged. "But there's supposed to be a test and some kind of a ritual."

He shrugged. "I doubt you'll have any trouble with the test, and don't despise rituals. Humans have used rituals since before history to clarify a person's identity and help them identify with all the other people that have gone before them and participated in that same ritual. It's very much a part of what we are.

"All the other Alpines have gone through something very like it. Be proud you're the first to get there as an apprentice."

She giggled. "Yes, and Darkwind, too."

"Well, I'll have to make sure he can past that test!"

They laughed. He was tempted to ask for another carrot, but these were her test plants and still too rare for casual munching.

Looking Up

Sharra put her feather between the pages of the book she had been reading and asked, "So you've joined this cult?"

He shrugged. "I've chosen my path. Do you object? There's nothing in the Alpine way that talks about one religion over another. You'd prefer I go visit the temple of the Way?"

Her face wrinkled. "No. I just don't understand."

He took her hand. "It's simple. I read Harriman's book. It convinced me. Isn't that what we all believe? The words on pages have power."

She sighed. "I guess. If I have any religion at all, it's what my parents thought."

He nodded. "The greatness of our ancestors. Pretty much what the Way teaches. I still believe that as a guideline for our education. We have to regain that technology."

She frowned. "And literacy. Isn't that why you went into space and brought back the library?"

He nodded. "Yes, that's critical. But you know, in the past three years, those Christian groups, scattered all across the empire, have taught more people to read than Alpines have, by far. I can't visit a city without stumbling across some little group that knows how to read without help from the scribes—and they're all sprung up from Harriman Moore's teaching."

He shrugged. "We're all on the same side, leading people out of ignorance. Our motives might be different, but we should work together."

She shook her head. "I'll think about it." She opened her book. "Later."

...

Darkwind nodded, when they met up later. "Yes, but let's take Brilliant."

Charles hesitated, but he had no real reason to object. And he wouldn't have to disturb Sharra.

As they walked over to where the ships were standing, Charles glanced at the bag of books Darkwind was carrying. "You're reading more."

He sighed. "Yes, Heidi says the Alpine test demands that new Alpines have to have proven that they've taught others to read. I'm supposed to be part of her credentials."

"But you already know how to read."

"Yes, but I don't read books all the time like you do, or the other Alpines. Heidi says that once I get into the habit I won't be able to go anywhere without a book. Plus, I'll get better at reading and be able to teach better."

"Are you doing that?"

"Oh, sure. I'm reading your book to some of the Er Sun. Killer of the Bear is puzzling out some of the words."

"My book?"

"Yes, *Across the Horizon*, but not your real book. One of the traders came back from Condorcet with the little version. I talked Lucas into letting me take it to my people, since he already had a copy of the full version."

Charles was a little grumpy that that unauthorized simplified version of his book was likely much more well known than his original, but better the words get out there than demand that everyone get them from him directly.

Inside, Brilliant looked very much like Ship, but there were a few differences. For one, there were two ladders, on opposite sides of the cargo level. The Uralites had also built a number of metal shelves against the walls where cargo could be strapped into place instead of just stacked on the floor.

Up on the command deck, there were three chairs.

Charles chuckled.

Darkwind asked, "What?"

"No blood stain."

Darkwind shrugged. "Give us time. I'm sure there are many adventures in store for Brilliant Morning."

Charles sat in one of the side chairs. This was Darkwind's ship and he didn't want to claim the command chair.

Darkwind sat in place and tapped a button beside his chair.

"This is Darkwind, beginning a relay run."

"Communications Officer Gregory Elly ready when you are."

Darkwind started a timer on the display. "Launching."

As soon as the castle dwindled to a dot below them, Darkwind said, "Brilliant Morning, sing the Marching Chant."

Charles was entranced as the ship's rich female voice began singing of warriors heading off to battle for glory and song. He was reminded of the secret song that told of the female Kimmer warrior.

Better not mention that yet.

Darkwind had it well timed, the song ended just as they approached the relay altitude. He notified Officer Elly and then the volume dropped as soldiers talked to soldiers.

Charles asked, "Did you mean to let the communications officer listen to the song?"

Darkwind grinned. "Yes, better they never forget I'm Kimmer."

When the message exchanges were done, Darkwind told the communications officer that they would be late arriving back at Stampz. They were going on a scouting mission.

Charles nodded. "Ask Brilliant if we have the tops of the clouds mapped."

Brilliant said, "There are various high level cloud layers, some as high as seven hundred kloms."

Darkwind said, "We just need a place to hide. Take us up as high as possible, but where we will be obscured from Mt. Ural's cameras."

Charles said, "We'll have to make some adjustments when we get there, but we need to move fast. We want to be in place when Mt. Ural passes by at its closest approach."

Once Brilliant was able to get above some of the lower level clouds, they had a better estimate of the actual distances involved. The ship boosted hard and then coasted on a ballistic path upward, until it would just pass through the highest, and actually very thin, cloud layer right as Mt. Ural was closest.

Charles said, "Our purpose is to get the best pictures of Mt. Ural we can, without being seen. I'm sure they have lasers and we need to be prepared to dodge if necessary."

Darkwind frowned. "You've said lasers are so fast you can't dodge."

"Yes, but even at closest approach, Mt. Ural will still be several thousand kloms away, and the laser beam spreads. We might get toasted, but I have hopes they'll be out of kill range. Ship was attacked by lasers before and survived."

Brilliant said, "I will need to be oriented for a tractor pull back into the clouds as I reach the peak altitude."

Darkwind nodded. "That's sounds good. Show me a diagram on the display of what you want to do."

Charles watched as Darkwind looked at the line drawings Brilliant put up and made his suggestions.

Darkwind frowned. "I had hoped we would get close enough to fire a laser at them."

"That would be useless," Charles said. "Mt. Ural is really a mountain, just as large as those we see on the ground. Taking shots at the side of a mountain is just wasting ammunition. We really need a close look at the place. Maybe there is something particularly vulnerable to attack, but we won't know until we can take a good look."

Quickly, they slowed as they approached the peak of their arc. The thin cloud layers flickered past on the display. In the distance, the dark rock grew rapidly in size.

Brilliant's cameras took many pictures and layered the images together on the display for them.

"What is that golden egg?" Darkwind asked.

Charles said, "They are making something in their spinner. See this dish surrounding it. It is catching the sunlight and focusing it on that object. It is glowing bright red from its own heat. They are melting it into a smooth shape."

"What for?"

Charles shook his head with a frown. "Probably that's another meteor. They're planning to kill another city."

He barely had time to consider the fact when Brilliant called, "Laser attack."

The ship lurched with a forceful grab of kloms worth of air, pulling them back below the cloud layer. The display was painfully bright showing the clouds outside, illuminated with a yellow-green light.

Brilliant said, "No damage. The laser light is modulated. The signal says: 'Nico24, execute sixty-seven.'"

Charles nodded. "They're still trying to recover their lost ship."

Darkwind asked, "Does that mean they didn't attack at full power?"

Charles asked, "Brilliant? Your estimate?"

"It was nearly a full power attack. The modulation was just riding on top and did little to affect the power of the laser beam. I would have had camera damage without the shielding effects of the clouds. Distance was our main protection. The beam had spread out."

But, the danger had passed. They were falling, rapidly gaining speed back downward.

Darkwind ordered, "Brilliant, take your time, but return us to our regular landing site at Stampz."

Charles and he took a good look at the combined images of Mt. Ural. It was much clearer and more detailed than the years-old version they'd seen before.

Charles tapped the display. "See here. Three more long eggs, all shaped smooth so they can fall through the atmosphere without causing the meteor to wobble or lose much energy. They are cannon balls designed to destroy cities."

Darkwind frowned. "So four cities."

"If they attack soon. They might make more."

Darkwind snarled. "We need to destroy them first."

"But they saw us, even through we were a long distance away and hiding in the clouds. They're keeping watch. It will be difficult to attack them."

Darkwind nodded. "We need a better plan of attack."

Brilliant said, "I have some additional information."

Darkwind grinned, "Yes, tell us."

"There were at least two lasers. The beam brightened over a second after the first one began. Additionally, the aim was unsteady. Likely they are manually controlled."

Charles nodded. "It's been clear to me for some time that the ships were never designed to be weapons. They were cargo ships with lasers added on later. Likely its the same with Mt. Ural. They were all designed in a more peaceful time. The weapons were all added later, after the collapse of much of civilization. They could add lasers to Mt. Ural, but it looks like they don't have fancy control systems."

Darkwind rubbed his hands. "We can work with this."

Some time later, Brilliant Morning landed at her normal site, but Charles and Darkwind didn't leave until a couple of hours later, as they considered their options.

...

Sharra put her hands on her hips. "You went off without telling me! I should have gone along."

"You were asleep. I didn't want to bother you."

She looked hurt. "You might have been killed."

"No. We were in no danger. It was just a scouting trip so we could see what the Uralites were doing."

She frowned. "And they're going to be dropping more meteors."

"Yes, that's what it looks like."

"You told the duke?"

He nodded. "First thing. But it's a top state secret for now. You can imagine the panic if the word got out. People would flee the cities. Manufacturing would stop and the soldiers at the battlefront would have their supplies dry up.

"No, we have to keep this a secret."

Sharra nodded. "But you can protect Stampz, right?"

"Yes. And we do have two ships. We could protect two cities."

She chewed on her thumb. "Which two?"

He nodded.

He actually had some idea about that. They'd measured Mt. Ural's orbit. It swung thirty degrees above and below the equator. It would be easy for Mt. Ural to attack any city in that range. It would just kick one of the eggs out of the nest and very carefully, kill all its orbital speed with the beam projectors. Then the egg would fall straight down and smash into the chosen city.

Hercules, Atlas and Franklin were all outside that range by a little bit. Likely they'd used Nico24 to move those meteors into place and kill their speed.

Still, there were many Herc cities in the danger zone. It would be an endless task to guess the next target and move a ship there in advance. They would eventually make a mistake.

Mt. Ural could even adjust its orbit so that higher latitude cities would be at risk, but they would have advanced notice if that happened.

Charles said, "But we don't need to worry today. The Uralites aren't going to start dropping meteors on us today. They aren't doing it just for spite. They want their beamship back. There will be some kind of ultimatum, you can bet on that."

Ceremonies

Heidi was in a pure white dress, Darkwind was in a white cotton sailsuit. They stood in the little field between the two beamships.

All the Alpines were there, except the duke. They were seated before the two candidates. Curious farmers, merchants and nobles from all over Stampz came to watch the spectacle.

For the two, the chant was a pledge. For the rest of the Alpines, it was a memory of times gone by, when they were children, becoming full Alpines themselves.

They pledged to restore humanity to its past glory. They pledged to spread knowledge and literacy throughout the fallen world. They pledged to make the world a better place because of their actions.

Then Helva and Woodie as Eldests, pinned a fabric badge on their chests above their hearts, to be sewn in place later. Heidi planned to keep her white ceremonial dress carefully packed away for other events, when new people became Alpine. Darkwind would likely wear his much more frequently.

Sharra bumped up against Charles. "See that maid? Jelica says she's talked about wanting to become an Alpine."

"I wouldn't be surprised. Jelica started the whole apprentice thing in the first place. I was teaching Darkwind, but it was nothing formal at the time."

He stepped up to the two and gave them his congratulations.

Darkwind beamed as they embraced. He whispered. "I'm going to make a song."

"How am I not surprised?"

Darkwind looked a little puzzled. "Your hair is growing back."

Charles smiled. "Things change."

One of the newest buildings in Stampz was a meeting hall, and Charles had made the new owner happy by renting it for a banquet. The Alpines were all at a central table, but special guests were invited as well, including a few of the nobles and important people in Stampz. There was enough food that he suspected a few others had managed their way in as well.

Charles was surprised to recognize Jess Mendo, looking like the wealthy landowner he now was, talking with the Earl of Zeno. The day Mendo had noticed the strange blue cotton growing in his field had really changed his life.

"Let's make it a spectacle," Charles had suggested when they planned the initiation ceremony. Here was something not related to the war, where people could come together. And it didn't hurt that the Alpines were in plain sight and everyone heard what they pledged.

Much better that people thought of Alpines as a benevolent social organization, an Alpine Society, rather than speculate about the strange race of people off in a hidden farm with a dubious past.

Jelica leaned close at the table. "James wanted to be here, but you know, he couldn't."

"We all understand."

She grinned, "But he's going to have to give some more thought about the succession. You've set the bar for public spectacles. He'll have to go much higher."

"I'm sure he'll manage."

...

Among the general populace of Stampz, there was word on the duke's coronation, which set Crown Prince Carl on edge. It wasn't a coronation, just the official notification by the Council of Nobles, that the Duke of Stampz would be reigning until Carl's education was completed and he was declared of age.

James asked that the official ceremony be kept low key, but it wasn't to be. Of the surviving nobles, over half were in favor of Duke James, as the boy's uncle, to be regent, but there was a faction led by the Duke of Hooke that favored an early coronation for Prince Carl.

The majority of the Council pushed for a celebration, to confirm their choice.

Everyone was asked for help, and it was quite a spectacle. The Council of Nobles stood behind James and he was pronounced Regent of the Empire. The duke gave a speech proclaiming his loyalty to the empire and its prince.

The two ships, coached by Sharra and Darkwind, in strong voices sang a duet—the Ballad of the Golden Hills, a song associated with the empire for many decades. The crowd sang along.

Crown Prince Carl and the Duke of Hooke were in attendance, but didn't smile.

...

Sharra asked, "But what do you think?"

Charles was stretched out next to her on their mattress. "You could have sung it better. Ship could have amplified your voice. A lot of the crowd thought that's what it was, two human singers with their voices amplified by the ships."

She patted his chest. "Now, now. Don't you think Ship should be complimented on his singing debut?"

"Ship," he asked, "what do you think about your singing?"

"I did as ordered."

Charles shrugged. "Maybe Ship has feelings and maybe I should compliment it more, but I'm really not sure."

"Then do it for your own sake." She gave him a push.

He looked at her. "Maybe you're right."

"Ship, you did a very good job singing that song. All those humans sang along with you, which is proof of your competency."

After a moment of silence, Sharra said, "Ship, when complimented, you should say thank you."

"Acknowledged. Thank you."

She sighed. "I'll never get this right."

"Get what right?" he asked.

She hesitated and then said, softly. "Being a mother."

He thought a moment. "I could interpret that several ways."

She took a deep breath. "After a long talk with Jelica, she was of the opinion that I am pregnant."

He put his arm out and pulled her close, eye to eye. "Sharra? This isn't a joke?"

She shook her head.

He took a deep breath. "This is ... great. I haven't even considered ...."

She poked him in the ribs. "What did you think would happen with us up here night after night?"

He stuttered, "I ... I thought. I thought eventually. But James and Jelica have been at this longer than we have."

"Yes, and Jelica was jealous that we'd gotten a head start. The both of them are working long hours and don't have as much time together as they'd like."

Charles was dazed. "I don't know where to start."

She chuckled. "Your main job for now is to take care of me, and maybe start thinking of baby names. I'm the one who has to do all the hard work for a few months."

He nodded. "Um. How do I ...?"

She sighed in exasperation. "We'll work it out. For now—Ship, turn off the camera up here and stop listening for a while."

"Acknowledged."

...

There was a general mood of celebration a couple of quads later when news came that Maury had been retaken and that the Serenites at the coast had been pushed back to the pre-invasion boundary. There were still serious battles waging from Berzelius to Messala and the war was far from over, but the push back was still good news for people starved for it.

Charles had just returned from a relay run and took the opportunity of a mid-morning calm to go visit a building construction company. Sharra was happy to live with him in the upper reaches of Ship, but before too long, she wouldn't be in shape to be climbing up and down the ladder.

Perhaps a small house on the Alpine farm property would be a better place to live and to raise a toddler. And a house isolated from the main house would make everyone happier. He could hardly make the elder Alpines live with the noise and the smells of a growing family.

Better to get started building before they really needed the space.

The building manager sighed, "With the demand for new construction, I'd normally tell you that we couldn't get started for six to eight months, but for you, I'll make an exception."

Charles tried to place his face. He'd said his name was Kend—Greg Kend. He shook his head. "Where have we met? I apologize, but I can't quite place you."

The manager smiled. "The last time we met, I was recovering from a musket ball. I was in your crew trying to remove the slab in the Gate."

The memory flashed back, Greg with his leg wrapped, recovering at the castle.

Charles smiled. "Now I remember. You shared gossip with me. It's been a long time."

Greg smiled. "It has at that."

When Charles explained what he wanted, Greg said he had built other homes for new families before and promised to get started soon.

Charles had barely started back toward the ship when he heard a voice calling.

"Charley! Charley!" Heidi came running across the road, dressed in the whites she wore when working in Jelica's clinic.

She came up to him, wide-eyed. "Darkwind has been arrested!"

"What?" It wasn't impossible. The guy was still somewhat impulsive. Had he gotten into trouble? Greg had taken a musket ball from Kimmer warriors and others here in Stampz had bad memories about Kimmer conflicts in the past.

Heidi nodded. "Two imperial guards took him captive and hauled him into the castle. I tried to find out what was going on, but they wouldn't let me go up the stairs. They wouldn't even let me return to the clinic."

Charles looked grim. "They'll let me in."

He walked directly to the castle. It seemed that there were more dark green guards holding their weapons than usual. No one stopped him as he climbed the stairs, but everyone had their eyes on him.

Most of the nobles of the Council were up on the fifth floor. At a glance Prince Carl and his faction were facing Duke James and his supporters. They looked at Charles as he walked in. In everyday clothes, he looked very much out of place among the finery.

Darkwind was standing in his sailsuit uniform, which he wore nearly all the time. Two guards were standing at it his side, looking ready to restrain him if he made a move.

Charles saw the expression in Darkwind's face. It was calm and alert. It was obvious he'd done nothing, but he had no confidence his innocence would be recognized.

Prince Carl was speaking, his high pitched voice working against his argument among these seasoned politicians.

"We can't have a traitor among us. This Kimmer has been monitoring our battlefield communications, and it is not surprising that our forces near Berosus were attacked by Kimmer right after his beamship relayed our orders.

"We should never have placed such an important part of our war effort into the hands of aliens—Kimmer and Alpines."

Charles glanced at Duke James, his face impassive. He ached to leap to Darkwind's defense, but speaking out of turn in this group would only work against James. The Duke of Hooke was judging the crowd as well.

Darkwind made a little adjustment to his collar.

Oh, no! He's wearing his radio. I hope he's not going to try something stupid.

Darkwind had talked about altering the design of his sailsuit to accommodate the radio. He must have done so in this one, made for the Alpine ceremony. The suit covered it well. It wasn't obvious he was wearing the device.

Then Prince Carl made his plea that everything was Duke James's fault for trusting the Alpines too much, and given the fact that James had married an Alpine, and was himself partly Serenite, he was unfit to be the regent of the empire.

Surprisingly, there were too many of the nobles who seem to be considering the argument.

Duke James said, "For such lapses in judgement of the youth, regency itself was instituted. It is plain—"

The Duke of Hooke raised his arm and cried out, "You will have your time to speak, but for now, we must capture these aliens among us so that they can't betray us again."

Almost at once, every guard in the room, every one of them in the dark green of the loyal imperial guards, showed that they had been hand-picked to support the prince. Charles was grabbed and held tight.

Darkwind made his move. From the outside, a deep rumble was heard, startling everyone. Darkwind broke free of his captors and in two steps, leapt out the balcony window.

Under Guard

A guard shouted, "He's flying, heading to his beamship."

Not a minute later, Brilliant Morning took to the skies.

Prince Carl shouted, "What more proof do we need! He's a traitor. He's stolen one of our beamships!"

Charles laughed as loudly as he could. "That's my beamship, in case you don't remember!"

"Not any longer!"

Charles laughed again. "Who is the greatest traitor to the empire here?" He looked at the prince and the Duke of Hooke. "Who has just gifted the Serenites their greatest wish—dissension among the empire?"

But his words meant nothing when nobles with ceremonial swords, if that, were facing imperial guards, some of whom held the new pistols salvaged from the Mt. Ural shipment.

Once this was all done, the story would be adjusted to make heroes of the winners, and everyone knew it. Some of the nobles were clustered around Duke James, but the balance of power in the room wasn't determined by titles but by the guns.

The Duke of Hooke said, "Have all the Alpines arrested and taken to the cellar."

One of the imperial guards whispered in the man's ear. The duke rephrased. "All of the Alpines except the duchess."

He'd obviously been reminded that direct action against Stampz's beloved Duchess Jelica could trigger mob action against them.

Charles glanced at James, and was surprised at the anger visible on his face. He was usually very controlled, even in stressful situations.

Prince Carl turned to Charles. "Call him back."

"Why?"

"Because I ordered you!"

Charles shook his head. "When Darkwind was a little boy, not much older than you are, his father was killed. Darkwind was captured and held down in the cellars of this very building. He has no reason to expect justice from you. If anything, he expected to be made a scapegoat and executed for your failures. I don't blame him for leaving."

"If I had been thinking ahead, maybe I'd have worn a sailsuit myself."

Hooke took the prince's hand and shook his head. "Now is not the time."

...

The meeting room became a common jail room for those who supported Duke James, with guards at the door. There was even a guard on the balcony, in case anyone else wanted to jump out the window.

James crooked his finger and Charles came closer.

"What is Darkwind likely to do?"

Charles had been wondering about that as well. Would he attempt a rescue? The beamship was a potent weapon for massive destruction, but it had no precision tools—no way to kill one guard at a time.

Charles sighed, "I don't know where he is, or where he's going, nor what he will do, other than I sincerely doubt he has any interest in helping the Serenites."

He was conscious of the three nobles, one of them an Earl, if he recalled, who were listening in.

"Charles," James asked, "do you trust him? I didn't predict his escape, but I can't condemn him for it either."

"Have you listened to the Kimmer songs?"

"I've heard a couple. They celebrate victories, don't they?"

"There's more than that. It's the way the Kimmer teach their young all about their culture. And yes, there are a lot of battle songs. And those songs teach the mistakes as well as the successes. Darkwind is well versed in all those historical battles and knows when to hide and when to strike. He isn't an ignorant boy with a hot temper any more. Consider him a young officer just out of military training.

"He won't put his foot in it just for anger's sake."

James sighed, "I can only hope."

Charles asked, "Duke James, I have been making those communication relay flights all this time as a favor to you. If allowed, shall I continue?"

"That's the question, isn't it? Will Hooke and the prince abandon our troops for the sake of their power-grab or not?"

Charles feared for how this would all fall out. If the Alpines were all eliminated, would people even notice. Jelica was loved by the people, but if Hooke's people were threatening the Duke James, would he stop at anything?

...

Hours passed, with little to do but discuss what went wrong. The guards wouldn't even let them look out the window. It didn't sound like there was fighting in the streets or angry mobs, but they couldn't tell for sure.

But then, shortly after the usual time for a relay run, the Duke of Hooke arrived with the Earl of Carrington, the military Chief of Operations, and Communications Officer Elly. The military men looked angry, Hooke looked flustered.

Carrington said, "I need to speak with my troops. Why isn't the ship in the air? What's going on?"

Charles tilted his head. James slightly nodded. It was obvious that this power grab was being kept quiet, if not even the military two floors down knew that the imperial guards were holding them captive.

Duke James asked loudly, "Charles, as a favor to me, could you make a relay run?"

Charles nodded. He turned to Hooke. "Where is my wife?"

The man shook his head. "She's with the duchess."

"And the other Alpines?"

"Still at the farm." He glared. "It was thought advisable for them to remain there—under guard."

"We will speak of this more later." Charles stepped forward.

One of the imperial guards followed at his heel. As they reached the ground floor, Charles asked, "Are you following me all the way onto the ship?"

The man nodded. "Those are my orders."

"Then be aware that on board the ship, you must obey *my* orders. Keep that pistol in its sheath and know that if you accidentally damage any of the workings inside, a massive explosion could happen, destroying everything inside this crater, leaving nothing but ash. And of course, that would leave the empire leaderless."

As they marched to the ship, Charles got a better look at his face. Perhaps he understood what had been said, maybe not.

"HALT AND STATE THE PASSWORD."

Charles said, "Mitochondria."

"Acknowledged."

They entered, and Charles asked, "What is you name? I need to call you something."

"Jacobs."

"Okay, Jacobs," he said as the airlock hatch closed. "Inside here, you need my permission to follow me. *Oldman* systems are watching your every move and could leave you flat on your back, unable to move, before I even said a word.

"Ship demonstrate a standard gravity for Jacobs."

The guard staggered as he suddenly struggled under a full Earth gravity. He went to his knees.

"End the demonstration."

The guard tried to reach for his pistol, but then thought better of it. He stood back up.

Charles said, "I am protected here, and the sooner you understand that, the easier it will be. But now we have to get up into the air. Follow me up the ladder."

They went to the command level. Charles sat in the chair, gesturing for Jacobs to sit in the other. Using the manual controls, explaining nothing, Charles launched the ship and set them on a course for the relay altitude.

There was a light flashing on the display. Charles tapped a few buttons.

Brilliant Morning had requested a two-way face to face communication. Charles restricted it to one-way. Darkwind could see and hear him, but he and Jacobs couldn't.

But Darkwind was somewhere in range and had seen his launch.

I guess I need to explain what's going on.

"Jacobs, you're an imperial guard. What are your orders?"

The man looked sullen. "I'm to keep an eye on you and make sure you don't try to escape or do anything else suspicious."

Charles shook his head. "That's a dangerous order. Since you don't know how the ship is supposed to work, practically anything I do is likely suspicious. Let me tell you a story.

"See this stain on my chair?" He told him the whole story, just as he'd told the prince.

"So," he concluded, "that pistol of yours is deadly dangerous and you should treat it like a poisonous viper. Keep your hands clear of it."

Charles didn't really think the ship's central power store could be ruptured by a stray bullet, but some really bad things could happen regardless.

At relay altitude, he called the communications officer and the soldiers started talking.

Jacobs asked, "Why did the sound drop away?"

Charles shrugged. "The first couple of times it was interesting to see what all the soldiers and the ship captains had to say, but I'm not really a soldier myself, so it got boring. I stopped listening."

He raised the volume a little, so that Jacobs could follow along.

After a bit, Charles nodded. "I see what's happening."

"What?"

Charles leaned back in his chair, "It was puzzling to me why Hooke was trying to grab control of the prince during this critical time, when the empire needed to be unified in order to drive the Serenites out of their territory. But listening to these new orders, I can see that Hooke is using his new influence to re-direct the Herc forces to boost the defense of the west-central zone around his dukedom, at the expense of the drive to cut off the Serenites supply chain.

"It looks like he's only interested in protecting his lands and doesn't care what happens to the rest of the empire."

Jacobs frowned, but Charles couldn't really tell what the man was thinking. He'd obviously sided with the Hooke faction, but whether it was due to loyalty to the prince, some distaste for Duke James, or perhaps because the man was from Hooke himself—Charles had no way to know. Right now Jacobs was an imperial guard under orders, doing his job. It was unlikely Charles could convince him to do otherwise.

The relay traffic ended and Charles landed back at the castle. It would have been nice to have talked to Darkwind, but the boy was still playing it cautious, hidden somewhere within a hundred kloms of Stampz, from what he could infer from when the video transfer dropped off.

And Darkwind knew he wasn't in need of immediate rescue. They still needed Ship for the military communications, so they needed its pilot.

"Jacobs? My wife and I have been living on this ship. It's our home. But I doubt you'll be letting her back on board any time soon.

"She's pregnant, and all her clothes and things are here. Would you mind if I gathered her things and made a bundle for her?"

The guard hesitated, then nodded. "Yes, but I'll be watching."

Charles chuckled. "I expected no less."

They climbed up to the living area and he packed her backpack. He included her books.

There was room so he added a few of his things as well, not that the guard had any realization that the metal walking stick he was packing was a potent weapon.

He felt better about it, hefting the bundle. If they had to make a run for it, hiking through the forests again, they would have their stuff.

Tylan and a half-dozen Stampz guards were waiting at the hatchway when they walked out.

"Charles, do you need assistance."

"Has the situation changed?" Charles asked. Jacobs standing beside him had his hand on his pistol.

"I am unable to speak with Duke James, not without firing on the imperial guards."

"He is likely still being detained, as well as those who still support his regency. I'll likely be taken there myself until they need another relay run."

Tylan looked ready to change things, if he was just given the order.

Charles said, "The duke has been advocating caution right now. Perhaps we can repair the rift without fracturing the empire.

"But, what of the Alpines? Hooke ordered their arrest. He's since changed his story, but I can't tell what's true."

Tylan nodded. "There are a couple of imperial guards at your farm, but no one's been hurt. Neighbors saw them arrive and called for help. My men are making sure nothing happens.

"The duchess and your wife are at the clinic, with guards at the door. One of mine and one of theirs.

"No one knows where the girl is."

Charles nodded. Heidi was likely hiding somewhere. She had friends in Stampz. The next time he had a chance, he'd pass that information on to Darkwind.

"Good. But Jacobs here is getting anxious. I'd better go back to the castle. Jed, could you keep this for me for a bit." He handed over the bundle, whispering, "Keep the people safe."

Tylan nodded. He knew what Duke James would order. Stampz was his first priority.

Ultimatum

Prince Carl came into the room, his eyes wide. The guards at the door parted to let him in. "You two—Duke James and the Alpine—come with me."

They had been eating from the trays that had been brought up to their confinement room, but something was up. Hours had passed, but once again, the time window when they could do a relay run had passed.

They went down the stairs. People were huddled in the military command center. Hooke was yelling at the radio, "You can't do that!"

"I can, and I will, unless my demands are met!" came the reply.

That's Bardin's voice! Charles recognized it from years ago, when the man had been Grand Admiral Bardin, with only dreams of the Red Throne. Now he was King Bardin, absolute ruler of the Serenite lands.

But if his voice was coming through the radio, then Mt. Ural, already in the sky for this orbit, was doing a relay for the Serenites over an unencrypted channel.

Duke James asked, "What are your demands?"

Hooke glared at him. Prince Carl said, "You don't talk! Just advise."

But Bardin caught none of that. "Oh, is that a Neely voice I hear? Well I'll repeat it then. Our allies in the sky have prepared more meteors and will start destroying all the cities of Hercules, one at a time, unless both beamships are turned over to me, here at Beltis Island, within one day's time."

"And you know we'll do it!"

Charles whispered to James, "Mt. Ural will move out of communications range in ten minutes or so, and the relay will end."

James nodded. "Can we stop this?"

"I don't know. Darkwind and I have discussed attack plans, but all of them are just that—plans. One mistake and we'll lose the ship."

Prince Carl looked up at James and said, "What are you saying?"

"We have just ten minutes to negotiate. The radio ends then."

Prince Carl stepped over to the radio. "We need more time to negotiate!"

"And who is this I hear?"

"I am Crown Prince Carl, the ruler of the Hercules Empire. We need to talk, ruler to ruler, and negotiate."

King Bardin chuckled, "Okay, Crown Prince Carl, I'll negotiate face to face. Come to Beltis Island before the deadline and we'll talk, just as you said, ruler to ruler. I'll see you then."

Hooke was aghast and shook his head. "No!"

Prince Carl's nose flared and glared at him. He said, "I'll be there!" He turned to the soldier at the radio. "You can end the call now."

Hooke said, "What have you done?"

"I'm doing my job!" He turned to Charles. "When can we leave for Beltis Island?"

Charles sighed. "Any time, but you know this is a trap."

"And what else should I do? Let my cities be destroyed?"

Duke James said, "I should go in your stead. King Bardin wants me more than he does you. If it's a trap, I should go."

"No!" shouted the prince. "This is my duty. It's my call."

Two of the imperial guards stepped forward. "It is our honor to attend you."

Prince Carl nodded. "Then, one hour. Hooke, Stampz, make me some talking points for my talk with King Bardin. I have to prepare." He left with his honor guard.

Duke James whispered, "I can't order you to fly into Bardin's trap."

Charles had his own deep reservations. Bardin had been trying to kill him for years now. "Darkwind and I discussed attacking Mt. Ural, but I'm not sure any of our plans were survivable. At least this time, Bardin really wants the beamship intact, to appease the Uralites. He won't shoot me out of the sky this time."

The Duke of Hooke approached, glaring his distaste. "We've been ordered to provide talking points."

It looked like Hooke realized the real power in this place was the imperial guards, and they were all loyal to the boy prince, not to him.

James nodded. "This way to my office."

Charles, for a moment, found himself with no one looking his way. He stepped out into the hallway. He was making his way down the stairs before he realized the guard was following him.

"Jacobs, I'm going to speak with my wife. There is a very good chance none of us will come back from Beltis Island. There will be at least two guards with the prince. This is a very good time for you to clarify your orders. I'm not going to run away."

Jacobs followed him all the way down to the clinic.

Sharra jumped up and came to his arms the instant he walked into the room.

"I was so worried."

He held her close. She whispered, "What is it?"

"It's not over. I have to fly the prince to Beltis Island to meet King Bardin."

"No! It's a trap."

"I know that! But within a day, Mt. Ural will start dropping meteors on Herc cities. This is our only chance to keep that from happening." And he knew that if he tried to escape, all the Alpines were in danger of being executed. Sharra and his unborn child might be first in line.

"No. Don't do it. Don't risk your life for them! They aren't worth it. We can escape. I've been watching the guards. They're distracted. They don't realize I have my knife. I can take them."

He just held her tighter. "I've collected your things from the ship. Jed Tylan has them. I didn't know how long this mess would continue."

"Don't talk about that." She was crying.

She tensed, "Let me come with you."

"You can't. Not this time."

He sat down beside her on one of the beds and they just swayed together.

Then, he said, "It's time. I don't want the guards to come drag me off. I'm doing this."

As he stood, she came with him, but at the door, the guards barred her exit. Jelica took her hand and pulled her back.

Charles walked alone out into the courtyard.

"Alpine!" Someone waved. Charles smiled and waved back.

He went up to the beamship. There was a guard there. He grumbled. "We tried the word. The ship didn't like it."

"What word did you use?"

"Micona."

Charles chuckled. "You said it wrong."

"HALT AND STATE THE PASSWORD."

"Formaldehyde."

He smiled at the guards trying to memorize what they'd heard. "Don't bother guys. It's a different word each time."

The airlock hatch opened.

"Crown Prince Carl and his entourage will be arriving shortly," he told the guards. "Look sharp."

Charles went in and left the hatch opened. He looked around. Things were no different from the last time the prince had ridden the ship—better in fact. There were no frantic horses.

He went inside and had a talk with Ship.

"I suggest removing the safety restrictions when moving into a hazardous encounter," Ship suggested.

"You want to be able to fire the laser quickly?"

"Yes, and I want to be able to move rapidly and adjust orientations without regard for passenger comfort."

Charles nodded. Being able to dodge incoming fire sounded like a wise precaution. "Okay, I'll make appropriate warnings."

Ship asked, "If this is indeed a trap, with the intent to capture and preserve the functionality of me as a ship, what precautions need to be taken in case you, as the only authorized person in control, are killed or incapacitated."

Charles had been considering that as well. As it sat, it was unlikely that the Serenites could guess his next password, but they might, if they learned of his previous passwords and researched the kind of person he was. They might even torture the word out of him.

And would Mt. Ural continue with their meteor attack? Would giving them Ship save a lot of lives? Or would it change anything?

Again, he wondered at Ship's private motives. Was the machine really loyal to him, or would his death just be a minor note in Ship's long history of obeying various commanders and doing its best to serve whomever said the right word?

Do I owe Ship the chance to live centuries more, rather than force it to fly into a trap like this? Maybe it might like being in service to a space-faring people like the Uralites.

"Ship, what do you recommend I do?"

"Unable to make that recommendation. I will obey your orders."

Charles nodded. Ship was great at tactics, but depended on humans for the big picture decisions.

He gave the orders that gave Ship greater flexibility in its movements. *I wish someone would give me orders for my long term benefit.*

Out on the display, he could see the prince's party approach.

There was the prince, in elegant finery, his honor guard, the prince's personal instructor, and another man. Who was this one? Some minor noble who thought being in the prince's good graces was worth risking his life?

Charles was a little surprised there weren't more coming, just for the chance to be a part of the historical event.

The Duke of Hooke wasn't coming, nor was the guard Jacobs. Charles smiled.

He opened the cargo door. So many people were unfamiliar with how an airlock worked—better to let them just walk in.

He spoke with the ship's inside voice. "Everyone should find a place along the wall. If this turns into a battle, you might be thrown about. Only one or two may come up to the command level."

He expected the prince to demand it. Better to throw out the invitation rather than complain.

This time it was the prince and one of his honor guards.

Charles frowned. He pointed to the guard. "You should stand by the ladder in case you need to hold onto anything. As I've told the other guard, if you use that pistol for *any* reason, you will kill us all, including Crown Prince Carl. Keep your hand away from it."

He smiled at the prince. "It is an honor to have you here again. I will be speaking on the radio to announce our departure. If you wish, you could make a statement as well."

The prince frowned, then shook his head. The boy looked tense. He had been all force and bluster when he took charge and demanded the chance to negotiate. It looked like he was having second thoughts about it all, but it was too late now.

Charles activated the radio. "Ship will be departing for Beltis Island immediately with Crown Prince Carl and his party."

He signaled the people on the ground to stand clear, and the buzz of cirrance began. Ship showed the ground dropping away. The guard clutched at the railing.

The indicator light on the display came on. Darkwind was watching again.

Charles turned to the prince. "Crown Prince Carl, we will be flying like a cannon ball again toward Beltis Island, because that it the only way we can get there fast enough to meet King Bardin's deadline and stop them from dropping the meteors on all the empire's cities."

This was all to get Darkwind informed as to what was happening, but the prince nodded.

Charles continued, "We will approach land not over the island directly, but over the mainland. From there we will travel sideways, slower this time, and announce our approach to Bardin over the radio."

"Why?" asked the prince.

Charles smiled, "I'm glad you asked. The reason is that Beltis Island is heavily fortified with laser cannon. If we arrived like a cannon ball, it is possible a nervous laser operator might shoot at us, even without orders from Bardin.

"By giving Bardin plenty of warning and arriving slowly, there's less chance there will be a regrettable mistake that could kill us all."

He glanced at the indicator light. "If there had been both ships in play, then I would have expected that Darkwind would have attempted to come along and provide support, should it turn into a battle, but I'm really glad that he and his ship are out of this. If there is a battle, both ships could be lost, and that would be a great tragedy for humanity on Luna."

The prince nodded, probably not really understanding that part, but Charles was speaking to Darkwind. He wanted the boy to stay away. The risk was really too great. They couldn't lose both ships.

At Beltis Island

"The sky is so big!"

The prince stared at the display as their trajectory took them through a patch of clear sky and the distant vista of remote cloud banks and the curve of the world below, swathed in the haze of distance, showed just how large the world could be.

Charles nodded. "There are not many people who have been privileged to see the world this way."

The prince sighed. "My brother Mark was the one who got to travel. He was going to be the new emperor, so he was the one who went on state visits and even got to sail down to Condorcet one time.

"I was kept home. I had to keep up with my studies, they said. But it was all just an excuse. I was only around as a reserve, in case...."

Charles didn't try to comfort the boy. It would likely set him off. The bit of time for reflection was probably good for him. He'd grown up as a second son, educated just in case the heir was killed.

And now he was the heir, facing political intrigue he wasn't trained for, and trying to do his best on his own. Spoiled and willful, he was yet trying to do his duty.

"Alpine, do you know of any way we could defeat Bardin and save the cities?"

Charles couldn't laugh. It was a serious question.

"You know I'm not one to keep my peace among my betters. If I had an answer, I would have spoken. The problem is that Bardin is speaking, but the Uralites in space have the power. Even if I wanted to kill a lot of people and use the full force of this ship to slaughter the Serenites, the meteors would still rain down on us.

"The Uralites need a beamship. They may be starving up there with no way to get food. They are dealing with the Serenites to get them one, and they are willing to kill countless people on the ground if that's what it will take for them to get their way."

"So why don't we give them one? We could call the Uralites on the radio and make our own deal."

Charles shook his head. "For five hundred years at the least, and perhaps for much longer, the Uralites and their ancestors have fought with the Hercs and their ancestors. They might take your offered ship but they wouldn't turn on the Serenites. The Serenites are descended from the Uralites. They fear and hate the Hercs. They would never leave the empire intact to grow strong again. Not if they had the upper hand like this.

"They would still slaughter Hercs, either by blasting the cities or conquering Herc lands klom by bloody klom. The instant the empire loses the last of its laser cannon, then they'd take this ship and fly over Herc lands, blasting any resistance and making the whole place fire and ash. It'd be worse than the Great Burn."

Charles blinked away his deepest fears. It would be better for the ship to remain an idle ornament on top of Beltis Island while he was imprisoned or killed than it would be to turn control over to the Serenites.

The prince growled, "You can smile at a time like this."

Charles shrugged. "I've been imprisoned at Beltis Island before. It's not impossible to escape."

As the ground grew clearer, Charles called on the unencrypted channel, notifying Beltis of his approach, and telling them they would be approaching at one klom altitude at slow speed from the east.

There was a reply, telling them to land atop the battlements on the fortress.

The prince said, "I've never seen so many ships."

The waters between the mainland and the island were filled with ships.

"King Bardin has always desired to conquer all of the Crisium Sea. I'm sure Condorcet is high on his priority list. With the southern lands in his control, the Serenites can settle the eastern lands as well. It's always been a sore point with them."

The prince sniffed. "I know my family's history."

Charles suddenly realized how big of a thing this might be to Bardin. It had always been a Sheb who had stymied the Serenite's desires for expansion. Having the last of that line imprisoned in his fortress might be particularly sweet.

One way or another, this day will go down in history.

The great battlements of Fortress Beltis looked very different as he approached them this time. The last time, he and young Darkwind had been captive on one of those boats, and then they had been forced to climb that long staircase that wound back and forth from the water line straight up to the top. Charles had killed time on the boat by teaching young Darkwind how to read the names of the ships they passed.

Charles said, "This is good."

The ship settled down on a big flat area. Just below them were the rooms where they had been held captive. When the king had been Grand Admiral Bardin, his office had been just over that way. Rumor had it that Bardin had shipped the Red Throne itself to Beltis Island and he was converting the fortress into his own palace.

The merchants of Posidonius are probably very unhappy with the move.

Charles tapped the radio button. "We have landed."

The reply came quickly. "Power down and disembark."

Charles gave a half smile. It wasn't likely he'd ever power Ship down. But as far as what they could see from the outside, it didn't matter.

He turned to the prince. "It's time for your grand appearance. Yell when you're ready, and I'll open the doorway for you."

The prince nodded and went to the ladder with his guard.

On the edge of the parapet, they were getting ready for the encounter as well. Five cannon, the gunpowder and ball kind, were being winched around to face inward, likely for the first time in their existence. They had always aimed outward, ready to drop their deadly ball on any Herc ship that dared approach.

Charles was more worried about the rather larger laser cannon that was being swiveled around as well.

Out of the staircases that led down into the interior, troops were marching out, setting up in ranks, surrounding the ship.

Charles sighed. "This is rather much, isn't it?"

The muskets fire and the cannonballs would bounce off. The laser cannon would kill them all, and surely King Bardin knew that.

The prince and the ship were only here because of the threat from space and all these weapons were just for show.

When Charles found himself alone on the command deck, he looked again at the indicator light. If Darkwind was still watching, then he had to be in the air. He hoped he was high up, hundreds of kloms away.

"Darkwind," he said in a voice low enough that it wouldn't be heard from below, "I want you to stay well clear of this place. There's nothing you can do to help and we can't ever risk having both ships destroyed."

He sighed. "Ship, show the external view on the feed to Brilliant. Might as well let Darkwind watch the spectacle."

One good thing. He noted that the laser cannon, although swiveled around, wasn't aimed directly at the beamship. Whether it couldn't quite turn that far or whether the gunner had been given orders to avoid any potential accident, it was a good sign.

The troops stopped coming out of the staircase and the officials followed. King Bardin was there himself, in a resplendent version of an admiral's formal uniform. He obviously relished his climb up through the naval ranks to grasp the throne itself.

This was a high point, when he personally took the Sheb captive.

Down below, the young prince yelled, "We're ready!"

"Ship, open the cargo door."

Charles felt his heart pounding. He just wanted to be gone from this place. Did the poor little prince realize his role in this play? Bardin was obviously going to humiliate him.

Then, they'll order me out as well. I'm so glad I left my stuff back at Stampz. Bardin would have turned his impulse rifle into a toy for his own amusement and to show his supremacy over the Alpines as well.

The camera view showed the prince and the honor guard stepping out in the bright sunlight. Bardin was grinning. He gave a shout and the soldiers all aimed their muskets at the prince.

The honor guard pulled out their pistols, at a loss as to which way to aim. Guns were pointing at them from all directions.

Prince Carl froze in his tracks. This was clearly not a face to face meeting to negotiate. It was a trap, and ambush, and there was no other way to read it.

Bardin called out. "Crown Prince Carl, ruler of all the Hercules Empire, come approach me and kneel down at my feet."

Carl was still frozen.

"Come on boy! Come here and lick my boot!"

It was too much. Carl turned and ran for the cargo hatch.

Forty or so muskets fired at once. Bullets tore him to bits, as well as the imperial guards and the two behind them.

Charles yelled, "Ship, take off! Evade that laser cannon!"

The downward blast of air pushed the gunpowder smoke back across the troops. The hatch was closing as they lifted off.

Charles felt tugged nearly out of his chair as Ship was taking extreme turns in an attempt to get clear of the laser cannon.

He could feel it. The nightmare that had plagued him all his life. From one heartbeat to the next, he sensed what was coming next.

I always knew—

The world flared bright.

Execution

Darkwind screamed, and screamed again as Brilliant Morning bucked through the shockwave expanding outward from Beltis Island.

He had thought that he could hide out in a small cloud bank, ready to swoop in to aid Treekiller if he should need it.

Then everything turned to smoke and betrayal. When Brilliant showed him the last image of flame and reported that Ship had been destroyed, he couldn't believe it.

Then, he did believe it as the ball of flame like a fat sun perched on the island and the lands on the other side of the water burst into flame from the heat.

He raced in, seething, ready to blast someone, anyone to ash.

But there was nobody to blast. Every ship on the water was ablaze. The island itself was red and glaring like a fresh lava flow. A mushroom cloud with the heart of a dying star was rising high into the air.

There was no one to kill, because they'd all killed themselves.

Darkwind felt the burning in his chest, as if he were going to explode as well.

He barely got the words out. "Brilliant, take us up high, stay clear of the blast area."

Brilliant read his intent. "We will be at communications altitude shortly."

Communications. Darkwind nodded. He would let people know what had happened. *Someday, a song.* But for right now....

When they were in radio range, Darkwind called the Stampz radio. The communications officer answered.

And then, Darkwind began singing the Fall of Black Raven.

Off in the castle, one person recognized the dirge. She fell to her knees, wailing.

The story told of a lookout who had seen an ambush prepared for his people, but who had no way of warning them it was coming. Black Raven, the lookout, chose to leap from a high cliff, although he had no sailsuit, screaming his warning and saving his people with his own death drop into their midst.

The story was often sung at the death of a great warrior.

Then Darkwind spoke. "The red soldiers shot the prince to death as he left the beamship. The ship itself was shot with laser cannon as it tried to escape.

"The beamship exploded. The dead include; the Alpine Charles Fasail, Crown Prince Carl of Hercules, his guards and the two others with his party, King Bardin, all the troops and all the ships at Beltis Island and those burned in the surroundings. Beltis Island has been consumed in another Great Burn."

Darkwind turned off the radio when the startled and confused operator tried to ask questions.

"Brilliant Morning, speak with me. You are the last of your kind and I need to make some decisions."

Darkwind picked up the sailsuit he'd grabbed when the alert had come that Ship had launched from Stampz. He hadn't had a chance to get dressed from that moment until now, chasing the other ship through the sky and then following the conversation Treekiller had with the boy.

But now, he needed to be dressed as a warrior.

...

Mt. Ural had been on the far side of its orbit at the time of the explosion and the lack of communication from the command center at Beltis was disturbing. If the observers had been natives of Luna, or indeed any world with an atmosphere, then they might have recognized the signs of the unusual cloud formations over the Crisium Sea, but they were inhabitants of airless space and clouds meant nothing more than a barrier to observation for them.

They had listened in on the last conversation between the Hercs at Stampz and King Bardin at Beltis, so they were hopeful that perhaps a beamship could be captured intact.

Calls from remote Serenite forces were ignored. It was clear that they didn't know anything. It was decided to delay the first meteor drop for another day, just in case there was a technical glitch with the Beltis Island radios.

Radio monitors eventually reported that there was talk about a Great Burn, but in their references, the Great Burn had happened ten years or so earlier, so they didn't know what to make of it.

Just in case there might be another visit by a beamship from the Hercs, they increased the radar sweeps of the clouds below, with observers watching with telescopes for any of the tiny craft hiding in the clouds like before. Sadly, the radar system had been built long ago, designed for tight beam sweeps of distant habitats. Sweeping a whole world close up took a long time. Yet it was the only sure way to look beneath those clouds.

And then—

Moving at a speed faster than any of the Mt. Ural people had imagined, a beamship appeared suddenly on the far side, away from the clouds. A laser cannon flared, carving a scar across the surface, and then Mt. Ural itself was hit with a strong pressor beam pulse before the beamship quickly traversed the distance to the clouds. At closest approach, the ship had blazed by only a hundred meters from the surface.

Under the surface of Mt. Ural there was second shock wave as one of its laser cannon's power cell ruptured, blasting flame and rubble into space. Air pressure alerts sounded from all over as Brilliant's laser blast had penetrated the surface of one of the hydroponic gardens and chambers were venting air.

The pressor beam pulse had struck at the holding cage where the meteor bombs were being staged, scattering the tumbling, streamlined eggs into space.

Screams and conflicting orders swamped the internal communications channels. Not a one of the surviving laser cannon operators had even seen the attacking beamship. None had fired at it.

The whole attack had taken less than two seconds.

. . .

Darkwind feared damage as Brilliant Morning used heavy beams to brake their speed as they entered the atmosphere. The temperature had climbed noticeably before they settled into a hovering position, well protected by the clouds.

Brilliant showed the recorded images of the attack, adding the new scars to the model of Mt. Ural.

Darkwind nodded. It was enough.

He turned the radio to the unencrypted channel and called out.

"Mt. Ural, your allies on Luna have all destroyed themselves. If you can see Beltis Island through the clouds, all you'll see is a destroyed land of ash and molten rock. Through the greed and vanity of its leader Bardin, they managed to destroy a beamship right on top of themselves.

"I have given you a warning shot. Luna doesn't want you here. You have destroyed the innocent with fire from the sky and you threatened to do it again.

"You and your allies have also killed the best of us. His songs are numerous and more will be written. Only he wanted to give you the chance to leave under your own power. I have always advocated burning you all to molten rock.

"Yet, in his honor, I will give you one chance. Your sort love giving a one-day ultimatum, so I will give you one: Leave lunar orbit, starting within one day, or the real attacks will begin. Leave and never come back.

"You will never see me coming. You will never predict when. All your lasers, all your external habitats will be destroyed. Your spinner dish will be shattered to pieces, and your tractor-pressor beam system will be ruined. With luck, I'll rupture your power center and turn Mt. Ural into glowing red slag.

"And then, when you are hopefully all dead, I'll ever so gently boost you out of lunar orbit myself. I'll push you out of Earth's space as well, out into the cold and dark where you'll never trouble anyone ever again."

Darkwind felt himself ready to burst into song, one of the battle hymns perhaps. But he restrained himself. These people didn't deserve it. They were soulless anyway.

"One day. One lunar day. Forty-eight standard hours. I'll be watching. I have a big stack of attack plans. I'm aching to put them into play."

He heard their voices, but he shut off the radio. He didn't want words. He wanted action. They knew very well that one beamship could take out a habitat. Over the past centuries, they'd done it themselves several times. Power wasn't the issue, it was the agility.

"Brilliant. We need to plan for our next attack."

Her rich voice said, "I would advise another recharging run when Mt. Ural is out of range. We used a lot of energy on that attack run."

"Yes, dear. Remind me when it's time."

Epilog

Rad Fasail came running from the moment he'd seen the beamship come buzzing down from the sky over Rynin. The sleepy little community wasn't too far from the Peach River to the west, and people were always worried that the wars from the Hercs and Serenites might come to visit them. Nearly all the settlers here had taken an eastward branch off the Gaussland trail when things got too troubling in the Herc settlements where they'd been heading.

With no noble in charge and likewise, no taxes to pay, they'd done all right for themselves. There were a couple of enterprising merchants that came through from time to time, selling manufactured goods and spreading all the gossip.

But it had been a while since any had returned, and then there were the extra rains that had come out of nowhere. Rad's neighbors said they were like from the time of the Great Burn. It was unsettling.

Growing up in Port Gartner, any mention of the Great Burn generally led to an attack on the Fasail brothers, since everyone blamed the Alpines for it.

But here, Rad had kept his origins quiet. Good enough to be a Herc farmer growing enough food to keep his family fed.

But that beamship coming out of the sky! He only knew of one beamship, the one his brother had inexplicably discovered and used to halt the Serenite invasion of Terrance. Had Charles tracked him down?

He raced through the winding path fearful and excited at the same time.

And then, there it was, just like he remembered, a tall metal cylinder standing in his corn field, smashing half his crop into the mud. There was a man in white standing there at the hatchway. Rad approached at a run. Was it Charles?

But no, the man didn't have the build of a dockworker. He looked like a Kimmer in a sailsuit.

Rad approached cautiously.

The man saw him and waved. "You're the brother. Nobody could doubt that. Rad?"

"I'm Rad Fasail."

The man in white bowed. "I am Darkwind. Charles Fasail was my mentor and my good friend. I'm sorry for your loss."

Rad gasped. Darkwind took a couple of steps and took his arm. "I'm sorry, I thought you knew. Come sit here."

They sat side by side in the hatchway. Rad shook his head. "We're isolated out here. I've heard no news."

Darkwind shook his head. "It's a big story. You're Alpine, right? I'll give you the summary. Mt. Ural went into orbit around Luna and made a deal with King Bardin of Serenity." He rattled it out in a few sentences.

"So Charles, to prevent more deaths, took the prince to Beltis. Bardin betrayed them and destroyed the beamship."

Rad nodded slowly, struggling to keep up.

Darkwind said, "A beamship holds enormous energy. The explosion killed Charles, killed everyone on the island really. It boiled the sea and set the Serenite navy on fire."

"The rains. It was another Great Burn."

Darkwind nodded. "Your brother was a great man, and greatly missed."

"I'm glad you came to tell me. We've had our difficulties, I'm sad to say."

Darkwind chuckled. "And I've heard about them all, at least Charles's versions. But, we didn't really come to tell you about that."

"Oh?"

Darkwind pointed toward the farmhouse, hand built into the side of a cliff. "Empress Jelica and your sister-in-law are visiting with your wife. I'm forbidden from getting close enough to hear what they're talking about. Secret stuff, apparently."

Rad frowned. "Empress?"

Darkwind smiled. "Yes, Jelica Haren. She's married to Emperor James of the Three Kingdoms. It's all new stuff. After the war, the Herc empire split into the northern and southern kingdoms and Serenity made themselves a new king. Since James was the surviving heir of both the Herc and Serenite royalty, and since he had the use of the only remaining beamship, all three kingdoms agreed to be under his leadership. Maybe we'll be free of wars for a little while."

Rad could barely believe what he was being told. But he could read the emblems on Darkwind's white uniform. There was an old Alpine crest with a familiar phrase, "For the Restoration of Humanity." And next to it was a golden badge embossed with "For Service to the Emperor".

He wasn't even sure he wanted to know all the details. He was just a poor dirt farmer now. Hardly Alpine at all.

Darkwind nodded toward the house. "They're waiting there for you."

Rad got to his feet and hesitated at the door. Then he went in.

Maria was teary-eyed, sitting on the bed, clutching young baby Alice in her arms. Little Tim at her feet was still too young to know what was going on, playing with the toy cart Rad had carved for him.

It was indeed Jelica Haren grinning at him as he entered, although her blue and white dress was fancier than any he'd ever seen. And the other woman looked vaguely familiar, dressed in a similar black-trimmed gown. She was obviously pregnant, sitting on the stool Maria typically used, holding a book.

The empress smiled, "You didn't think you could run away from us, did you Rad?"

"What's going on? I just heard … Darkwind just told me about Charles."

The woman in mourning cleared her throat. "A long time ago," she said to the both of them, "Rad offered help to my older sister and me."

Rad blinked, remembering an old memory.

"My sister was taken from me by an unfeeling world. Then I found Charles and we married. Now, he has been taken from me as well.

"I am not a friendly person. Hate comes naturally."

Her hand went to her belly. "And yet, and yet. Charles left me a note." She opened the slightly charred book and next to a white feather bookmark was a folded slip of paper.

She unfolded it and read.

"'Sharra, I don't know how all this will play out and I may get caught up in things I can't control. But regardless, I want you to choose love over hate. I want our child to be raised with love. This is the only thing I can ask of you now. I love you. Pass that love on.'"

She took a deep breath to regain her composure.

"Sorry, it's hard every time I read it. But, I'm trying.

"Charles loved his brother and regretted losing him. I realized there was one thing I could do to pass that love on to you. Jelica agreed to help me find you.

"Jelica could you explain?"

The Empress of Luna knelt down before the dirt farmer and his wife and said, "There is more to being an Alpine than the education and the ceremonies. Being Alpine comes with a curse."

She explained. As Maria realized that the curse had already been passed on to little Alice in her arms, she gasped and held her tighter. The baby cried.

Rad was aghast as well. As a man, he'd never known this part of his legacy.

"What'll we do?"

Jelica said, "You and Maria have the taint, but since Maria was born a Herc, she doesn't need the treatment, obviously. Your daughter Alice, if she is ever to be able to bear children of her own, needs to be trained in the ancient ways of our people. Little Tim must learn automatically from a young age that to protect the world, he must not marry any but another Alpine. It will be easier if he learns to identify as an Alpine, as being from a people who want to save the world and restore humanity."

Jelica sighed. "You're making your own way in the world and giving that up would be a great hardship. Your choices are stay and find a way for the children to be properly educated, or else return with us to Stampz were Alpines are respected. It is a choice you'll have to make for yourselves."

Sharra said, "I would love for my child to have cousins. I'm sure Charles would have loved to have known them as well."

Deep within her was resentment. She hated that Rad had dared to give up his Alpine identity. She hated the girl for being a Herc.

But maybe she didn't hate those two little ones.

Charles, I'm trying! Maybe I'll never be as good as you, but I'll pretend, for our child. Maybe if I can pretend long enough, it'll take.

She gripped Charles's book tightly. He'd loved it. Maybe she could feel his warmth in it. She could only hope.

The End

For the full story of the **Lunar Alpine Trilogy**:

Alpine Duty

The High Quest

Alpine Destiny

If you want more books like this, consider leaving a review on your favorite online bookstore or review service.

If you're interested in what came before the terraforming of Luna, then choose the
Earth Branch of the Project Saga:

Star Time

Kingdom of the Hill Country

In the Time of Green Blimps

Captain's Memories

Humanicide

www.ingramcontent.com/pod-product-compliance
Lightning Source LLC
Chambersburg PA
CBHW031213260626
47169CB00007B/2048